DOMINO DIE

Michael Woodman

Connlaswell Publishing

Copyright

This edition published in 2020 by Connlaswell Publishing.

Copyright © Michael Woodman 2020

The right of Michael Woodman to be identified as the author of this work has been asserted in accordance with the Copyright, Designs and Patents Act 1988. All the characters in this book, with the exception of those already in the public domain, are fictitious, and any resemblance to actual persons, living or dead, is purely coincidental.

All rights reserved. No part of this publication may be reproduced, stored in a retrieval system or transmitted in any form or by any means without the prior permission in writing of the publisher, nor be otherwise circulated in any form of binding or cover other than that in which it is published without a similar condition, including this condition, being imposed on the subsequent purchaser.

Woodman, Michael. Domino Die.
Connlaswell Publishing.
www.connlaswell.com

ISBN 978-1-9160095-4-7

WHAT AMAZON READERS ARE SAYING:

★★★★★ "A fast paced, tense, gripping story of espionage that will keep you well up past your bedtime."

★★★★★ "…a complete thrill ride starting on page one."

★★★★★ "Incredibly well-written, this is a book that gives us the readers great moments and a feeling of loneliness when it ends."

★★★★★ "A genuinely exciting and intriguing story by an expert storyteller."

★★★★★ "I had no intention of reading it cover to cover in one day but I did!"

★★★★★ "The plot is absolutely brilliant, and the characters are highly believable and realistic."

★★★★★ "Full of action and suspense, this novel takes you down many twists and turns and leaves you wondering who to trust."

★★★★★ "…Absolutely compelling, grabs you, holds you in close and doesn't let go."

★★★★★ "It is difficult not to get engulfed in this kind of storytelling. Terrific start to the CJ Brink series."

★★★★★ "A must read. Loved all the players. Wonderful women. Devastating losses. Brilliant writing."

WHITE HOUSE STATEMENT

May 13, 2019

WASHINGTON — At a meeting of President Trump's top national security aides last Thursday, Acting Defense Secretary Patrick Shanahan presented an updated military plan that envisions sending as many as 120,000 troops to the Middle East should Iran attack American forces or accelerate work on nuclear weapons, administration officials said.

USA

One

Should I kill him?

CJ scribbled the question on a napkin, then unfolded it and smoothed it flat, brushing a few crumbs off the counter to make room. He studied it as he drank his coffee, looking up from time to time, although there was not much to see through the convenience store window other than a parking lot and a dusty blacktop with plenty of dirt, rocks and mountains beyond it. This was what his life had come down to. A question. All of his past had brought him to it and all of his future depended on his answer. He drew a vertical line underneath it and wrote *Yes* to the left of it and *No* to the right. Someone had once told him that this was how Winston Churchill used to make his tough decisions.

World War Two. Yes or no?

Something like that.

CJ had believed it too, at least until Alex had disputed the fact, insisting that it was not Winston Churchill but Benjamin Franklin. They'd argued about it, of course.

1

They'd argued about everything. CJ doodled arrows, decorating the napkin, lost in the moment as he recalled his dead friend.

If only Alex were still around to argue with…

Lieutenant-Colonel Vance Preston, the *him* in the question above, was the man responsible for Alex's gruesome death. Not his killer exactly, but the author of his fate. He hadn't scripted that ending, but he'd set the stage. Preston was the CEO of Tratfors, their former employer, a shady guns-for-hire outfit masquerading as a private security and geo-political risk organization.

Should I kill him?

CJ sipped his coffee and looked around the store. It was a quiet morning on a quiet road in Nevada. A few customers were paying for gas and picking up coffees to go, all of them getting a cheery welcome from the sales clerk, a young woman way into her pregnancy. He went back to his list. He was stalling and he knew it. The question was too easy. The *Yes* column was a no-brainer, with reasons to kill Preston streaming through his head like a Wall Street newswire. But check out the *No* column, as stark and empty as the desert outside. That should have made it easy, but it made it hard. What was the point of a choice with only one answer?

A car skidded to a halt outside and CJ looked up—an old Ford in need of a paint job. But whoever was in such a hurry to get to the store must have changed their mind because no one stepped out of it.

CJ went back to his napkin, but the paint job Ford had cut the thread of his thoughts.

Choice… that was it.

Once, as a kid in a foster home, he'd been offered a choice of dinner menu—*eat it or leave it*—and that had pretty much framed his approach to life. He had *chosen* to join the Marines, although that had been more of an escape hatch than a choice, preordained after a childhood of institutions. And since then? Iraq and Afghanistan. Wars that had left him qualified for one thing only, a job with an assault rifle and a bulletproof vest. Then came the betrayal in Iraq and its aftermath of pain and blood, followed by a trail of vengeance. Killing Preston was more of the same, a future dictated by the past.

Less of a life… more of a ricochet.

CJ shook his head like he was warding off an aggressive fly. He was nobody's victim. His life was no ricochet.

Eat it or leave it?

All he had to do was make the call and…

"Leave it!" He blurted the words out loud, looking around to see if anyone had noticed. But there was only one other customer, a man in a brown jacket, and he was up by the cash desk getting directions to the washroom from the sales clerk. Inappropriate social behavior like that was part of CJ's life now, a legacy of the experimental surgeries that had brought him back from the dead. It was the cost of his resurrection, according to his military doctors, along with hallucinations. There was a dividend, though—enhanced hearing, morphine-like pain tolerance, and neurotransmission speeds usually only found in cats.

He finished his coffee and made the call again, silently this time. It was time to move on and reclaim his life. Enough was enough. He'd pass on payback. Preston was more than worthy of the executioner's ax. But on this bright Nevada morning, he'd gotten lucky, and his death sentence had been commuted. CJ screwed up the napkin. There was no trash bin nearby, so he jammed it in his pocket, planning to flush it later. Not a good idea to leave assassination plans, even abandoned ones, on a convenience store counter.

So what next?

With his business agenda cleared, there was only one task left in America. Alex's family. His parents had both passed and his sister now lived in the family home. He wanted to meet her. He wanted her to know what had happened all those years ago. How some heroes were made of hype, but her brother was the real thing. He called her, but as it rang through, he pulled the phone away from his face.

Is this a mistake?

Families got wounded by death, and their pain often bled into anger and blame. CJ and Alex had been a team in Iraq. They'd had each other's back. So how would she read that? The phone was answered with a simple hello. But it was enough to convince him to take the chance. If a whipping was due, he'd have to take it. Lord knows he'd whipped himself often enough about those final moments.

"Jeanine?" he said. "It's CJ, Alex's buddy from Iraq."

He waited for an answer, a few seconds as clocks count, but they stretched into an age for CJ.

"Hi, CJ." Her voice was husky, warm, but wary.

"Did you get the photo?"

"What photo?"

"Oh… maybe it will get there tomorrow. I sent it the other day. Me and Alex. When we first met." He was trying to sound upbeat, cheerful even. But it sounded wrong, like it was a holiday snap he was sharing with her. He took a beat, drifting with the somber reality of it all. "I wanted you to have it. Someone in his family. It's a great photo. We've got all our kit on, and…" He trailed off. "I hope that's okay."

"That's fine. Thoughtful. Thank you."

"I'm in the US," he said, encouraged by her reply. "I had a business thing planned, but it got canceled. So I've got time before I head back. I was hoping we might meet." He waited. But she said nothing—no enthusiastic reaching out to grab his invitation—a nothing that made him nervous. "I was there at the end, and…" He stopped, no idea where that sentence was going.

"I'd like that, CJ. I really would. Where are you now?"

"In Nevada. There's a bus. I can be in California tomorrow."

"I'm working tomorrow, but we could meet afterwards. I get off duty at two p.m. We could meet before I pick up my son."

"Duty? Are you in the military?"

"I'm a cop."

"Oh… that's great." CJ hoped it didn't sound as hollow as it felt. There'd been talk about an extradition warrant to get him sent back to the UK to face a phony murder charge. Maybe it was just talk, but CJ would have felt a lot more comfortable if she'd been a soldier, or a nurse, or any other profession that called work *duty*. "And you've got a son. That's wonderful. I'd love to meet him. How old is he?"

"He's thirteen, going on thirty." He could hear the pride in her voice.

They wound up the call with CJ noting the diner where they planned to meet, and he was slipping the phone back in his pocket when a car door's slamming hit him with a jolt.

No ordinary slam, that. More like a starting gun.

He looked out the window.

It was the paint job Ford. There'd been two slams, in fact, synchronized so they got squeezed into one. Two men were pacing towards the convenience store, not side by side, but separated by about three or four body widths. One was a teenager, short and slight, wearing pants and a long-sleeved top that were both fifteen sizes too large, so they flapped around him as he walked. The other was older—not by much—but he was bigger by plenty, his baggy top padded out with a belly, his round face hardened with metal studs.

Trouble.

CJ had spent a lifetime recognizing it and either avoiding it or confronting it, according to circumstances. It wasn't so much the look of the men as the sum total, the way they walked like Batman and Robin closing in on the bad guys, the way they carried themselves, and most of all, the gap between their pulling into the lot and their synchronized exiting of a car whose doors they failed to lock. There might be plenty of reasons to stay in a parked car, but one was surely to wait until the rush of customers he'd seen earlier had cleared out. Another might be to smoke a breakfast pipe and get pumped. CJ hadn't survived combat and years as a bodyguard on the world's most dangerous streets by second-guessing his instincts. Fight or flight was a decision best made tactically, not emotionally, and with warrants pending, this was no time to be a hero.

Good advice.

Not that CJ was overly gifted at taking such. Growing up an orphan, he'd been bullied and picked on, and it had left him both scarred and stronger, with an irresistible compulsion to even up score lines. So as he ducked down an aisle, heading for the back door exit, a doubt nagged him: the woman at the cash desk. CJ was far from expert, but she had to be seven months gone, a good-looking woman with a rosy glow about her cheeks that in his unprofessional opinion augured well for the health of her child. He was feet from the washroom and the nearby fire exit when Batman and Robin burst open double doors and the woman let loose a yelp. CJ ducked down, peeking out from behind a special offer of windscreen washing detergents. Robin had a revolver, held loosely at his side. No pointing, no threatening. That was Batman's job. He was obscured by a stack of canned goods, but the semiautomatic pistol pointing out beyond it was unmissable, and so was the voice booming threats. That got to CJ, the big-man swagger as he threatened the woman. Two armed men versus an unarmed pregnant woman…

No way.

But as CJ swiveled away from the exit and went to stand, the washroom door opened and the man in the brown jacket stepped out. He stopped mid-stride, his eyes on the men. Then he reached under his arm and dropped into a combat stance with both hands aiming a pistol.

"Police. Drop it. Down on the floor."

God bless America… an armed off-duty cop in the right place at the right time, a hero in the making, and a load off CJ's back. But then the shooting started.

At that moment, half a planet away, Vance Preston, the target of CJ's scribbled to-kill-or-not-to-kill soliloquy was enjoying the afternoon and sipping a cocktail on the terrace of his Spanish home. He was looking beyond the pool, through wooded hills that cleaved apart as the valley met the sea, towards North Africa, a hazy smudge of clouds and mountains on the horizon, and his thoughts were far from CJ Brink. He knew that he was out there, of course. A trained assassin with Preston's name at the top of his list was hardly something he was likely to forget. But on this afternoon, the threat he posed was theoretical, not existential, like an earthquake. It could happen here on the Costa del Sol, but no one was losing sleep over it. Besides, Preston was in his fortress, his guarded compound in Alcazada, Europe's most luxurious and secure urbanization in the hills above Marbella, and he had a far more pressing issue to deal with…

Domino.

It was the crux of a deal he was brokering between two natural-born enemies, Nazar Moshiri, an expat Iranian, a gilt-edged hustler based in Monaco, and Mark Schilder a mouthy New York billionaire whose fast track to fame had been the creation of market trading software with world-beating artificial intelligence. It needn't have been like that. Nazar was hardly a Koran-thumping mullah. He was more the shifty playboy type gone to seed. His business, OneOil, was billed as an oil services company. In reality, it was an umbrella of interlocked offshore corporations, washing money and lining the pockets of corrupt politicians and bureaucrats. With all that going for him, he had plenty of common ground with Schilder. According to *Forbes* magazine, he was a genius, another Harvard dropout who'd "done good." But in Silicon Valley, he was known as a shark, a man who never saw a shortcut, however gray, he didn't like the look of. Two smart men, both self-made billionaires whose intelligence deserted them when each was faced with the other. There was something chemical about their antipathy, like that high school science experiment mixing yeast with hydrogen peroxide. It makes heat. Every time. No exceptions. Despite this, Preston had kept the deal alive, but now, with the Domino exchange days away, he was getting antsy.

"Sir…" Tony stepped out onto the terrace. "You'd better see this." He was holding a tablet and cuing bad news with a furrowed brow and watchful eyes. Tony was Preston's PA, but his boss liked to think of him as a Mr. Fixit, as adept at solving problems with a pistol as with a pen.

Preston took the tablet and played a video news report while Tony waited apprehensively.

Sharof Moshiri was arrested in New York today following an investigation by FBI special agents of the Financial Crimes Section. In a reported… Preston tuned out mentally, his eyes glazing over as the news bulletin played out.

That dumb bastard…

Not Sharof. He was just a name to Preston, someone he'd never met, but he was Nazar's brother. He passed the tablet back to Tony, who disappeared into the shadows as Preston put the call through to Nazar.

"I told you." He leapt up as soon as he heard the Iranian's voice, pacing aggressively out into the sun. "This was always going to happen… prancing around New York, sucking up to celebrities to get his face on Instagram. Why didn't you stop him? This guy's got Fredo written all over him and you act like it's okay to…"

"Who's Fredo?"

"What?"

"Fredo who?"

Preston groaned, his eyes closing as they panned up at the blue sky. Back on the phone and back in control, he stepped out of the sun into the shaded part of the terrace. "It doesn't matter… it's not the Godfather's brother who's the problem. It's yours."

"Don't concern yourself. I haven't spoken to him for years."

"FCPA," Preston shouted, losing it again. "Foreign Corrupt Practices Act. Government contracts. Bribery."

"That was fifteen years ago. He ran some errands for me in Africa. Relax. He knows nothing about Domino."

"Is that what I'm supposed to tell Schilder? *Relax!* Stop jerking me around. The feds are not interested in your pipsqueak brother. It's you they want. And when they offer him a get-out-of-jail-free card, he's going to serve you up like a slice of toast."

"He's got nothing on me."

"He'll make something up, or else they will. Give me some good news for Schilder, something to keep this deal on track. Where's the Domino?"

"It cruised over the border into Pakistan a few hours ago."

That was excellent news. At fifteen thousand feet, the frontier between China and Pakistan—the Khunjerab pass—was the highest in the world, and even in May, closure due to snow had been a risk. Now the load would be heading to Gwadar, a Pakistani port on the Arabian Sea. Nazar's technician was scheduled to meet with Schilder's man there to check the Domino and witness its loading onto the freighter.

"Schilder will use your brother's arrest as a lever. He'll want something more."

"I want something more too. The final payment in diamonds. No more US dollars."

Nazar's demand was not unexpected. Upping the ante as soon as the other side had skin in the game was a tried and tested tactic, and Schilder had already coughed up the initial payments. The final payment was due on delivery.

"What's wrong with your money laundry?"

"It takes too long… placement, layering, integration."

"So what's your hurry? It looks bad, right after your brother's arrest. This could be a dealbreaker."

"The laundry basket is full. That's all there is to this. If Schilder balks, tell him I'll find a new buyer."

Preston left it there, and he was back in his chair, sipping his cocktail and worrying, when Tony joined him. "I called the office," he said. Preston didn't need to ask which one. *The* office meant Tratfors HQ in LA. He waited for the news. *Not good, not bad.* He could read it already on Tony's face. "Brink's vanished. Maybe he's gotten it out of his system."

That was possible. Brink had logged an impressive body count of Tratfors employees. Maybe he was done, but Preston doubted it. He was the last guy in the world who'd quit on a mission. But he might have crept off to lick his wounds, and if he could stay vanished for a few weeks more, that would be enough. Domino would be done.

"Tell them to keep their antennas tuned in," he said, "just in case. After Domino, we can dial up the heat."

Tony replied with a cocky smirk, and he disappeared off the terrace, leaving Preston alone with his thoughts.

Cocky.

That was the last thing he needed to be. Brink had left a trail of cocky corpses in the aftermath of that Iraq fiasco. As for *dialing up the heat*, Preston had no illusions. He was an amateur. Brink was its master.

Two

It?

The hero cop had said "Drop *it*," not "Drop *them*." He hadn't seen the kid, and when he did, it was too late. The kid fired, and the cop took one in the chest. He spun back, catching another round on his way down, his gun slithering away over the tiled floor. CJ glanced at it and made the call in an instant.

Too far…

No way could he get to it. They'd nail him before he even got close. So he stood up with his hands above his head, and in a blink, both guns were aimed at him.

"Don't shoot. I'm a customer. I'm unarmed."

The kid edged closer to CJ in a series of loping steps as the big guy whirled towards the cash desk. "Get away from that alarm." CJ couldn't see the woman, but she had to be petrified.

"This guy's still alive." CJ edged towards the cop but kept his hands in the air.

"Get away from him," the kid said, pouncing forward, but still out of CJ's reach.

"Get the gun," the big man said without taking his eyes or his weapon off the woman. She was whimpering, fearful sobs eking out from beyond the racks of food-to-go.

The kid scurried over to the cop's fallen gun, and as he picked it up, CJ said, "He's still alive. I can save him. I'm a paramedic." The kid stood up straight, brimming with two-gun confidence. "He's still breathing. Maybe I'm wrong, but this looks like a robbery to me. So this would be a murder in special circumstances, and this is a death penalty state. Please…" He moved towards the cop. The goons exchanged a look and the big one nodded. CJ crouched by the cop, who was lying facedown, slipping his hand under the man's throat.

No pulse.

"He's still alive…" CJ barked it out triumphantly. The difference an aggravated killing of a cop would make if they were ever caught had to mean something even to losers like this. Of course, the *if* in *if they were ever caught* was a big one. And CJ had plans to make that wholly unnecessary. He closed the man's eyes surreptitiously as he rolled him over onto his back, then busied himself like a paramedic, opening the cop's mouth and checking his airways before performing mouth-to-mouth resuscitation. After a few breaths, he worked on chest compressions, using both hands and skipping over the cop to get more room in the narrow aisle. At least, that was how it was supposed to look, but he was now much closer to the kid, just feet away.

"Bitch." Batman screeched it. "I told you not to touch that alarm."

The woman screamed as he cuffed her, sending her crashing through shelves and breaking open the glass counter. The kid checked it out, and as he turned his head, CJ launched himself from the crouch. He grabbed the kid around the knees, upended him and crashed him headfirst on the floor, an instant red card on the rugby field, but here in Nevada—just the ticket. The kid's gun went off as he lost balance and his arms flailed, then one more time as he hit the floor and his collarbone cracked like a dry branch with both guns spinning aside.

CJ kicked the closest gun beyond the aisle as he ran for cover and the big boy lurched into action, shooting at the empty space behind him. CJ ducked out of the aisle, keeping on the move as he picked up the gun. It was the kid's five-shot .38, so there were three rounds left. Now that they both had guns, it was down to a peekaboo game, or a straight shoot-out. CJ's vote was Wild West. Roll the dice. The wager was simple. He was backing himself. He was a better shot than the big boy. Practice and experience count.

He jumped out at the end of the aisle and the man whirled on him too late. CJ's first shot hit him in the chest and his arms flew aside as he stumbled back. The second hit him on the nose and his face folded in on it as he fell feet away from the woman, who was lying unconscious in a pool of blood. CJ ran to her and checked her vital signs. Her pulse was strong, but frantic and irregular. Hard to see where that blood was coming from. Her head was cracked open and she'd been cut by glass.

Then there was…

CJ touched her belly with his fingertips.

What was he doing? He didn't know a damn thing about miscarriages. He caught some movement on the edge of his vision and looked up. The kid was dragging himself towards the cop's gun and his hand was just inches away from it. CJ scooped up the big boy's 9mm and took the shot on the fly. It looked good, and the kid slumped motionless. But his hand was already on the weapon. CJ sprinted down the aisle and kicked the gun away, sending it skidding out of sight under a rack of shelves at the end of the store. Then he checked the kid. That didn't take long. His shot had caught him on the neck, right where it fits to the skull. CJ rushed back to the woman. Her pulse was still strong. She was going to live. He was sure of it. But what about her kid? Only one thing for it... he'd have to make that 911 call.

Police, ambulance, trouble.

He was reaching for his phone when a voice stopped him. It might have been an imaginary voice, one of those hallucinations his doctors loved to talk about. But sadly, it wasn't. He was standing with his back to the entrance and his hand in his pocket, looking down at the fraught scene... the bleeding woman, the wrecked counter, the big dead man with the red sun on his chest. The voice was faint, muffled by the numbing impact of recent gunshots in a confined space, and it was soon followed up by an image, served up as a reflection in the broken glass counter. A uniformed police officer was standing right behind him with both hands on a pistol, aimed at his back.

"Drop the gun."

The alarm...

The woman must have hit it.

CJ crouched and placed the 9mm on the floor, kicking it out of reach.

"Face on the floor."

CJ inched his way down, wondering about that napkin in his pocket, and ricochets, and where the hell this one was going.

As CJ was processed through the system, news of his arrest was picked up by Tratfors HQ in LA and relayed to the boss. Preston was fixing himself a cocktail at the bar in his villa when Tony took the call.

"Brink?" he said, when Tony had hung up.

"He's been arrested."

"Where? What for?"

"Nevada. They haven't charged him yet, but they've got hell of a shopping list of options. Felony murder. Robbing a convenience store. Killing a cop. He'll end up in a max facility. We can get someone to…"

"Knocking off a store?"

"They got him with a smoking gun… literally."

"He wouldn't be stupid enough to rob a convenience store."

"Maybe he ran out of money."

"Then he'd rob something worthwhile and he wouldn't get caught. Did he have anything on him?"

"Like a memory card?"

Preston nodded. He wasn't even sure that such a card existed, but if it did, it was doom in the making, the key to a data vault in the cloud that catalogued Tratfors' black ops going back years. There was enough in it to get Preston locked up for a thousand years, if he was lucky. More likely, he'd get disappeared by one of the many clients he'd shafted and spend the rest of his short life eating gruel in some gulag and breaking rocks for fun.

"No card. But he had a napkin." Tony hesitated. "Reasons to kill Vance Preston. For and against. With the *yes* column running top to bottom on both sides of the page."

"And the *no* column?" It was a stupid question, but it was already out of his mouth.

Tony shrugged… *Please don't ask.*

Preston went silent. The idea of Brink coldly plotting his death with an itemized list of justifications was gut-churning.

"Was there anything else?" Preston said.

"He made a call to Jeanine Solo before it all went down."

"Solo?"

"Yeah… it turns out Alex had a sister."

"What do we know about her?"

"She's a cop. A single mom with a teenage kid."

Preston mulled it over. There was something wrong with this story. Brink was a killer. But a cop killer? No way.

"I was thinking we could wait until he gets sucked into the system," Tony said, "then get some con to do him."

"If he ends up locked in a Supermax or waiting in line on death row, we can forget about him. He won't be a threat anymore. But I don't see that happening." Preston sipped his martini. "There are only three ways this can turn out. Brink gets released, or he gets indicted, or…"

"He disappears up some US Marshal's ass into WITSEC."

"You got it. Witness protection. He'll trade that goddamn memory card for a clean slate. He'll get a new ID. I'll never see him coming."

"So how?"

"The cop, the sister. She could get to him. What if she calls the lead detective—cop to cop—and tells him about her brother, Brink's cherished buddy. The detective will see her as an asset, a cop with a personal connection."

"What then? She blows his brains out in the interrogation room?"

"I was thinking something sneaky… *Putinesque*. So she won't even know she's killing him."

"Like that defector with radioactive shit?"

"That's too dangerous, and we'd never get it. That other guy in the UK, the spy."

"Novichok… we could get that stuff?"

"Maybe not. But something like that. Something that kills through the skin. She could tell Brink she's got him a lawyer and give him an envelope with the lawyer's client agreement. So Brink thumbs through the papers and signs it. Then he pops it back in the envelope, and bingo—he's a dead man walking."

"It's so complicated… and how do we get her to agree?"

"Kidnap the kid."

"The cop's kid?" Tony said, rolling his eyes.

"A mother's kid. I'm betting she's more mom than cop. And even if she refuses, that kid's my bulletproof vest. Brink is sentimental. He'd never touch me if he knew I had the brat-nephew of his dear buddy Alex."

Preston finished his martini and went back to the bar to make another. He didn't offer Tony a drink. He never did.

"It's super risky." Tony was still shaking his head.

Preston waved his objections aside.

"Alex Solo's nephew is Brink's kryptonite, and I want him."

"But who's going to do it? We don't have people who do that kind of work."

"There must be someone. What about that Belgian pimp?"

"Ernald?" Tony's face screwed with disgust.

"Find him. Get him on it. And work on that black-ops fairy dust. Some Novichok thing."

"That's going to take time."

"Then you better get moving."

Tony went to go, but Preston called him back.

"Anything you need, Tony. Whatever it takes. And remember... Putinesque."

Three

The twenty-four hours following his arrest went quickly, with CJ always on the bumpy stretch of a learning curve. *Probable cause,* for example, a new legal term for CJ's American lexicon. That was how the officer justified the arrest, referring to the dead bodies and the smoking gun he was holding. Despite that, they hadn't charged him, although that had less to do with his presumed culpability and more to do with the muddled crime scene and his convoluted account of how it had gotten that way. CJ had spent the time in a gray building in Las Vegas, the sort of place you know you're not going to escape from anytime soon with plenty of thick concrete and windows not designed to take in the view. Mug shots and fingerprints were taken, questions posed, and explanations provided, the latter delivered by a uniformed officer in a monotone voice and articulated so slowly that by the time he got to the end of each sentence, CJ had forgotten the beginning. The next step was a criminal complaint—he understood that much—and it would be provided by the district attorney. That was a logjam that would soon get unblocked by forensics and/or the testimony of Poppi Brightwell, the cash desk clerk. She'd been in surgery for hours and CJ's solicitations concerning her welfare had gone unanswered. That was a worry. They wouldn't even tell him if she'd lost her kid.

You have the right to an attorney….

That was an option that gave him pause. Everyone gets one in America. He'd seen it a thousand times in movies and on TV. They'd even offered him one for free, and he had the right to remain silent. He'd had a good think about that one, but in the end, he'd turned down both the attorney and right of silence with some naive sense of justice propelling him forward. He was, after all, innocent and he was convinced that the truth—or at least a severely edited version—would save the day. The trick was to remember exactly what he'd said earlier so he could repeat it when asked to do so, and that was a given. Besides, although the DA was waiting on forensics to build her case, CJ was anticipating the reverse. Those scumbags had fired weapons. There'd be gunshot residues, spent cases, angles and impacts. Plus, they'd looked pretty comfortable robbing a store and shooting people like it was their main line of work, so they probably had police records.

As time passed, there were incremental changes. The big bump at the beginning was that CJ was a cop killer. The off-duty cop who'd been shot was a visitor from New York. So thankfully, not a personal friend of any of the arresting officers. But he was still a cop, and while no one beat CJ with a phone book, the detective in charge, Phil Kazan, looked like he wanted to. Overnight that changed, and so did the questions. They'd obviously gotten detailed files on him by that point, his military service and special ops background. They brought him sandwiches and coffee and reminded him that he had a phone call, even if it wasn't to a lawyer. He thought hard about that one too. Jeanine Solo was heading for a meeting in a diner he'd never be able to make. *But what to do?* Call her and say he'd been arrested for killing a cop and not to worry because it was all a misunderstanding. Better to contact her after he'd been released and make some excuse. Or in the worst case, call her after he'd been charged and scream… *Help!*

CJ was thinking about just that when he was joined by Detective Kazan. He was in his fifties, with the heavy build of a man who had once been serious about the gym but had long since moved on. CJ saw at once that something had changed. Kazan didn't take the seat opposite as he had so many times before. He just stood there with his arms crossed on his square frame, a smile creeping over his face. Then he added a nod as if in some quiet agreement with himself.

"I always had the feeling," he said. "But you know how it is… you got to go with what's there, and that was a gun and a lot of dead people."

"She made it?"

"She more than made it. Her baby boy did too." CJ slumped back in his chair. With tension cranking up since the arrest, the relief turned him into jelly. "That blood was mostly from the cuts on her body when she smashed through that glass counter, but her son's going to make it. And so will you." CJ flashed him a look, way too hopeful to dare ask. The big detective finally sat down, leaning forward with his elbows on the table. "She validated your story—the attempted robbery, the intervention by Officer Gomez, our courageous New York colleague—and she gave us enough on you to realize we've got the wrong man sitting here. Her statement pretty much clears up everything. Who shot Gomez, who assaulted her, and who was robbing the store."

"Pretty much?" CJ couldn't help but notice his qualifier.

"Nothing to be concerned about. If it was up to me, you'd be on your way."

"Then who?"

"The prosecutor is a bit of a tight-ass about details." Kazan waited. He seemed reluctant to say it, and that only magnified CJ's apprehension. He hadn't spent years in the military without learning that when someone says "nothing to be concerned about," you'd best hit the deck. Kazan tapped the back of his head with two fingers. "The kid. The coroner says he was severely injured already when he was shot in the back of the head in what looks like an execution."

"He had his hand on the gun." Even as the words came out of his mouth, CJ knew he was wasting his time with the truth. "I kicked it away." He pressed on anyway, his mind's eye seeing the gun skidding down the aisle and disappearing under a shelf of Asian sauces. "And he'd killed Officer Gomez."

"I know... he sure as hell deserved it."

"Did they check the entry wound? The forensics? It wasn't an execution. I made that shot from twenty feet away. It was a nice shot too..." He broke off, zipping it tight. That last part had been a mistake. This was no time to brag about marksmanship.

"The lab work is on the way. We'll straighten this out." CJ sagged in his chair. Who'd have thought of a thing like that? *Go find that gun, wipe your prints off it, and stick it in the murdering lowlife's hand.* "Cheer up, mate." Kazan's take on a British accent was right out of a Monty Python sketch, and it was oddly effective. It made CJ feel like someone had his back.

"I'm not very good at gray," he said. "I'm more of a black-or-white guy."

Detective Kazan chuckled, "You and me both, pal, and we're pretty big on self-defense in Nevada. It's a stand-your-ground state, and the law backs you up for the most part. You were not the original aggressor. You had a right to be there. You were not engaged in criminal activity. And you believed the aggressor posed an imminent threat."

"Exactly…"

"The tricky part is… did you inflict no more force than necessary? Some people might say that the bullet in the back of the head of a severely injured man is more like murder than self-defense. But his hand on the gun changes that picture, and who wouldn't kick it away? Besides, Ms. Brightwell would most likely have died without your intervention, her child too." Kazan eased forward and rocked himself up out of his chair. "CJ, the team out there"—he jerked his thumb over his shoulder—"they want to give you a medal. It'll be okay. You've got the good guys in your corner." He reached over and squeezed CJ's shoulder. "We'll get you out of here. Don't worry." He went to go, then turned back. "You need any more coffee. Another sandwich?"

As CJ was ruing his hasty dispatch of the kid, Preston and Schilder were facing the doglegs of Alcazada's golf course.

So far, so good.

Preston had passed on the good news about the Domino's progress through Pakistan and its imminent arrival at the port of Gwadar, and that had been well received. The mood was upbeat, their conversation relaxed. The name Sharof Moshiri had not arisen. So either Schilder hadn't yet heard about the arrest of Nazar's brother, or he hadn't thought about the consequences, and since Schilder was the thinking man's thinker, the possibility of the latter was negligible.

Preston was setting up his shot, and Schilder was leaning on his club watching him when he said, "It's all about waves." He pointed out to sea. "It's not just out there. Everything is waves. Markets, societies, individuals. We're all slaves to waves."

"I thought we were talking about America First and 9/11," Preston said.

"We were. Osama Bin Laden is the granddaddy of America First. That's my point."

Preston let the shot wait, giving Schilder his full attention. "So how'd you figure that?"

"9/11 flipped the switch on the progressive wave that started back in the sixties. All that make-love-not-war stuff. Fifty years later, the boomers aren't singing 'Imagine' anymore. Screw John Lennon. Now it's *me-first* and *we-first*."

"And Domino?"

"It'll kick off the fifth wave, the big one. There'll be wars all over the Middle East. Markets will go crazy. My software will rip it up, and you'll do pretty good too."

Schilder left it there and Preston went back to his shot. *Pretty good* was a lot less than he was planning. Tratfors had once held billion-dollar US defense contracts, but they'd been cut short when its contractors killed a bunch of terrorists who were later reported, by *fake news* outlets, as being innocent women and children. Schilder's AI-generated models had never been wrong. When the Domino toppled, the US and Russia would end up duking it out through proxies and the rest of the world would line up on either side. The good old days of the Iraq Wars would be back. Regimes would tumble and nations crumble, and Tratfors would rise like a Phoenix from their dust. He took his shot. A good one. He'd birdied the hole, but that wasn't so good. He was already too far ahead. If he wasn't careful, he'd end up beating Schilder and deflating his vast ego. No point in that.

"Nice shot, man." Schilder turned to his bodyguards who were standing off at a discreet distance with Tony. He indicated the golf cart, then said to Preston. "Let them take it. You okay to walk?" He tapped his love handles. "I need the steps." He walked off without waiting for a response. Preston followed him, giving the younger man a cold-eyed military appraisal. He might be a genius, but to Preston he was an apology of a man. Arms and legs like sticks, saggy shoulders and soft belly, he was a living commercial for *bring back the draft*. Preston swallowed his contempt and caught up. He'd had a belly full of Schilder's opinions, but listening to his sermons was eminently preferable to making excuses for Nazar and begging the little prick to stay in the deal.

Schilder was setting up his shot at the next hole when one of his security team barked out, "Sir," and held up a phone. Schilder set the shot aside, handing off his club to a bodyguard and apologizing to Preston with a shrug and an obsequious smirk that said *when you're the smartest man in the world, you have to put up with this shit*. He sat in the cart and took the call as Preston stepped away to give him some space. But he didn't get far…

"What?" Schilder screeched it and Preston spun around. "Hey, Preston… come here!" Schilder waved his arm after him like he was an errant dog.

Preston smothered a surge of anger. He wanted to run at that cart and tackle him. He could see it all. He'd knock the fat, oily little toad out of that cart and pummel him into the manicured turf. He took a long breath instead and sauntered back casually, smiling like Vlad the Impaler.

Schilder hung up and did a self-control thing too, his teeth grinding and his eyes rolling.

"So when did you plan to loop me in on the *good news*?"

No point in acting dumb with the smartest man in the world, so Preston went straight to it.

"It's not that big a deal. Nazar and Sharof have been estranged for—"

"It doesn't matter how long. They'll bust his balls till they get something, then they'll pick up Nazar. They'll get him for parking violations. Anything. Just so long as they can pick him up and threaten him till he gives them someone else. *Someone more important*." He labored his bellowed punchline by pointing both index fingers at his own head.

"They've got nothing. They're—"

"Potato pickers. The feds are potato pickers. They pull one out of the ground and it's game on. They keep pulling on those roots, going from one potato to the next." Preston sighed as he squeezed into the cart beside him, his brain racing, figuring out ways to calm him down. But Schilder was far from finished. "What?" he said. "You think we're going to play golf now? We're done playing golf. And we're done with Domino."

He went to get out of the cart, but Preston stopped him, looping his arm around him, masking a physical restraint as a one-arm buddy hug.

"I didn't want to share this with you, Mark, for your own protection," he said. "But I've taken steps…" He paused, partly for dramatic effect, but mostly to figure out a convincing lie. "Like everyone else, Nazar's brother has important people in his life. It makes him"—Preston stopped again, this one pure milking—"open to persuasion."

"He's not married, is he?"

"I think it's important that you maintain deniability as far as the details go. Let's just say that if I'd stapled his lips closed, I couldn't be more confident that he'll keep his mouth shut."

Schilder eased back in the cart, visibly relieved, and Preston released his buddy-lock hug. "Listen… I got a bit excited there," Schilder said. "It's just that—"

"We're all on edge. I understand. But that arrest makes no difference to us."

Schilder seemed placated, a crisis averted, and they were soon back playing golf, with Preston tidying up operational details. It was getting dark when they wound up and bade farewell, with Schilder thankfully declining Preston's invitation to dinner at the gourmet clubhouse restaurant. So Preston headed back to his villa, oozing smug. He hadn't managed to broach the delicate subject of Nazar's getting that last payment in diamonds, but his spur-of-the-moment fabrication of a threat to Sharof Moshiri's loved ones had been a masterstroke. He was sitting in the back of the Mercedes next to Tony as they pulled into his villa and his PA took a call.

"It's on," Tony said as he hung up.

"The cop job?"

Tony nodded, checking his watch. "Right about now."

More smug-fodder for Preston, who headed directly to the bar. This called for a bottle of something special.

In California, Jeanine Solo was waiting in the diner, holding the photograph CJ had sent her. It was mounted in a metal frame, a cheap one, but the photo itself was priceless. She ran her fingertips over the glass as though she could touch the men depicted beyond it. On the left was her brother, Alex, a US Marine outfitted for combat. At his side was CJ, another Marine, but wearing a different uniform. British. It was a buddy photo, shot in a war-torn street in Iraq. They were bristling with weapons, dirtied up and disheveled, but smiling through it, thick arms draped on broad shoulders. She was looking forward to meeting CJ. That's what she told herself and that's what she felt. But then again, she was dreading it. She put the photograph on the table and checked her watch.

He was late.

Her mixed feelings were no kind of commentary on CJ. Alex had trusted him with his life, and not just in combat, but after the war, when they'd worked together as security contractors in the world's most dangerous conflict zones. And he'd seemed nice enough on the phone—nervous, perhaps, apprehensive about their meeting like her, sharing the same forebodings. The issue wasn't Jeanine or CJ. It was the baggage that came with them.

Alex.

It seemed shameful to think like that, referring to her big brother as baggage. But the pain of those years when he'd been held hostage by terrorists was overwhelming still, the anguish and uncertainty, ending abruptly with his horrific death. Years of healing since had done their best to repair the unrepairable, but CJ's call had reminded her just how thin that scar tissue was.

Damn it! He's very late.

She thought of calling him back, but she called for the check instead. Something had obviously come up. They'd have no time to talk now anyway, and they could always reschedule. She looked back at the photo, at her brother, and swallowed a choke of tears, her eyes skidding around the diner to see if anyone had noticed that. No one had. It didn't matter anyway. She wasn't in uniform. She'd changed at the station at the end of her shift. She tucked the photo away, her emotions churning, paid for her coffee and stepped outside. But when she reached her car, her phone buzzed an incoming message.

CJ. It had to be. Some excuse.

But it wasn't. It was her son, Aidan. At least, it was his phone.

We have your son. He is safe. Come immediately. Come alone. Do not contact 3rd parties. GPS will follow.

She staggered, catching herself on the car. She read the message again, her brain gears disconnected, years of cop training neutered by a single fact.

Aidan's been taken.

But that was impossible. He was in school—a protected environment—waiting for her to pick him up. School wasn't even out yet. None of this made any sense. She flipped over to her contacts, and she was about to call the school when another message buzzed through from Aidan's phone.

The GPS coordinates.

She ignored it and called Aidan's number. It seemed to ring forever before going to voicemail.

Another message.

Call this number again, we kill him. Call anyone, we kill him.

That was followed by the GPS coordinates a second time.

It took her only a moment to find the location, a patch of dirt between La Cienega and South Fairfax up in the Baldwin Hills, a non-urbanized district surrounded by sprawling cities. Part of the area was recreational with hiking trails and lookouts, but plenty was scrub, littered with scruffy oil installations, their pumpjacks still working one of LA's biggest oilfields. Something mechanical switched on inside her, bringing her back to her senses, and she found herself striding to the car. Then she was driving, heading south.

Realistically, did she have any options?

She could defy them and call it in. Theoretically, that was an option, but it was never going to happen. What if they followed through on their threat? She shuddered and shook the thought out of her head. Her priorities were clear. She had to verify that Aidan was alive and make sure it wasn't a hoax, and the first step on that route was to check out that GPS location. Within thirty minutes, she'd found the spot. Most of the area was fenced off, with locked gates opening onto dirt trails linking scattered pumpjacks and tanks. There was an open gate at the GPS spot she'd been directed to and a busted padlock nearby.

Nobody.

She followed the trail beyond it, snaking around a spur and coming to a dead end with a silent pumpjack next to a tank on concrete blocks. It was a great location for an ambush, hidden from the main roads with plenty of ridges and gullies strewn with the leftovers from eighty years of pumping oil. She stopped the car and got out, drawing her weapon and crouching behind the door. She trained her gun on the tank and the disused equipment adjoining it. There was no sound beyond the buzz of distant traffic and the dull rhythm of pumpjacks on nearby hills.

Still no one.

She got down low and peered under the tank, spying the thick tires of an off-road vehicle.

She pulled herself up and leveled her gun.

"Come on out…"

She heard a car door open and shut and a man appeared from behind the tank. He wasn't creeping or surreptitious in any way. He walked with one hand raised above his head and the other partially raised but weighted down by a large can with a metal handle, like a paint can.

"Stop right there," she said.

The man stopped.

"Put the can down and step away from it, then lay facedown on the ground."

He put the can down and took a few steps to the side. He bent as if to crouch, but then he stopped and said, "I'm only the messenger." He had a foreign accent, maybe British, maybe not. "You know what they say about not shooting messengers."

"On the floor."

He was a tall man, skinny and cadaverous with long, gangly limbs, insect-like as he folded them and eased towards the ground.

Thwack.

The paint can exploded in a shuffle of sounds. Not a bomb, but a bullet whose impact split the can open, blowing red paint against the rusting tank. The insect man had stopped halfway to the ground.

"That was the first part of my message," he said. "It's a Steyr SSG 08. Or so they tell me. Chambered for .338 Lapua Magnum. I have no idea what any of that means, but I'm sure you do. And I've got the shorthand version too." His chatty, neighborly tone shifted gears, now sinister, threatening. "Whether you're wearing a vest or not, that sniper will drop you in a split second." Jeanine looked at what he'd done already. That paint can was in shreds and there was a fist-sized chunk of concrete missing from one of the blocks under the tank. A rifle like that could take her out from a thousand yards or more with the right shooter looking through the scope. She was exposed, surrounded by hilly scrubland specked with unattended or abandoned installations. He could be anywhere.

"Who are you? What do you want?"

"A small errand. Nothing more."

"How do I know you've got him? He could have lost that phone."

"My principals foresaw that question, and they have authorized me to play you this message." He pointed to his pocket. "My phone." He reached his hand into his pocket, pulled out a phone and played a recording. She was expecting Aidan and steeled herself for the reaction, relief on hearing his voice combined with an overwhelming urge to shoot this man in the head. But it wasn't Aidan, it was Marta. Jeanine knew that voice. Marta was an admin assistant at Aidan's school. And evidently, today she was answering the phones there, her cheery Texas twang greeting the caller with a warm welcome. Jeanine knew the caller too, and as she listened to the conversation, she lowered her pistol, not consciously but distractedly, as she slowly eased upright out of her combat stance.

The voice was hers.

"Scary, isn't it?" he said. "Technology. The things they can do. Deep fake, they call it. Years ago it would have been called magic." He held the phone up high and edged it closer to her. Jeanine listened to herself explaining how she was working late and that Aidan would be picked up by someone called Harriet. "I'm Ernald by the way," the man said as he clicked off his phone. "Harriet is my partner. She's a trained nurse. So don't worry."

Jeanine felt weak, confused. Everything was still the same—the distant hum of traffic, the thud of pumpjacks, LA's lifeblood getting circulated in real time. But nothing was the same. She'd fallen down Alice's rabbit hole, her gun useless now, dangling at her side, this creep Ernald cast as the White Rabbit. The man seemed to sense her acceptance, or maybe he mistakenly took it for submission. He smiled. Crooked teeth, overlapped like he had too many of them, or else his mouth was too small. They were all stained yellow too, more on the right than the left. Most probably a right-handed smoker. That observation was a comfort. She was noticing things again. Details. That was good. It meant her cop brain had turned back on and the shock was wearing off.

"Tell me what you want," she said. He'd used the word *errand*, obviously playing it down. There had to be one hell of a big ask coming to set all this up. Who were these people? What did they want? It couldn't be money. She was a cop. That made no sense. Information. It had to be. Access to law enforcement records. It was all she could think of.

"Set up a meeting with CJ Brink."

"What!" That was so unexpected it made her giddy. "Brink?"

"You didn't know?" The man looked surprised. "I thought you cops knew everything. He's being held by police in Las Vegas."

"What for?"

"That's what they're figuring out. Felony murder is one possibility. He was robbing a store. Three persons dead, including a cop. Serious stuff. And as Brink called you just before it all happened, the investigating officers will be interested in talking to you too. In fact, they will most likely contact you, but we'd like you to short-circuit that option. You have a personal connection to Brink, and you're a cop. They'll let you in. You could be useful to them."

"But why?"

"We'll explain all that later. Right now, all you have to do is call Nevada's finest and talk your way into getting into the same room as Brink."

This made no sense. None of it. CJ accused of killing a cop! Alex had been a fine judge of character, and he couldn't possibly have been that wrong about CJ. So many questions. But for the moment, only one option. Play along. Appear to cooperate to keep Aidan alive.

"Okay. I'll call them."

He tossed her a phone. "You contact them on this phone and keep it with you at all times. And that concludes our business. I will message you with further instructions." He smiled again. "I don't like to threaten. So I'm going to call this a promise made to you by my principals." His face fell into a scowl, his crooked-tombstone teeth grinding out a sneer. "Do anything stupid, and they won't kill Aidan. That would be such a waste. They'll give him to me."

She jerked up the pistol, but before she could aim it, a sniper's round blew the empty shell of a paint can up in the air in a cloud of dirt and smashed it into the tank. Her elbows buckled and her hands dropped.

"Thank you for your cooperation." Ernald sickly-smiled one last time and disappeared behind the tank.

Jeanine heard him enter the vehicle and start it. Then a Ford Bronco appeared from behind the tank, the plates were taped over. She noticed that, even though she hadn't particularly been looking. She'd seen enough already to know that they weren't going to make any kind of mistake. They had Aidan, and they had her. And she knew then and there that she was going to do exactly what they'd told her to do. That wasn't submission. That was calculation. She was going to get Aidan back. For sure she was. Priority number one. But that wasn't going to be the end of it.

It was getting dark in Marbella by the time the good news reached Preston. Success. The cop mom was in his pocket. He congratulated himself as he went upstairs to his office, his bonhomie only slightly besmirched by his team's failure to find a suitably Putinesque execution method for Brink. Too bad. But having Solo's nephew was enough. Even if Brink was released, he'd be powerless. That kid was a Brink liability life insurance policy *par excellence*. And the good news didn't end there. Gwadar had gone well. Schilder's techies had met with Nazar's man. The Domino had been verified, and the freighter had sailed. Countdown… that's all it was from here on out with days to go before the final exchange.

On reaching his office, Preston stood in front of a mural on the wall, a Lichtenstein original, his Pop Art rendition of an American flag. There was a mirror next to the artwork, and he touched his hand to it and the mural slid to the side, revealing a steel door that clicked open. Preston went through into an annex, shut the door, and sat at the workstation there. This was his steel-lined panic room, and much more, a nasty boy toy shop of weapons and spy-gadgets. It also served as a secure communications center for day-to-day operations thanks to its snoop-proof copper-wired walls. He fired up the computer and was soon studying a live map of global maritime traffic. Powered by AIS, the automatic identification system, it showed the position and heading of all commercial vessels over three hundred gross tons. Preston zoomed in on the Arabian Sea, fiddling with filters to remove the stream of vessels squeezing in and out of the Persian Gulf to the north. He soon found the object of his interest, a boat-shaped icon, heading southwest. He hovered his pointer over it and read:

Viking Prince

Cargo Vessel

Rotterdam

Seeing it made it real. The Domino was on its way. No more hurdles to navigate, no more *what if this* or *what if that*. Congratulations were in order, and Preston was not humble about taking the credit. He'd been right not to rock the metaphorical boat by confronting Schilder with Nazar's demand for diamonds. He'd ducked it until now, waiting until the vessel had sailed and it was too late for Schilder to back out. But now, that delicate conversation had to happen. He composed himself and put the call through to Schilder.

"So… everything went well in Gwadar?" he said, starting their conversation on a positive note.

"Perfect." Schilder sounded uncommonly chipper, doubtless still swooning after sharing a geekfest of techno-drivel with his rocket scientist in Gwadar.

"Your guy made his inspection?" Preston decided to milk his good mood for all he could get.

"It's the real deal alright."

"There is one other small issue," Preston said, like he'd just remembered it. "Nazar's got a problem washing the money, so—"

"They're locking his accounts? He's been indicted already?"

"No, no. It's an accounting thing. Anyway, he just needs the final payment in diamonds."

"*Just?*" Schilder laughed. "Absolutely not."

"He thought it might be easier for you since—"

"What? I'm a Jew? Like I've got side curls and a beard? This has nothing to do with accounting. It's about the feds. By the time that money gets washed, he'll be a fugitive already, and he knows it."

"I give you my word. I can control outcomes here."

Schilder went to speak, but it died in his mouth like he'd had unexpected second thoughts.

"Okay, I agree," he said, his sudden conversion hitting Preston as mightily suspicious. "But if he can change the deal, so can I."

"What do you want?"

"Peace of mind. I don't trust the bastard. Why can't you hold the activator? So on D-Day, all I'll need from him is the targeting code."

That wasn't much of an ask. To go live, the Domino had to be primed for a target. That meant jacking into its control panel with a physical device, an activator, and entering codes to unlock its preprogrammed targets. So without the codes, the activator was worthless. It seemed like more of a token, something to ask in exchange for a concession granted, a face-saver. So Preston readily agreed. Nazar would have a hard time refusing.

After the call, Preston went back to the computer screen, looking for the *Viking Prince*, but for some reason he couldn't find it. *Some glitch with the display…* that was his first thought. Maybe he needed to refresh the screen. But no. That didn't work.

The *Viking Prince* was gone!

He called Nazar.

"The freighter. It's gone. No signal."

Nazar fumbled for answers as Preston elaborated, explaining how he was tracking the ship via AIS.

"Oh, that… what does that matter? It's probably some technical thing. Schilder's man put a transponder in the container. He's not complaining, is he?" Nazar had a point. Schilder's techie had tagged the container itself, and he'd only spoken to Schilder minutes before. If that signal hadn't been coming through, he'd have screamed bloody murder. Even so, Preston ignored his question. He wasn't going to let him off the hook, and it was worth pressing the point just to put Nazar on the back foot. That way he'd have a hard time refusing Schilder's request. "I'm sure it's nothing," Nazar said, breaking the uncomfortable silence. "But I'll make a call and see what I can find out. In the meantime, what about my diamonds?"

"There's a condition. He says I've got to escrow the activator. No diamonds unless I'm holding the activator. So on D-Day, it's a simple exchange between you two, diamonds for codes."

There was a long silence before Nazar said, "Okay, I'll get it to you."

Twenty minutes later, Preston was staring at the screen when the icon reappeared, and soon after that, Nazar's call came through.

"It was something to do with the VDR," he said.

"What the hell is that?"

"The black box. Like on planes. They fixed a fuse, and it's all good now."

It wasn't all good. Preston hated crap like that. But he could see the ship was back on track now and he hadn't heard a squeak out of Schilder. Ships have electrical issues, especially an old freighter like this. So there was nothing more to be said.

"What about the activator? When can you get it to me?"

"Well… I'm hardly going to send it by FedEx. I'll fly down myself."

They made the arrangements, then Preston hung up and went downstairs to the bar. He was planning on making a martini, but he changed his mind and pulled a bottle of Petrus from the wine cabinet instead. He drew the cork and took it out on the terrace, where he doused the lights everywhere except underwater in the pool. He slumped into a lounger and looked across its eerily lit glow and beyond the darkness of the valley towards Africa and its black mountains starred with pixels of light. He'd forgotten the wineglass. No matter. He swigged the premium Pomerol from the bottle like a pirate with a bottle of rum, his brow furrowed with deep lines. It was still a good news day, but it had lost its shine. It wasn't just the vanishing freighter that was troubling him. It was Schilder's speedy acquiescence. Sourcing that amount of diamonds was a pain with all that clarity and cut business, carats and certificates. Preston had been anticipating a knock-down, drag-out fight for that one, but Schilder had hardly even squealed. Something was wrong about that. Something was wrong about a lot of things. He could feel it in his bones, and no amount of French plonk, even the three-thousand-dollar-a-bottle kind, was going to change that.

Jeanine was in her home, a bungalow in West LA, one of the few remaining on a street of condo buildings. She was in the living room sitting opposite a silent TV, with two phones on the coffee table in front of her.

Choices.

Which phone?

She could do the proper thing. Some might say the right thing. And call it in. That was the *her phone* choice, the head choice. Or she might do the crazy thing and pick up Ernald's phone and call Nevada, the heart choice. She'd been so certain in the Baldwin Hills, but following through was ripping her apart, doubt paralyzing her, with every which way fraught with downside. One of the phones chirped. That son of a bitch Ernald's phone… a message reminding her to call Las Vegas police. They knew she hadn't called yet. The phone was bugged. Of course, it was. They'd be tracking her every move, and every word she said on that phone would go straight back to them. For a moment, that did it, banging her up against a wall like that. Anger exploded inside her, then bubbled out. The phone was in her hand and she was dialing… *her phone*. She was calling it in, already rehearsing the details she'd relay to her colleagues. Within minutes, the blue brotherhood would be on it and she wouldn't be alone anymore. But she never finished dialing that number, rehearsals abandoned, stripped from her head by an image of Aidan. That blue-suit camaraderie would not make a damn bit of difference to him. He'd still be alone. He'd be counting on her. She grabbed the other phone. And even as she waited for the call to ring through, she knew it was the right thing, the crazy thing maybe, but the only choice she could live with.

After some preliminary exchanges, she was patched through to Detective Kazan, who told her that Brink hadn't been charged. But before she could explain anything, he was called into a meeting with the prosecutor, leaving her with a promise to call back within twenty-four hours.

No sooner had she hung up than she got another message, telling her to make two more calls.

Tricky ones.

To her boss at the station and the principal of Aidan's school. Prior to making these calls, she had to come up with a plausible sob story about an out-of-state relative who needed care. In this way, the note explained, she could get time off under the Family and Medical Leave Act. So now, she had to lie not only to an unknown detective but to people who trusted her, people she respected.

That hurt, but she did it.

It was only going to be for a week or two, the note said, and after she'd done it, she felt better anyway. With her mind clear, she could think this through and try to make sense of what was going on. Who were these people? And how was CJ involved? She went back to the photo he'd sent her, staring at her brother and his best friend.

What the hell was all this about?

Four

CJ had never been much of a second-guesser with weasel words like *if only* never passing his lips. But on this day, with the winds of fate blowing at hurricane force, they were hard to resist.

Timing.

It was all down to the clock.

Three hours.

That's how long it had taken the DA to green-light his release, and after a flurry of paperwork was signed off, he was on his way to freedom when his path was blocked by two men in blue jackets with US Marshal written on the back.

So that was it.

The missing three hours.

He would have been on his way to California to see Jeanine Solo. But that hadn't happened, and all because he'd kicked the cop's gun away. He'd been pretty sure the kid was dead, and another bullet would have been—what had Kazan called it?—*more force than necessary*. So safety-first, his military reflexes in overdrive, he'd cleared the gun before checking the kid. Only cops and crooks thought about evidence. So now, instead of the bus to California, he was getting a ride to…

"The UK?" he said, interrupting the torrent of boilerplate legalese from the lead marshal, a small man with wavy hair and pointy, foxlike features. "You're extraditing me?"

"Yes, sir, pursuant to the treaty of—"

"You have a warrant?"

The marshal held up a piece of paper. "All duly processed and signed off by the US Attorney's Office."

CJ ignored the document, his eyes zinging back and forth between the two men, the small, skinny one who continued his recital and the big one who was eying CJ speculatively.

"Judge?" CJ said, picking out a key word in the flow of verbiage. "I can see a judge?"

"A magistrate judge…"

"And have a trial?"

"A hearing. The judge checks the paperwork to determine if you are extraditable and certifies your extradition. That then gets passed to the secretary of state, who decides whether to surrender you."

"So what are my options?"

"You got one." This was the big marshal. It was the first time he'd spoken, a different accent, deep south. He leaned in on CJ. "This all has been fast-tracked like… *whoosh.*" He demoed a plane taking off with his hand. "That means someone important wants it to happen. That means it will happen. So you can choose to spend a few days as a guest of the federal government and stuff dollar bills in some lawyer's pocket while he dicks around filing this and that. Then, you'll get sent home. Or you can waive your right to a hearing and we'll get this signed off and you'll be on your way. Either way, you're going home, boy."

Fox-Face had listened to his colleague's improvised counsel with a grave expression, and when it was done, he said, "We are not authorized to provide legal counsel but to take you into custody and inform you of your rights. Do you understand your rights?"

CJ looked from one to the other in scant hope of a ray of joy, but there was none.

"Yeah… I got the right to get shipped back to Blighty and stitched up for a murder I didn't commit." He held out his arms ready for the restraints. "Let's get on with it."

Getting the extradition "signed off" was not quite the *whoosh* the US Marshal had promised, and even uncontested, his fast-lane paperwork took another day to get done. Even so, his point was well made. Between them, the marshals had more than forty years of experience in extraditions—both interstate and internationally—and neither of them could remember anything like it. That was the takeaway. So CJ spent the time lying on a mattress in a tiny cell, letting the marshal's judgment sound off in his head like a perpetual echo.

That means someone important wants it to happen.

On the face of it, it was the UK government. They wanted to bring him to justice. But that was a possibility he rejected out of hand. Even if they believed he was guilty in the UK killing—which they surely didn't—why fast-track it? There was something else going on here, some connivance between US and UK intelligence services. But who was driving it?

Someone important?

Someone like Vance Preston, a man with tentacles wrapped around powerbrokers in London and Washington.

When the formalities were completed, CJ was back on the road with the same two marshals in the same unmarked sedan, but this time they were joined by a uniformed officer who did the driving. An hour later, they pulled into an airport with a range of aircraft lined up in slots close to hangars. None of them looked big enough to make it across the Atlantic. They stopped by a plane where three men were waiting at the foot of the steps. The skinny marshal stepped out of the car and went to the men. IDs were flashed, and he went on board with one of them while the other two approached the car. CJ's cuffs were swapped for a new set that were hooked to a body belt. He didn't complain about any of this. It was no time to be a smartass. That'd be a fast track to a Hannibal Lecter mask.

As soon as the skinny marshal appeared at the top of the steps with a bundle of documents, CJ was boarded and the plane took off. He was expecting a Hollywood Con-Air plane rigged with cages. But this was your everyday executive Learjet with comfy seats and handy tables. He had the cuffs on, but otherwise his only restraint was the seat belt. One officer was sitting next to him, one across the aisle and one directly behind him. They were British alright. He'd heard them speak. But there was a lot wrong with what was going on, and it wasn't just the plane, although there was plenty wrong with that. Aside from its limited range, there was the expense. The cash-strapped British government would hardly be stumping up this kind of money to repatriate anyone, not unless he owed them a few million bucks and had the vault keys in his pocket. Repatriated offenders flew commercial, like everyone else, their tickets bought wholesale at cheapjack-airways.com. Even more troubling were the accompanying officers. Fetching home bad boys was a task left to regular cops with special training—stuff like fuselage restraint tactics, bodycuff usage, dynamic risk assessments and the paramedic skills to revive an offender accidentally strangled while being restrained. But for all that, they'd still be regular cops with that stoical I've-seen-it-all glow about them. No way did these guys fit that frame. They were twitchy, watchful, more like undercover cops, guys distracted by a secret.

CJ waited until the flight was well underway before voicing his doubts, tackling the issue with his usual blundering subtlety.

"I used to work with cops from your outfit. That was way back. You're Special Branch, right? No… wait. What do they call it these days? Counter Terrorism… thingummy?" No one spoke, but they all looked—first at him, then at each other. "So you still run errands for Mischief Incorporated?"

Nice one that, guaranteed to get a rise. Mischief Incorporated was a reference to MI6 and MI5, the UK's counterparts to the CIA and the FBI's counterterrorist units. Elite cops love that—to be called second-rate intelligence operatives.

"Is this bugger going to shut up, or do we have to gag him?"

It was the cop in the aisle opposite, a Scot, and clearly a no-nonsense one.

"You might as well tell him. He'll find out soon enough…" This from the cop in the seat behind.

The officer sitting next to CJ took a long breath like he was prepping a speech, but he barely managed a sentence.

"We're taking you to location in the US where—"

"Texas," the guy behind added. "*Yeehaw.*"

"Where what?" CJ said.

"Where some ugly bastard with scars on his face will stick a cattle prod up your arse until you sing soprano." That was the Scot again, his contribution quickly sanitized by the soft-spoken cop at CJ's side.

"You'll be debriefed by intelligence officers. Then you'll resume your trip to London, escorted by UK police officers."

"If you're bloody lucky," the Scot said.

So that was it. The fast-track extradition, the spiffy jet, the elite cops, it all added up to a simple piece of advice.

Hang onto your balls, CJ.

As CJ contemplated his sudden reversal of fortune, Preston sat on the terrace of his Spanish villa and fidgeted. He had demanded hourly updates on the Brink business. It was becoming a mess, a troubling distraction, but try as he might, he couldn't let it go. His festering anger made sure of that. He couldn't get it out of his mind—Brink doodling death plans on a dirty napkin in some tacky Nevada liquor store like he was some smalltime crack dealer who'd stepped out of line. Anger was screwing his judgment. He knew that too. His Putinesque gambit was absurdly ambitious. Ridiculous, in fact. How many martinis had it taken to come up with that? *Novichok on a lawyer's contract.* What was he thinking? Not only had his team struck out with Novichok, but all the alternatives were unworkable too. Ricin had to be breathed. Thallium looked promising at first, but the isotope they needed had to be injected. In other words, the cop sister would have to be in the loop. She'd have to know she was killing Brink, and that was sure to be one twist of her arm too far.

"Sir," Tony said, announcing his arrival as he walked out onto the terrace.

Preston spun around. "Well?"

Tony had this way of declaring bad news with his face. He'd have made a great town crier.

"What…? Dammit…"

"Brink's gone."

"What do you mean… *gone?*"

"Disappeared."

"This is not South America. They're Nevada cops. Not the CIA. They don't disappear people."

"They released him. Then he got arrested by US Marshals with extradition papers."

"So they're holding him?"

"No. They ran it all at warp speed and signed him over to British cops, who put him on a jet."

"No court hearing?"

"It gets weirder…"

"He's not *gone*, though." Preston leapt up out of the chair and it fell back, clattering on the marble. "He's in the UK, or on the way. Call Masterson in London, and—"

"I already did. That's the weird part. Here's what he says…" Tony whipped out his phone and consulted it. "*The CPS.*" He looked up at Preston. "That's the Crown Prosecution Service."

"I know what it is, dammit."

Tony went back to the message, reading nervously, "*Have withdrawn the warrant based on the strength of the evidence.* Then he adds this bit in parentheses. *This stinks. Watch out!*" Tony put his phone back in his pocket.

"The Brits jump through all these hoops to get him back, then decide they don't have a case. No way. What about air traffic control? Where did that plane end up?"

"We're on it. Nothing yet."

There was a long, empty pause after that. Preston composed himself and picked up the fallen chair. This wasn't like him, losing his cool. When he was settled back in the chair, Tony said, "What about the cop kid?"

Preston pointed an admonishing finger at him. "He's my insurance policy."

"But the Putin thing. That's a blowout."

"Forget that. But we keep the kid."

"And the mother?"

"Keep her sweet. String her along."

That damn phone…

Jeanine glowered at it. She was sitting at the kitchen table with four objects on it—the creep's phone, her 9mm pistol, her cop badge, and the framed photo of Alex and CJ. No photo of Aidan. She didn't need one. Aidan was there inside her like a living presence, even more now that he was gone, it seemed, than when he'd been growing inside her. That damn phone had become her life. Detective Kazan's twenty-four hours had come and gone and she was about to call him when it finally rang and she snatched it up. But it wasn't Kazan, it was Ernald…

"I called Nevada," she said. " I'm still waiting."

"Yes, nice work and all that. Only he won't be calling back. Brink's been extradited to the UK. Rather unexpectedly."

"The UK?"

"For murder, apparently. He gets around."

"Then you can release Aidan. I can't get to see Brink now. I won't file a complaint. Why would I? It'd be stupid."

"Yes it would. But my principals have not authorized that course of action."

"Why not?"

"Brink called you before he was arrested. Why?"

Since they knew about the call, there was no point in lying.

"He wanted to meet me, to tell me how Alex died."

"Call him back."

"Okay, sure. Like the British cops taking him back to the UK are going to let him take calls. They're only extraditing him for murder after all."

"Ever heard the word rendition?"

Jeanine ignored his question. "Let Aidan go. I can't help you. Brink's gone. He's out of US jurisdiction."

"That's exactly the issue. He's gone. But where? He left Nevada, but there's no trace of him since. Apparently, he's been extradited via the Bermuda Triangle."

Jeanine wobbled for a moment, cop curiosity wondering about that.

"Look, I don't know what your issue with Brink is, but it doesn't concern me or my son. And if you let him go now, I'll—"

"Shut up, woman, and listen. Open your mouth again and I'll drag your son to the phone and you can hear him scream while my partner pours scalding water on him. She's really good at that sort of thing."

Jeanine shut up, the blood draining from her cheeks, draining away like her strength, sucked into the black hole of fear opening up inside her.

"I'm listening," she said, meek and compliant through gritted teeth.

"That's better. I want us to get along. Aidan is fine at the moment. He is... *untouched* in every sense of the word. Harriet is taking good care of him. All is well. So concentrate on helping us, and it'll all be over soon. Our goal is killing Brink, but we can't find him. *Inconvenient...* you might say. That's where you come in. That's why I want you to call him. If you get through, act dumb about his arrest and extradition."

"And if I don't get through?"

"Keep trying. But he'll probably contact you anyway. They tell me he's the type who keeps promises."

"Okay, I agree to do it, but I need to see Aidan. If I get to see he's okay, I'll play ball."

There was silence and Jeanine steeled herself for a welter of abuse, but it never came.

"Very well," he said. "I'll arrange something. I'll call tomorrow."

He hung up and Jeanine called CJ, but as expected, there was no response. So what now? More waiting. That was what she was facing—a whole day to watch seconds ticking away while she waited for the only thing that might give her temporary relief from the emptiness twisting her guts. Aidan. Just seeing him, hearing his voice, knowing that he was alive and well would at least give her strength.

She picked up the photo of Alex and CJ and thought back to the coffeeshop where she'd stared at it, waiting for CJ, the sadness and joy she'd felt, two conflicting emotions spliced into one. Now all that was gone, replaced with a simmering anger. Ernald had filled in the blanks, the why of it all. They'd taken Aidan to get to Brink. Her son had become collateral in a feud between

Brink and Ernald's so-called principals. That was a revelation with plenty of ride-along baggage. Since Brink had spent most of the past decade in a coma, it had to be something going back to Iraq, and that pointed the finger at Tratfors.

For a second, she got excited about that—a connection, a suspect. Maybe she should call it in. But then, she set it aside. Even if Tratfors was behind it, they'd hardly be keeping Aidan in a filing cabinet at their downtown office. In fact, they'd have nothing to do with it. They'd have farmed it out to contractors. Alex had always told her about his concerns. The money in Iraq was great, but Tratfors was always a company that walked the line between legal and criminal with an unsteady gait. If she reported the kidnapping and pointed them at Tratfors, Aidan would be killed within minutes and his body buried so deep she'd never find it. If playing dumb and being useful was going to keep her son alive, then that was her future.

She picked up her pistol, her comfort pillow, and checked it. Ernald had mentioned that call from Brink. How did they know about that? Her eyes went back to the photo of Alex and CJ.

Brink, Brink, Brink.

If he hadn't contacted her, maybe none of this would have happened. She lashed out, smacking the photo frame off the table with the gun barrel. It was a stupid, uncontrolled act, and she regretted it even before the sound of glass smashing on the floor brought her to her senses. She put the gun down, took a long breath and held it before blowing it out slowly through her mouth. That sometimes worked, and it did help a bit this time. Something else that might be useful was a shot of JD.

Jeanine wasn't much of a drinker, but then this wasn't much of a day.

She took a bottle of Jack Daniels from a cupboard, splashed a generous measure on a few cubes of ice and sat at the table, staring at the mess on the floor. That hot temper again. How many times had it gotten her in trouble? She had to learn. She had to change. If she kept losing it like that, Aidan was a goner. She sipped the JD, the burn in her chest steadying her nerve. Then she set about cleaning up the mess. That precious photo. She'd get a new frame—something classy—and find a good spot for it.

She picked it up and carefully removed the remaining shards of broken glass still wedged in it. She was anxious not to damage the photo, but in the end she damaged herself, a glass fragment slicing her thumb. She put the frame on the table and washed the cut, then dried her hands on a paper towel and used it to sop up some blood too. It wasn't so bad and the bleeding soon stopped. She sat back at the table, finishing her whiskey in a long cool swallow before turning her attention to the photo.

Blood.

The photo had not escaped injury. CJ was now bloodied. It was nothing, really. She could wipe it off, but it was oddly upsetting. She cleaned out the rest of the glass, removed the photo and wiped it. There was still a faint stain there, but she didn't want to use a cleaner that might damage it even more. As she put the photo aside, she noticed something stuck to the frame's cheap cardboard backplate with Scotch tape. It was a SD memory card, the kind they use in cameras and tablets. Her first thought was, *That's it.* This had to be what they wanted from Brink. She fetched her tablet and slid it into the slot. But it was empty, the system prompting her to format it to make it usable. Why would CJ hide an empty memory card behind a photo of him and Alex and give it to her? It made no sense. She called CJ again, but there was still no reply.

She checked her watch. Only one hour had passed since Ernald's call. Almost a whole day to go. She took her gun to the bedroom and lay next to it on the bed, endless questions marshaling in her head…

But no answers.

Five

CJ didn't get that call from Jeanine, but she was in his thoughts. His phone was tucked away in his knapsack along with his passport and a roll of cash, all of which constituted the sum of his worldly goods. He looked out of the window as the plane taxied to a halt close by a ramshackle hangar built out of corrugated tin. The plane stopped, but the engines didn't, and CJ was still in his cuffs when he was deplaned by two of the British cops in a swirl of dust. They handed him off—along with his knapsack—to two men who had emerged from the hangar. One man stood back, holding a micro Uzi loosely in front of him where CJ would be sure to see it. The other man took CJ's knapsack and his cuff keys from the cops and led CJ by the arm towards what, on closer inspection, was more of a big shed than a hangar. And that was it. No roads, no pylons, or telephone poles. No sign of civilization.

Welcome to Texas.

Every armchair geographer knew Texas was big, and this place felt like it. Not real desert, but getting there. A wilderness of dirt held together by creosote bush and its drought-friendly cousins, bordered by low-rise mountains on a distant horizon. The double doors of the hangar were open, and CJ was led into the cool of its interior. No planes here, just a metal workbench serving as a table set between two chairs, and tall racks stocked with rusted bits of engines and aviation gear. From somewhere, a generator hummed, powering strip lights hanging on chains from its corrugated roof. There was a door at the back and windows on either side of it, and CJ could see a woman outside there, talking on the phone. He could tell by the antenna that it was a satellite phone, and no doubt she'd slipped out of the metal hangar on the south side to get a clear line of sight to a geostationary satellite. She was facing that way with her back to the hangar, her free hand gesturing as though her interlocutor was in front of her.

CJ didn't need to see her face. This was Alicia Colby, and CJ knew immediately that the plane's bumpy arrival was going to be the smoothest part of his ride all day. He was pushed down on a chair at the bench-cum-table and the two men took up positions behind him. CJ listened in on the conversation beyond the glass, but it wasn't easy. The cavernous building had strange acoustics, and the whine of the generator and the roar of jet engines outside didn't help. But by fine-tuning his amped-up senses, he caught a few words, although they didn't mean much to him.

Yes, I meant it … don't say that … we will … when this is over … I promise. Colby looked over her shoulder and saw CJ. *Brink's here … let's do this.* She hung up and strode out of the office, leaving the door ajar.

"Hello, Alicia," CJ said, upbeat and chummy, like they were old friends. They certainly had a history, but all of it was bad. They had met twice, both encounters shot through with mistrust. All he knew about her was that she had once been an MP in Iraq and she'd worked forensics on the site where he and Alex had been held hostage by terrorists. Later, she'd found her way into some sort of intelligence role. He'd pegged her as a CIA operative attached to some special activities group. She was part of a transatlantic double act, partnered by an MI6 ooze-bag called Ashford.

She ignored his greeting, picking a satchel up off the chair opposite, sticking it on the table and dropping her phone inside it. She studied him awhile, big brown eyes coasting up and down, before taking off her suit jacket and arranging it neatly on the back of the chair. She was wearing a shirt with vertical black-and-white stripes, collar undone, and a red silk scarf hanging from a tight knot at her throat. There wasn't too much to that scarf, and in the gaps between it and the shirt—where the skin might have been—CJ spied the matte black of her Kevlar vest. The small-frame 9mm on her hip completed the getup, not so much government agent as a Wall Street banker heading for a meeting with a cartel capo. She stepped around to CJ's side of the table, reached back as though she was going to get something from the satchel, but twisted back suddenly, smashing her fist into his face. She hit him so hard his chair toppled backwards, but she grabbed his jacket with her other hand and jerked the chair upright. CJ coughed and spluttered, spitting blood at her as she walked back to her side of the table. She opened the satchel and took out some tissues, tossing a few towards him and using the rest to wipe blood off the table.

"Undo the cuffs," she said.

As one of the men followed through, the other one pointed the Micro Uzi at CJ's head. It had now been accessorized with a compensator—not exactly standard issue for US law enforcement types, but pretty much a weapon of choice for clearing a building the size of this hangar, or stitching a line of holes in his back. In Las Vegas, there'd been talk of his ending up on death row—a bad-news future to be sure. But everything's relative, and compared to a shallow grave in the desert before sundown, it hadn't been such a bad option after all.

The men stepped back and CJ picked up a handful of tissues and mopped up the blood from his mouth. He went to speak, but it was more of a splutter…

"What was that for?"

Colby pulled out more tissues.

"Old times' sake." She tossed them across the table, then made a fist and waggled her thumb. But it wasn't a thumbs-up. It was a reminder. She'd pulled a gun on him in LA, and he'd snatched it off of her. Her thumb had been a casualty of that encounter, and evidently, it had not yet found its way into her forgive-and-forget file. "It wasn't meant to be that hard. I guess you just bring out the best in me." She sat down. "Besides, we don't have much time, and I remember well your love of witty repartee. So I thought that might help us cut to the chase and establish the parameters of our new relationship."

"Relationship?" CJ could barely speak through the wads of tissue in his mouth, but that word had to come out.

"There, you see, it already worked. You're engaged." CJ grunted, his eyes following Colby as she took two envelopes out of the satchel and put them on the table. "Here's the deal. Either you cooperate—in which case you get a new ID and a clean slate—or you don't, and you get back on that plane and continue your trip to London."

"That plane already left."

"Oops… I'd say that narrows your options."

"You can't rendition me? I'm an ex—"

"Human being… you no longer exist. Do you have an ID?"

"Sure. A passport." He nodded at the Uzi man who'd taken his knapsack.

Colby kept her eyes on Brink and flicked her fingers, beckoning her man over. He put the knapsack on the table and Colby retrieved the passport. She thumbed through it, disinterested, before pulling out a lighter. It had a flame like a mini blowtorch, and when the passport was burning up nicely, she tossed it in the dirt by his chair.

"Not anymore," she said. "And word is—the UK government is not going to be giving you a replacement anytime soon."

CJ watched it burn as he peeled bloodied tissue paper off his busted lip.

"Not much of a relationship from my point of view, is it?" he said.

"It gets better." She opened an envelope and tossed a passport on the table.

Guinness…

That was CJ's first thought when he saw the harp on the cover. But this was an EU passport, not a bottle of stout.

"Irish?" he said.

"Calan Jake Flynn. So you can still be CJ."

"Is it real?"

CJ picked it up and examined it.

"So long as you're not planning a trip to Dublin anytime soon." Colby took a Visa card out of the envelope too and placed it on the table.

Calan? He liked the name. Much better than his own hated Christopher, and the passport certainly looked real.

He put it back on the table. There was no price tag hanging off it. There didn't need to be.

"I'm not an assassin," he said.

"Oh really? So what explains the body count in your vicinity?"

"I was serving military back then."

"I'm not talking ancient history or long-forgotten wars. I'm talking last week in Nevada and Los Angeles."

CJ's eyes kept drifting back to the passport. It was a ticket to freedom, washing away bad-boy Brink's dirty deeds with a single stroke.

"Who?"

"Do you need me to tell you?"

She was right. There was only one candidate.

Lieutenant Colonel Vance Preston.

"Where is he?"

"Spain."

CJ torqued his head, catching the sound of a distant plane, and judging by the grind of its single propeller, it was a lot more Buddy Holly than Learjet. Colby checked her watch.

"It'll be here in about ten minutes. In case you were wondering. That's how long you've got to decide. That plane will hop over the border and you'll be in Mexico. From there, you'll head down to Panama, then you fly to Madrid. Here's your itinerary and tickets." She reached into her satchel one last time and tossed an envelope on the table.

"And Calan... what's his story?"

"He's a best boy."

"C'mon…"

"Seriously. He works for Icon Dreams Inc., a movie equipment and staffing agency. He's a best boy grip. He's responsible for all the other grips and for making sure the right equipment is at the right location at the right time. You'll report to the production controller. Her name is Paz." She waited, but CJ stayed silent, mulling it all. This was big money. A fake movie company? That was brilliant. Ever since the spaghetti westerns, Hollywood had been making action films, supposedly set in the US, in Spain. Movies needed lots of equipment, boxes full of stuff. Sometimes they needed explosives and weapons, and other items hard to explain. And it wouldn't be the first time US intelligence agencies had used a fake company. Iran-Contra was a history lesson for CJ, but it was one he'd read more than once. In the Reagan era and under the auspices of the National Security Council, the US had sold arms to Iran and funneled the proceeds to rebels in Nicaragua with both legs of the operation illegal under US law.

"Eight minutes," Colby said.

CJ didn't need eight minutes, or even eight seconds. Back in the day when he was a philosopher scribbling on napkins, he'd planned to walk away, but philosophers were dreamers. Passports were real, and he couldn't keep his eyes off this one. Too bad about the caveat. It was so obvious it might have been written on its Special Observations page. He'd been selected on merit. He had a motive. His grievance towards Preston was documented. He was expendable and could be taken out in a tidying-up operation when the mission was accomplished. And failing that, he was blamable. He was suffering from PTSD. He hallucinated ghosts. His brain was the weak link at the end of a chain of traumas and accidental surgeries that it had no right to survive.

Best boy?

He was more like patsy-supremo. So maybe he would kill Preston and maybe not, but one thing he was not going to do was say no.

"What's to stop me doing a bunk," he said, "disappearing with my nice new passport?"

"Why would you? Tratfors is hunting you. We could always help them find you. Besides… what about your ghosts?" CJ's face clouded over. "I've got your complete medical record. Those ghosts are never going to let you rest. You survived. They didn't. You're their strong right arm. You're an inheritor. Their scores are yours now, and until you settle them, you'll never find peace. I think you know all that." CJ's eyes drifted down to the table, unable to face her. She'd pulled out a trump card. It was true. He'd daydreamed in Nevada about a different pathway to peace, and reaching out to Jeanine Solo had been part of that. But can such a past as his be purged by turning your back on it? "If you play ball, we'll keep your new ID secret."

"Who's we?"

"Me, of course. And Paz."

"She's with the agency?"

"She's a contractor like you. You'll need her. She's local."

"You trust her?"

"With my life."

CJ fingered the passport again. "What about Ashford?"

"Don't worry about him."

"But I do. I worry about you too. You guys used to be in bed with Preston. Now you want him dead. Why?"

"He hasn't worked for us since his guys killed those civilians way back in Iraq. The media shitstorm all but buried us."

"So why now? Closure? All those times Preston got his hands dirty keeping your hands clean."

"No comment. Disclosure's done. Ashford's in Europe. He's there if we need him. But you report to Paz, and she reports to me. In other words"—she stood up and leaned across the table, towering over him—"I own your ass."

CJ rolled his eyes up at her as he licked the blood off his lips. This was another good moment to keep them zipped.

Colby eased back and checked her watch. "If I don't call that pilot now, he heads back to Mexico. And we"—she glanced at the two Uzi men—"clean up, and kick off plan B."

The message couldn't have been plainer.

CJ nodded and Colby headed out the back door with her satellite phone. He stood up casually and stretched, then pocketed his new passport and Visa card and reached over the table to drop the ticket into his knapsack. That's when he saw it—an exchange between the Uzis. No words. Just a glance and the slightest of nods. CJ sat back on the chair as though he'd seen nothing. But it wasn't a nothing. It was a big something. He played it back. Something had changed. No more relaxed Uzis. Now they were keyed up and ready. The deal was done. He was on the team. So why was the tension ratcheting up? He'd seen enough men primed for action to know the signs. An exchange like that was usually the prelude to a noisy finale. He was still wearing the restraint belt where his hands had been pinned to his belly. He reached around his back and unbuckled it, placing the belt and the cuffs on the table in front of him but keeping his hands on them, his eyes on Colby as she came back through the door and stopped, his worst fears written all over her face.

At that moment, in California, Jeanine's smoldering anger was about to burst. She'd done everything Aidan's kidnappers had demanded. She'd called Brink repeatedly, using the kidnapper's phone as well as her own in case he was not picking up for the unknown caller. Either way, there'd been no response. She'd done her side of the deal. But then, nothing. The insect had said twenty-four hours, but this was closer to forty-eight. So where was that video call they'd promised her?

What if it never came?

That was the new fear tormenting her. She'd curse herself for not phoning it in.

Waiting, waiting…

Time was a torturer, sending her mind spinning. It wandered relentlessly, navigating a zigzag path between planning and wishful thinking. She'd get Aidan back. That was the gist of it. She'd set up a meeting with Ernald and ambush him. She'd get him under her control. Then he'd talk. He'd tell her where they were keeping Aidan. He'd even volunteer the best way to get him back. He'd be more than helpful. She'd see to that. She had a power toolkit in the garage. She'd see how long he'd last with his elbow in a vise and a metal drill bit buzzing through it.

Jeanine jumped up off the couch, shaking the latest revenge fantasy out of her head. She had to get a grip. She was losing it, her professionalism, even her humanity. Rage and anxiety was breeding hate.

The phone rang. She snatched it up.

"These are your new instructions," Ernald said.

"I'm listening."

"Hang tight."

"That's it?"

"Your son is—"

"You show me him alive and well right now, or that's it. I'm calling it in."

"I don't believe you."

He'd called her bluff. But was it a bluff? She had no idea. It had just come out of her. She was a cop. She knew the stats. This was a stranger kidnapping of a child—a pretty rare event, with only a few hundred a year reported in the US—and the chances were good, with a survival rate of ninety percent or better. But how many went unreported? No statistics on that. Stranger abductions were classified by type according to the goals of the perpetrators, and the two things she knew for sure about this one were a comfort and a terror. They had a specific want. If she complied, she'd be highly likely to get Aidan back unharmed. That was the comfort part. But it was the terror part that ravaged her. The sniper, the deep fake voice stunt. This was an organized crime operation, the most likely perpetrators to use violence if thwarted. And finally, the horror stat... seventy-four percent of abducted children who are eventually murdered are dead within three hours of being taken.

"He's dead already," she said. She didn't believe it— she couldn't—but she had to say it.

Ernald took a long time—forever by Jeanine's reckoning—but then she got what she wanted. He told her to download an encrypted message app and said he would call back. She wanted to threaten him again, give him a time limit. But thankfully, she held her tongue.

Fifty minutes later, she was sitting at the kitchen table when the call came through, but it wasn't what she wanted. It wasn't interactive. It was a canned video. So she couldn't comfort her son and that was a loss that hit her hard. But at least it was current. Aidan was standing in a driveway of white stone chips with a wall on one side and oleander bushes on the other. He'd been crying and the tracks of it still wetted his face. He was wearing clothes she'd never seen before. A woman was standing beside him, holding his hand, with only the lower half of her body visible. In her other hand, she held a tablet computer, tuned in to CNN's web page. Jeanine took a snapshot of her phone screen, getting a permanent record. She could check the CNN site later, but it was obvious from the headlines that the video was made today.

The woman yanked Aidan's hand, some sort of prompt, and he winced and said, "I'm okay, Mom." Another yank and he yelped before saying, "They want me to say you should do what they tell you." Jeanine fought a mounting rage. That woman. She wasn't going to forget her in a hurry. She had no face to remember, but what she could see was fleshing out her personal identikit wanted poster. That loose skirt, those ankle boots, socks, and bare legs. Her hands. No rings. No jewelry. Her skin. Its color and condition. Nails, knuckles. Jeanine was stacking the details away, and it was damn hard to stop those fantasies from spinning. She'd find that woman one day, and break both of those arms.

Preston cut a lonely figure as he awoke in his four-poster bed, summoned by the chirping phone at his side.

He slid his sleep mask up on his forehead, rocked onto his elbow and snatched it up.

"Tell me."

Tony's call in the night was always good news. He wouldn't dare wake Preston for anything less. "We got a hit from air traffic. Brink's plane touched down in Texas."

"Let me guess… a few miles from nowhere."

"You got that right. Down by the border. A ways out of El Paso. An airstrip that never made it onto Google Maps. The DEA ran a sting on some guys there a few years back, and from there it found its way into a government inventory of useful places that don't exist."

"No roads, no trails?"

"Yep, you get there with wings, or else you crawl."

Preston checked the clock on his phone, studying the preset time zones and calculating. It was still afternoon in Texas, and it would be night before he could get that airstrip checked out.

"What else do we know about the place?" he said.

"Not much. There's some makeshift building. It was abandoned way back, so it's beat up."

"Contact LA. I want a team there at first light—"

"He sure as hell won't be there then. My guess is—"

"We don't know that. And there might be a lead if he's not."

"Okay, so what's the deal?"

"Four guys. Dawn. Fly by and report. I'll take personal control from there."

"Fully operational?"

"What else?"

Preston tossed the phone aside and stretched out on the bed. He slid the red silk mask back over his eyes, but sleep was elusive, slipping in and out between strings of muttered abuse.

Brink... you bastard.

Six

Double-cross...

CJ read it on Colby's face even before she went for her gun and that first round hit her. He dived under the metal table and upended it as a welter of 9mm rounds chewed up his chair and pockmarked the table. He readied himself and glanced back at Colby. She'd gotten off a few shots, maybe four or five, but that was over now. Automatic gunfire was pounding her vest and knocking her backwards, her arms flailing, her gun slithering in the dirt.

CJ burst from cover, rolling and jumping as he flung the restraint vest and cuffs at the lone gunmen. Colby had evidently made her few shots count and taken out the second Uzi. The man dodged the vest and in that split-second, CJ was gone, slipping behind a rack of engine parts. A cascade of bullets followed him, ricocheting off rusting metal. Then the shooting stopped. CJ couldn't see the man, but he could hear him. He was sliding a new clip into his Uzi. He could see Colby, a glimpse through machine parts. She was on her back, her hand making small movements as though she was reaching for something. Her gun, maybe. But that was yards away, and anyway her shooting days were over.

CJ dodged around the next rack and then two more rows. There were eight racks in total, some heavily loaded with parts, others stacked more sparsely. It was a maze, but not a big one. They could play hide-and-seek for a while, and that was a game where CJ's inhuman hearing range gave him an edge. But sooner or later, the Uzi would get lucky. He was working the racks methodically now, no more wasting rounds with random bursts, but stalking back and forth along the aisles. CJ had to change the game or die. If he could get to Colby's gun, it would help. But even if he made it, he'd end up with a handgun with no cover in a gunfight with a guy blasting twelve hundred rounds a minute.

CJ darted another row back and grabbed an engine part off a shelf. He didn't know what it was, but that didn't matter. It was the size and shape he was looking for, a shaft with a lump at the end giving it the shape of a club, although going up against a submachine gun with an improvised club was not what he had in mind. He tossed it so it flew up above the racks and tumbled down somewhere around where the Uzi was pacing. Where exactly didn't matter. He wasn't looking for a miracle, some random chance that he might take the guy out. It wasn't a diversion either. It was a mask, hitting the top of a rack and skidding off, dragging something with it in a chained clatter of sounds. CJ used it to scale a rack, changing the game and shifting the odds.

Now he had two things going for him. The most comforting was the thick steel shelf he was lying on. It was built to support aircraft engines. There were bullets that might go through it, but they weren't in a 9mm Uzi.

The high ground gave him offensive opportunities too. That odd-looking shaft-club he'd tossed was not the only throwable weapon. There were boxes of steel junk of all shapes and sizes, much of which could be dropped or tossed. He lay flat, listening. With little ambient sound, the gunman's muffled footfalls made it easy to map his progress. CJ looked around, noticing that the closest rack was not stacked in a logical way, with heavy objects like engine blocks on the bottom shelf and lighter objects higher up. It was top-heavy, with the upper shelves loaded with heavy gear.

The gunman was two rows away. He got to the end of his row and paused, then slowly paced it, ghosting from side to side as he checked the blind spots. CJ was crouched, counting his steps, waiting until he was in the middle of the row. Then he leapt across the aisle onto the overloaded top shelf of the next rack, expecting his flying 230 pounds to topple the rack. There was a burst of gunfire as he hit the rack, and for a moment, it all seemed to have failed, with the rack rocking unsteadily. But then it hit the point of no return and over it went, crashing into the next and triggering a domino effect, the neighboring racks tumbling in turn as CJ rode the chaotic jumble of crashing steel. The gunfire stopped abruptly and CJ scrambled off the debris.

No gunfire. No screams.

CJ surveyed the wreckage. No sign of the gunman, hidden somewhere under a mess of steel. He raced back to Colby. She was motionless, her throat shot out, her silk scarf in tatters. He picked up her gun and switched the clip for a fresh one he found in her pocket. A sound caught his attention and he looked beyond the open doors as a small plane approached the makeshift runway. He was about to head out towards it when another sound stopped him. A groan. That second gunman was alive. CJ stuck Colby's 9mm in his belt and picked up the Uzi of the gunman she'd shot, then clambered over the debris of fallen racks and engine parts and soon found the gunman. He'd been trapped by two shelves, with one pinning his legs and the other his arm. His body had miraculously escaped damage. The man's eyes flared as CJ kicked a box aside and aimed the Uzi at him. He'd evidently lost his in the melee.

"Please," the man said. "My leg's broken. Help me. I got money. Anything."

CJ lowered the gun and peered closer. The man's leg was well broken, with bones poking through skin. He was sweating profusely, his face pulsing with pain.

CJ crouched next to him. "You need help," he said, "and so do I."

The man whined and rolled back. "Just get this damn thing off me and I'll tell you anything."

"I was thinking more along the lines of… you go first."

"I can't think. I can't talk."

CJ put the Uzi aside and found a square steel bar, an axle. "This should take the weight," he said, sliding it under the rack and levering it with a good heave-ho. The man went to grab his leg and pull it free as the shelf eased up. But CJ dropped the rack with a jolt. The man screamed and writhed.

"Sorry, mate," CJ said. "It's a bit heavier than I thought."

The man's screaming died into sobs. CJ waited as he sobbed out his pain and self-pity, standing soberly, the axle held like a staff in one hand. "Tratfors?" he said finally.

"What?" The man's voice was barely a whisper.

"You're working for Tratfors, right?"

The man screwed up his face. "The security guys?" he said. "Hell no." He sucked down air in rasping gasps.

"So who?"

"I don't know. I hang out in an invitation-only chat room on the dark web. People hire me. They pay with crypto. I don't know who the hell they are. I swear."

It was plausible. The dark web was an anonymous network created for American spies, enabling them to bypass WWW by using a new system called The Onion Router, or TOR. But since that had meant anyone using it was a spy, they'd made it public to cover their tracks, and now it was the platform of choice for kiddie porn peddlers, illicit drug and gun sales, and evidently, rent-a-killer.

"What's it called?"

"Wetslope…"

"How come Colby didn't spot you?"

"She was told there'd be two guys to back her up. That's all."

"So where are her guys?"

"In back," he said, nodding towards the other end of the hangar. "What the hell do you care anyway? You've got your passport, and I can give you hundreds of Bitcoins. Move this rack off me and help me out of here and your net worth goes up a million dollars. We could work together. I need a new partner anyway."

He wasn't the only one. With Colby dead, Ashford would be half a team, and what did that mean for his assignment to head to Spain, hook up with Colby's contact and kill Preston? The assault of the Uzis had left CJ unscathed, but he was still bleeding from Colby's auld-lang-syne punch. He wiped the blood from his mouth as he stared down at the man, wondering if he had any more to give him.

"See what she did to me?" He showed the man the blood he'd wiped onto the back of his hand. "I should hate her. She was a real hard case, but I liked her. The truth is I fancied her, although I could see that wasn't mutual…"

"C'mon, man. The bitch is dead."

"I know… you shot her throat out…"

"Screw her."

"And I was next."

"We're both alive. Let's move on. Do the smart thing."

Beyond the hangar doors, the approaching plane was calling time on CJ's efforts to get to the truth. He glanced back towards Colby, then down at the gunman.

"The smart thing?" he said before raising the axle and looking at it thoughtfully. "Like helping you instead of killing you… some bastard who knows my new ID, who hides behind a computer and sells his loyalty for Bit-things. You got me all wrong, pal. As I told Colby, I'm not an assassin. For me, it's never business. It's always personal. Besides, I want you to deliver a message to your unknown employer on behalf of CJ Brink and Alicia Colby." He hefted the axle above the gunman like a spear and rammed its squared-off point through his belly until it cracked hard on the floor. The man pincered up, then slumped back, eyes and mouth gaping, a silent scream of blood oozing from his mouth.

CJ let go his spear. He could hear the plane close to the hangar doors and wondered about the pilot.

Who would he expect to come walking out that door?

Just him, according to Colby, but surely not carrying a submachine gun. So he left the Uzi. Colby's 9mm pistol was a much more easily concealed carry, and with that tucked in his belt, he stepped out into the sunlight and headed towards the plane as it taxied to a halt.

When dawn came to the silent Texas airstrip, Preston and Tony were in the panic room of Preston's Marbella villa. Tony was sitting behind the computer, working the keyboard, and Preston was pacing, stopping only when the first live camera feed popped up on the wall monitors. He was pumped, doped up on caffeine, that ragged sleepless night long gone. The big screen in the middle was first to fire up with the feed from Max's headcam. He was the team leader. Tony set up the rest of the connections and when all four streams were coming through, he flipped on the audio and Max delivered his report. They'd flown by twice already, then made a low pass, hedgehopping to get eyeballs into the building. There was no sign of life. No planes, no vehicles, no personnel. They had a drone on board and Max wanted to know if they should deploy it to take a closer look, but Preston dismissed the idea, telling them to get down there.

After a jarring landing, the team entered the building, and as Preston watched the images, the energy pump that had had him pacing like a panther only minutes before wheezed to a halt. He'd seen this mission as simple. Like a coin flip. Either the team would find the airstrip empty, the trail stone-cold—or they'd find Brink and whoever else and deal with them appropriately. But instead, he had this…

Chaos.

It looked like a tornado had passed through the hangar, and this being Texas, that might have been the case were it not for the bodies and the bullet holes.

"Is one of those bodies Brink?" Preston said, his faint hope twined with creeping doubt.

No Brink, just his aftermath.

It was sickening, and what made it worse was this eerie feeling that he'd been through it all before, that this wasn't a live show but a recording, somehow familiar, a forgotten nightmare making an encore. The Brink effect...

"Chaos." Preston repeated his judgment out loud. Brink was contaminated with it. The man was a human wrecking ball aimed at Preston and the organization he'd spent almost three decades building.

"Looks like this one got caught by the Uzis," Max said. "Black. Female." The commentary was hardly necessary. Preston and Tony could see for themselves as he rolled Colby over. "She's got a vest on, but she took it in the throat." Max checked her pockets. No ID. But Preston didn't need one.

"Alicia Colby." He intoned it like a snooty maître d' announcing the arrival of an unwelcome guest.

"What's she?" Tony said.

"She turned up in LA with a Brit spook." It took Preston a while to get there. "Ashford. They were trailing Brink. Or that's what we figured anyway. But I always wondered if it was me they were really after and Brink had just stumbled into the frame." Preston nodded, confirming his own thoughts as he watched the search in the rubble.

Colby?

He'd been right, not paranoid. They had to be using Brink to get to him.

"There's another one," Max said as he clambered over a tumble of fallen racks. Preston studied the dead man with an axle poking out of his belly, his legs and arms crushed by a rack.

"It's not Brink," Max said. "Looks like falling debris got this one."

"Idiot," Preston hissed to Tony. "That's Brink's work. He might just as well have signed it. Straight through the liver. Look how the flesh is burst open. That shaft was slammed home, then pumped like a jack."

"So Brink got the jump on them?" Tony said.

In the company of such heavily armed escorts, that hardly made sense. Then again, nothing about Brink made sense, and if not him, then who?

They watched the search forlornly until Max found a leather satchel and they both perked up. Max checked inside and pulled out a satellite phone.

"Jackpot." Preston slammed his fist into the palm of his hand. "Check it out. Last calls." They waited impatiently, following Max's progress as he stepped outside through the back door. He soon found a signal and checked time stamps and calls.

"Country code 34," he said, although they could see the numbers for themselves. "Same number. Plenty of calls." Tony used his phone to shoot a photo and capture the number. "And a couple of calls to 44. What do you want me to do with it?"

Preston made no reply, his jackpot moment gone at a stroke. Those +34 calls were to a Spanish number. No doubt about it now. Colby was setting up Brink to take him out.

"Spain," Tony said, "we can link that to an ID."

It was a nice thought. Burner phones didn't exist in Spain. Ever since the 2004 Madrid train bombings, an official ID document had been required to purchase a SIM card, and the cards issued were PIN-locked. But Preston was less than hopeful.

"Dream on," he said sourly. Whoever Colby's Spanish contact was, they certainly weren't using a phone linked to an ID. As for 44, the UK, that had to be Ashford.

"What now, sir?" Max said.

"Keep looking for Brink's body. Don't leave until you've checked under every nut and bolt. When you're done, leave an incendiary. I don't know what all this means, but I sure as hell don't want someone else figuring it out." That was a lie, or half a lie anyway. He knew what was behind this strange assignation in the Texas wilderness. Ashford and Colby had actioned an unofficial, but government-sponsored, hit on him, and the timing, one week before D-Day, meant that they knew about Domino and planned to stop it. But that still left the mystery of what had happened here.

He waved instructions, fingers across the throat… and as Tony shut down the links, he said, "Get on air traffic again. If Brink survived, he'd have taken a plane south of the border. Find him."

Seven hours later, Preston was eating a sparse and lonely dinner at a banquet table when Tony interrupted him.

"You were right," he said. "Brink went south. There was a blip. Then it was gone. Just a hop over the border."

"And the phone numbers?"

"The Spanish number dead-ends at the UK embassy in Madrid. It was part of a bundle. Diplomatic immunity. So no IDs required. The UK number was a burner."

"Any trace of Brink?" Preston had already guessed, but he had to ask.

Tony shook his head.

So that was it. Brink was on his way. A few days before, he'd been a vague threat, motivated and dangerous, but still just one man. Now he had backing, intel and gear, provided by the world's most sophisticated intelligence agencies. If it weren't for Domino, Preston could go to ground, bury himself so deep he'd be safe; instead of that, he was about to host a mammoth party. Covering up the Domino exchange with a massive social event had seemed like a good idea. Now it looked suicidal.

"We've still got the kid," he said, reassuring himself as much as reminding Tony.

"We could lure him in and kill him," Tony said.

Preston was thinking more along the lines of using him as a Brink repellent, but Tony's idea had merit. "Get the kid over here," he said.

"Whoa… a kidnapped kid across borders?"

"Sedate him, stick him in a trunk and fly him out of Orange County in the jet along with his babysitters. And I want Max and his team on the same plane too. We're going to need reinforcements."

"And the mom?"

Preston had no ready answer, pacing back and forth, running scenarios. Then he stopped and said, "Tell her to pack her suitcase."

Jeanine snatched up the phone. She lived for that phone now, her heart soaring with hope each time it rang.

"Anything?" It was Ernald, the voice she waited on, the voice she both hated and hoped for with an abiding passion.

"He still won't pick up the phone."

"Keep trying. He's been flying. And you're going to join him. Book a ticket to Madrid."

"What? *Spain* Madrid?"

"You know any other?"

"Is this a joke?" Jeanine's words were cut with anger, with the pain of waiting, of not knowing, and more and more, she was angry with herself for not calling in the abduction on day one.

"Your son is in Spain, or he will be by the time you get there, and I'm authorized to arrange for an interactive video call between you both as soon as you arrive. Until then, you get nothing. No contact, no updates."

Her thoughts raced. *Our goal is killing Brink.* That's what they'd said. Did they expect her to do that? A police officer? By threatening Aidan with some unimaginable horror if she didn't? Fear made her tremble. Something new. Not a fear for Aidan—that was a constant—but something even more terrifying, casting a shiver right through to her soul. She'd do it. That was the fact of it. To save Aidan, she'd kill Brink.

She forced herself to take control, trampling her fears with reason. They wouldn't ask her that. The outcome was too uncertain. These people were calculating monsters. They'd go for something they could control and get guaranteed results. She was bait. That was it. They'd use her as bait to get to Brink. They'd use Aidan too. Then—whatever the outcome—they'd both be killed. The realization calmed her. They weren't the only ones who could calculate.

"Is this still about Brink?" she said.

"He planned to meet you, then he didn't show. When he starts something, he finishes it. So he'll follow up on that for sure."

"And he's in Spain?"

"So I'm told."

"So he calls me and I say, *Gee, what a coincidence! I'm in Spain too. Let's meet up.*"

"Try it. Maybe it'll work. If not, tell him you're in Spain because your son has been kidnapped and that he will live only if Brink abandons his mission."

"What mission?"

"He'll know, and you don't need to."

Jeanine was stumped, her brain reeling. "That's it?" she said.

"Do whatever is necessary. Beg him. Seduce him. You're a woman for God's sake. You need a roadmap? Brink is a knight in shining armor. So play the maiden in distress. Tell him your son's life depends on him. He'll offer to help you get the kid back. Connive with him. Say anything, do anything. Just get close to him—"

"And then?"

"You'll get your son back."

"What if he refuses to meet me?"

"Oh dear… are you sure you want the answer? Hint, hint. There's a ready market for virgin white boys in Morocco. Or so I've heard."

She had to fight after that, struggle to stay in control and not rise to the bait.

"Okay," she said finally, "I'll do it. I'll get to him. I'll kill him if I have to… but I'll stop him."

Ernald went quiet on hearing that, and Jeanine was pretty proud of her theater.

"Now you're talking," he said.

It was CJ's first trip to Panama, and it was a short one. He was waiting in the departure lounge at Tocumen International Airport, having just made it in time for his flight to Madrid. He'd hopped over the border only so far as a dirt field in the mountains. From there, he'd been driven in a truck off-road to a blacktop that grew into a highway and ended up in Monterrey, where he'd dumped the gun before taking a commercial flight to Panama. All of which had taken twenty-four hours and given him plenty of time to think. He had a fresh ID. He could disappear. The plastic they'd given him would be useless, and his bank accounts would be locked up. But he had his bankroll, enough to get him started. The problem with that was the itch troubling him ever since he'd stepped out of that hangar in Texas. Someone had taken out Colby and tried to take him out too. Logically, someone who wanted to stop him from killing Preston, and the most obvious candidate was Preston himself. Back in Nevada, he'd chosen to walk away from the vendetta. But now Preston had played him back into the game. All this was spinning around in his head, but so was Panama.

In a hurry to get lost?

Panama's your place. The Pacific on one side, the Caribbean and the Atlantic on the other, the whole of the Americas to the north and south, and everywhere else just a boat ride away. Panama is the Cadillac of bolt-holes. It was enticing. But what about that itch? He took a long last look at the ticket, still juggling options. Then he checked into the Madrid flight, and with that scratch sorted, he turned his attention to the other itch that had been troubling him ever since his arrest in Nevada. He bought a phone and made the call.

"Jeanine… at last."

"CJ?"

"Sorry… I got arrested."

"Are you in Spain?"

"What! Who told you that?"

"They took Aidan…" CJ was about to say *Who?* when the answer came to him. "I'm on my way to Spain," she said. "That's where he is. And they said that if you don't quit—"

"They'll kill him." There was an icy silence following that. "Jeanine?"

"What the hell are you doing that's worth my son's life?"

"Tell 'em I quit. We can fix this." He wanted to sound convincing, but the lie wasn't easy.

"I think they could do it, too… actually kill a child."

"They won't. Don't think that. They need him alive. I'll back off. We're going to get Aidan back. Keep telling yourself that."

"Why do they want you dead?"

"They said that?"

"They want me to seduce you, then kill you." CJ was stunned. Not by what she'd said, but the fact that she'd said it upfront. It told him a lot about her smarts as well as her character. She had to know there was no way these people would let any of them live. Even so, her son had been abducted because of him, but she was still reaching out and trusting him.

"Don't beat up on yourself. You did the right thing." No doubt about that. But there was something weird about this revelation, a timing thing, and it took him a moment to spot it. "When did they take Aidan?"

"Right after you were arrested. Before you were extradited." That didn't make sense. If Preston already had Aidan—a hostage guaranteed to stop CJ in his tracks—then why stage the killings in Texas? That had to be someone else. "Who are these people? Why do they want you dead?"

"Because some things I don't forgive."

"Like what?"

"Alex."

The last call for CJ's flight echoed in the background and he signed off, overriding Jeanine's questions with hurried words of reassurance before rushing to make the plane.

His pulse was still racing as he stared out the window and watched the Americas disappear, the *why* driving all this churning in his guts. Kidnapping a cop's kid, the killings in Texas. This was something much bigger than the enmity between him and Preston. This was massive, and now Aidan had been tossed into the maw of it. That meant killing Preston was off the table. Aidan was the top priority now. He had to get him back. CJ could only imagine the nightmare Jeanine had to be living, the loneliness of it. He closed his eyes, marshaling his resolve.

You're not alone anymore…

ANDALUSIA

Seven

MR FLYNN

The words were big and bold, written with a red marker on a whiteboard, but CJ almost missed them. He hadn't been Calan Flynn for much more than a day, and the fit was still uncomfortable. Besides, he was expecting a *her*, not a *him*.

So where was Paz?

CJ didn't ask. The driver was Spanish, with all the right vibes. But after Texas, CJ was wary, so he sat directly behind him. He'd spent many vacations in Spain, but like many a beach-loving Brit, he'd never visited Madrid. Spain's capital was a splendid place by all accounts, with more bars than any other city in the world, although CJ knew within minutes that he was not going to be partaking of their delights as they were soon heading south on motorways clogged with traffic. When they left them, the taxi pulled into a suburban shopping complex and stopped at Corte Inglés, a department store, where

CJ said his *adios*, stepped out and waited, his knapsack hooked on his shoulder.

Within minutes, an off-roader pulled up and the woman driver said, "Get in." He sat beside her, and she pulled out of the parking lot as he buckled up.

"I'm Paz," she said, offering him her hand. Rather formal. "So you're the best boy?"

"That's me." CJ said as he shook it. "How long's the drive?"

"All goddamn day. Down to Marbella."

She offered him a bottle of mineral water. CJ took it and sipped, eyes measuring her in casual glances. Not Spanish, despite her Spanish name. Her accent was British, London or thereabouts. She was wearing jeans and a shirt, and it was all a tight fit on a skinny frame with long limbs. She looked lithe, strong and flexible, like she might do yoga and be a dab hand at crawling through tiny windows.

"Everything okay back there?" she said.

"Which back where? I've been on the road for days."

"Texas. We never heard from Alicia."

"She was supposed to call?"

"Then fly on over. She's my handler. I got worried. I had to call it in."

"To Ashford?"

"Who else? The toady one. He said he'd look into it."

"Everything was okay when I flew out in the crop duster." CJ had no idea why he was lying, but this was clearly no time for the truth. "What's with the film company?"

She nodded at a bag on the back seat.

"Check the brief."

Once upon a time, a brief was a sheaf of paper documents. But this bag had just four objects, and the only piece of paper was a pink Post-it note stuck to the screen of the phone with its PIN. That was the second thing he found. The first was a Glock pistol and a spare magazine. Paz winked at him. "Welcome to Spain."

CJ logged in on the phone and he was soon lost in it as they hit the A4 and headed south.

"Why DOMINO?" he said, pointing at the screen.

"It's the code name of the weapon. They're smuggling it out of China through Pakistan."

"Whose they?"

"The three *bandidos*. That's what I call them. My little joke. Because they're *one-percenters* like the motorcycle gang. You know what they say—ninety-nine percent of bikers are law-abiding citizens, and one percent are outlaws. So my update on that is ninety-nine percent of billionaires are decent human beings and one percent are bandidos. So here we got Vance never-saw-a-war-I-didn't-like Preston, Nazar how-to-bribe-dictators-and-rape-the-poor Moshiri, and Bobby I-really-am-God Schilder wheeling and dealing their way into ownership of something to kick off a war."

"What kind of weapon?"

"One big enough to start World War III."

"You're kidding... a nuke?"

"Not that kind of war. The kind that drags on and on and mints cash for bloodsuckers like the bandidos."

"Where does this intel come from?"

"Different places. It's like a jigsaw with bits missing. They've been working on it for months—Ashford and Alicia—piecing together scraps. The bandidos are super careful about comms."

So far, so logical. War in the Middle East had always been a money spinner for Preston and Nazar, but...

"What does a software guy like Schilder get out of it?"

"He doesn't sell his AI software. He leases it for a percentage of the trading profits. Markets will go berserk. Some will skyrocket, others crash. Banks and hedge funds trade trillions of dollars with his platform. Up or down. It makes no difference. They'll make profits and he'll get a cut. It's a financial mafia, and he's the Godfather. Right now, he's the third-richest man in the world. But after this, he'll be able to buy out the top fifty with his pocket change."

Now it all made sense. This setup. Icon Dreams. The expense. And hiring CJ Brink too. A criminal indictment against players at this level needed concrete evidence, not snippets of intel, leaving no option but to sanction deniable executive action. In other words, get some crazy bugger like Brink to do it. That Nevada arrest had been a gift that must have played right into their plans.

CJ went back to studying the file. The film company had leased a villa on Preston's exclusive urbanization, a gated community with guards packing .44 Magnums on regular patrol with dogs. Effectively, the task was to kill a guy in a rich man's jail with no escape route. Even without the sidebar complication that he could not kill Preston and somehow had to leverage the release of Aidan Solo, her plan sucked.

"Any more questions?" she said as they turned south onto the E-902, cruising towards a baking sun.

He nodded. "You bet. But I'm more hungry than curious."

"I've got some food at the house," she said. "But I'm not much of a cook."

"I wouldn't say that. You cooked up a crock here alright." He nodded at the file.

She glanced at him, a knowing smile on her soft lips. "There's a bit missing… we'll hit the coast soon. Let's eat some tapas and have a few beers, and I'll fill in the blanks."

They went quiet after that, following the sun and turning westward. CJ eased his seat back a few notches and crossed his arms, hiding his eyes behind the sunglasses he'd picked up at the airport. It was time to play the weary traveler, time to figure out how to kill Preston without killing him, and somehow save Aidan's life. Another conundrum begging a solution was Colby, the news of her demise no doubt en route and likely to hit town with a bang. Marbella might be a playground for the rich and famous, but for CJ Brink it was going to be a battlefield.

Paz pulled over when they hit the suburbs and led him to a bar tucked in an alley and deserted save for a few locals, a perfect spot for a discreet *tête-à-tête*. They picked simple tapas at the bar buffet and ate them at a corner table while sipping ice-cold beer. Between mouthfuls, Paz sketched in the missing bits. It took her some time to get through it all, but when she was done, CJ summarized it in a sentence.

"So you're shagging Preston's gardener?"

Paz skewered a chunk of *pulpo* with her fork and waved the octopus tentacle in front of his face before sticking it in her mouth. "José. He pops in for a quick one on his way to work three times a week."

CJ nodded. The honeytrap was a classic, tried and tested since the days of the Bible and still working like a treat.

"G-o-o-o-o-l." CJ flashed his eyes up at the TV riveting the attention of the patrons at the bar as the soccer match commentator let loose a stupendous rendition of the word. And for a few moments, he watched the accompanying celebrations, but his thoughts were soon back on other goals. The job was set for the following day, with CJ gaining access to Preston's property in the gardener's vehicle while Paz was "distracting" him.

As the celebrations quietened down and the play resumed on the TV, CJ got back to their conversation.

"Why does it have to be tomorrow?" he said.

"Preston's security works in teams of two. Plus, there's Tony, his PA. But every ten days, he gets a fresh crew, and on that day, there's only one guard in the morning. Tony usually subs for the missing guard."

"Two guys?"

"Exactly. Tomorrow the shift rotation coincides with the gardener's day. So it's perfect. And if we miss it, we won't get another chance. He hosts a party on his yacht every year in Majorca to celebrate the Es Firó festival. They're closing the Domino deal on board the night of the party. So he'll be heading there within a day or so."

"So during tomorrow's quick one—and not too quick I hope—I borrow his truck and drive to Preston's place. Then what? They wave me through at the gate. I take it your gardener is a reasonable lookalike for a six-foot-three-inch English bloke with mousy hair and an ugly disposition."

"No one's going to check. That's the beauty of the armed guards at the main gate. Preston's security know the routine. They expect the gardener on certain days and they know he has to have gone through the checkpoint at the gate."

"But it's a risk."

She shook her head. "I bugged the van with a camera. I gave him a Saint Christopher medallion on a chain to hang from his mirror and keep him safe."

"You bugged a saint?"

"This is Spain. It's crawling with saints. They're everywhere, so no one sees them anymore. And hanging up there by the windshield, the camera records everything. They never even look. They wave him through."

CJ swept his plate aside, wiped his hands on a napkin and finished his beer. He'd gotten it wrong. If all this was true, it was hell of a good plan, at least for killing Preston.

Too bad that wasn't going to happen.

In the hills above the city where CJ and Paz were planning his future, Preston was contemplating an important step closer to D-Day. He was about to get the activator, and when Nazar's limo arrived, he stepped outside to greet him.

They shook hands. No words. No greetings.

Then Preston led Nazar through the house and out onto the terrace, where his rent-a-butler was waiting with two glasses of champagne on a tray, Preston having furloughed his housekeeping staff for security reasons until after D-Day. They touched glasses, then sat at a table by the pool amid flaming torches and drank as they talked about anything other than the business at hand while the butler and his team loaded up the table, decanted a bottle of red wine and served the first course, *jamón ibérico.*

"Pork and alcohol," Nazar said as he tucked into the acorn-fed Spanish ham and washed it down with Rioja. "What would the ayatollahs say? Corrupting a good Muslim boy like me."

They shared the joke, eating leisurely, two rich men with all the time in the world. Nazar's ancestry made him a distant relative of the Pahlavis, the dynasty that had pillaged Persia throughout the twentieth century until the shah was dethroned by the Islamic revolution, and although he'd only been a child at the time, he had a dreamy fixation on his lost inheritance, casting the mullahs as the evil monsters who had deprived him of his birthright. Preston liked to humor his fetish, always serving up pigs and liquor.

After dinner, the butler served coffees and Belgian chocolate liqueurs, and Preston dismissed him.

From now on, it was strictly business.

"The activator?" he said.

"Assuming I brought it…" Nazar was always like this when he'd had a few drinks. All it took was a glass or two of red and he became a preening, supercilious smart-ass, a persona no doubt perfected at that posh British boarding school he'd attended.

"Schilder's anxious," Preston said. "In view of your brother's situation, it's a reasonable enough request. And what do you care? He's agreed to the diamonds."

Nazar gave it a while before taking a blue felt jewelry bag out of his pocket. He dangled it by its drawstring teasingly before passing it to the American.

Preston opened it and took out a Latin cross made of copper on a chain necklace. He frowned, wondering what to make of it, but then he saw the hairline of a removable cap at the bottom of the stipe. He pulled it off and found a memory stick.

"USB," Nazar said. "But I fancied it up for him. Captures the sense of drama… the biblical theme and all that. I'm sure dome-head will love it."

"It doesn't seem like much."

"You stick it in the Domino, open the control panel and poke in the codes he'll get on D-Day."

Preston held it in the palm of his hand, studying it in the flickering light of the torches.

"I don't get it. It's just a USB stick. Why all the drama? Why couldn't you just copy the files and send them to me?"

"Oh sure… like our Chinese friends are that dumb. This is not… *just a USB stick*. It's an operating system. You can't copy it, and if you try it will self-destruct. It's locked up and booby-trapped."

Preston nodded, impressed, then hung it around his neck, arranging it on his chest with solemn precision like an award, a medal perhaps for extreme treachery.

Nazar appraised it as he reached for another chocolate liqueur.

"Amen," he said, his smiling cheeks lit red with Rioja. "A-bloody-men."

<h1 style="text-align:center">Eight</h1>

On leaving the bar, CJ and Paz headed to the Icon Dreams villa in Alcazada, the road meandering up from the coast into the hills. The security gate was a breeze. Paz's car was immediately recognized. But they stopped by the office anyway to confirm that CJ was on the list of crew members who'd need access. They continued to the villa, a somewhat less imposing affair than Preston's but still an awesome property with an impressive list of must-have amenities for the billionaire set. But with time so pressing and CJ's stay so short, Paz skipped the guided tour and led him straight to the kitchen, where she pulled out a tablet and passed it to him.

"Take a look," she said. "Courtesy of Saint Christopher."

CJ played the videos. They were hard to follow when the car was in motion, the dangling medallion catching random flashes of the road, the hedgerows and José's face. In the mornings, following his sessions with Paz, he'd be wearing mirror shades and a baseball cap with the logo of a pesticide company, and he'd check himself constantly in the mirror, all grin and flashing teeth. The gate to Preston's villa was always open when he arrived, although there was invariably a guard on the path to the villa. Most mornings the guard was reading something on his phone and he'd look up and wave the van through. He'd never once stopped it or checked the occupant. Between his arrival and departure, the camera was mostly idle. But now and again, Preston's security would pass and trigger it to record. CJ noted all the faces, the times and the locations.

When he was done, CJ slid the tablet to one side.

"Checking the time stamps," he said. "I see that the gardener spends at most thirty minutes with you, and on one record-breaking day he was in and out in seventeen minutes. So…"

"He's definitely no marathon man."

"But I can't get it done in that time frame. It'll take me that long to get up the road and back."

"I've got a plan for that. Two plans, in fact. One option is to Mickey Finn his coffee. I've got loads of Rohypnol and he always has a cup."

"And number two?"

"You kill him."

CJ gave this one time to settle in. Part of that was dealing with the numbing disbelief that she'd said it.

"I can understand your frustration—what with his quick trigger and all—but isn't that a little harsh?"

"Seriously, he's a loose end. The only problem is getting the body off campus. But I was thinking we could leave in his van and take it with us."

"Only he'd be dead."

"The van's full of gardening tools. We'd have no trouble burying him. He's even got a handheld digger.

That's very important in Spain. The ground's rock-hard. You'd never dig a grave with a shovel."

CJ was impressed, with the planning, if not the plan.

"Tell you what," he said. "Why don't you just Mickey Finn him, and I'll take care of him afterwards." CJ had no idea how, but he could always dump the bewildered bugger somewhere and tell him he'd gotten his just deserts for cheating on his wife.

"Your call," she said, standing up and checking her watch. "I'll show you to your room."

She walked out through the dining room, and as they passed through the lounge, she flicked on the lights…

"Aaagh!" Paz yelped and threw out her arms. CJ was a pace behind her but tall enough to see over her shoulder. Sitting in a wingback chair by the fireplace was a man aiming a pistol with a silencer directly at them. "Damn you, Ashford." Paz put her hand on her heart and heaved down air. "You couldn't have called? I didn't even know you were in Spain."

"Step away from him," Ashford said, waving the gun, then training it back on CJ. "Drop the knapsack, kick it towards her and step away from it." He waved the gun again. CJ followed through, and Paz picked up the knapsack. "I assume you already issued him with his gun." Paz nodded and she took it out of the knapsack. "Take a seat, old chap. You've had a long day."

CJ dropped into the armchair opposite, a huge affair with soft upholstery, the kind of chair it would be difficult to get out of in a hurry. Introductions were unnecessary. CJ had met the man twice before. Ashford had identified himself as MI6 when he'd visited CJ in the hospice where he was recovering from a coma. He'd showed up in LA too. Once again, with Colby. Different countries, different agencies, an odd couple, but one team. That was how they'd played it. Ashford had come over as slippery, a guy all too easy to distrust, and now here he was, aiming a pistol at CJ's belly. Ashford looked to be in his late forties, a Gen Xer, but he was a throwback to a bygone age, a retread old-school Brit in windowpane tweed who'd kid you that all a deal needed was a handshake and the word of an Englishman.

"Get the gun," Ashford said.

Paz did it with a few grunts and groans, clearly puzzled by his sudden appearance. "Do I get any clues on this?" she said. "Or am I supposed to guess what the hell's going on?"

"Perhaps CJ can tell us," Ashford said.

CJ shrugged, still acting dumb. It had worked with Paz, but something told him it had a shelf life and it was about to expire. That was confirmed when two quick shots struck the back of the chair, missing CJ by inches and littering his shoulders with yarn and fluffy white padding. It was nice shooting, like a fairground trick, and that was a surprise coming from Ashford. And not just the accuracy, but the casualness. That one-handed grip with his elbow propped on the wing of the chair like he was drinking a cup of tea. *I'm not a pencil pusher. Pay attention.* That was the message, and to underline it, he followed it up with a grin, oily and sanctimonious, his face all hamster jowls and aquiline nose. He'd have made a great clown, and the face worked pretty good on a killer too.

"That airstrip in Texas," Ashford said. "It looks like a barrel bomb hit it. It's burnt to the ground." Paz was standing a few paces off CJ, his pistol hanging loosely at her side. "And since we haven't heard from Alicia, we can only assume the worst…"

"Bastard." Paz leapt at CJ, bringing the pistol down hard on his head. He whipped up his arm at the last moment and it took most of the force, but the blow still landed with a crack.

"Paz." Ashford was on his feet and across the room. "We need him to talk." Ashford took the gun from her. She stepped back, glaring at him, eyes like fiery coals. "Outside." Ashford pointed at the door. "Get a breath." But she didn't move. She stood there, staring down at CJ, her jaw sliding from side to side in a slow grind of hate. "Go." Ashford amped up the volume, and she left, still snarling defiance.

"I didn't do it," CJ said as he wiped his head wound with his hand to check it out. Blood. But it could have been worse; having metal plates in your head is sometimes a bonus.

"So what did you do?"

CJ told him the truth. Why not? It was as good as any lie he could think of.

"So who?" Ashford said.

"Who what?"

"Killed Colby…"

CJ had moved on from that. He was wondering who'd come by later and cleaned up the place. "You've obviously got a mole on the team," he said, suddenly realizing that this was the opportunity he needed to delay the hit. "So what else do they know? Tomorrow? Do they know about the hit? Am I walking into a trap?"

Ashford called Paz and she rejoined them. She was visibly still shaken, but in control.

"Alicia recruited Paz," Ashford explained. "She was her mentor, so they were close." CJ nodded and looked at her appealingly. Ashford turned his attention to Paz. "I don't believe he had anything to do with it. He was in custody for days before it happened. And besides, he followed through. He came here. If he'd disappeared, it would be another matter. So we must have a leak. Someone tipped off Preston."

"You think it was him?" she said.

"Who had the most to gain?" Ashford said. "It has to be him… or Nazar, or Schilder, and Preston is the one with the resources. Either way, we can't take a chance tomorrow."

"It's off?" Paz said.

"No choice… until we figure this out."

"What about José?"

"Keep screwing him with a smile on your face. He's still our entry pass to Preston's villa. We're not quitting. We're reassessing." He turned to CJ. "And you can make yourself scarce while she's at it."

"So what?" Paz said. "I report to you now."

Ashford shrugged, then tucked his gun in a shoulder holster. "We hardly have a choice." He got up and passed CJ's gun back to Paz. "He won't need this for a while." She went to take it, but he didn't let go. "But we still need him. Is that clear?"

Paz nodded, calming down, and he let her take the gun. When Ashford had left, CJ repeated his account of what had happened in Texas, getting into the detail he'd skipped with Ashford. "Telling you back on the road when you picked me up didn't seem right," he said. "It wasn't a planned deception. I don't do deceit." She seemed to accept it for what it was, but she was clearly unhappy. She waved for CJ to follow her. "Come on," she said, his gun swinging at her side as she turned to go. "I'll show you your room."

When they reached it, CJ said, "Whoever leaked Texas probably knows about this place too. Two guys with

Uzis. Are you going to be comfortable handling that if they wake you up in the night?" She looked down at the gun in her hand and took a beat before passing it to him.

"Don't make me regret this."

Less than two kilometers away from the drama playing out between CJ and Paz, Preston was about to turn in when a message came through from Schilder. The digital prick was demanding a video conference. Why couldn't he just make a call and get it over with? Why did he have to grandstand and announce his coming like a second messiah? *Lo and behold… I will burst forth from the video screen in thirty minutes.* And what would the call be about? Nothing, essentially. He'd want Preston to hold his hand and comfort him. That's not what he'd ask for, but that's what he'd need. A nanny. Preston had been here many times with corporate types, men whose bellies outweighed their balls by a considerable measure. He'd offer them a key to an express elevator, but every key had a price, and not always payable with a bank account. There was an ethics ledger too, a gray book, its pages devoted to what you could get away with versus what was legal. Maybe an entry in it was troubling him, costing him sleep, so he needed his nanny to comfort him. Preston had studied many things, but none with more passion than his fellow man. Earth's most elevated species, he'd concluded, was driven solely by fear and greed, commodities that Schilder had in abundance. Whatever the problem was, all Preston had to do was hit one of those buttons and Schilder would be sleeping like a babe.

When the video call came through, Preston was sitting in the annex, viewing the wall monitor.

"I got the activator," he said as soon as Schilder's face popped up on the screen.

"You have?" Schilder's eyes lit with excitement. The monitor was so big, the resolution so high, and Schilder so close to the camera that the hairs in his nose looked like brush that needed clearing.

"What about the diamonds? How's that going?"

"The diamonds. Yes. They're on the way. But I was thinking…" Schilder stopped, his face oddly grave.

"What?"

"That you should end up with the diamonds. Not Nazar."

Preston went quiet. That was a charming thought, but loaded with implications. Its provenance too was shocking. This was Schilder, *Time* magazine's Nerd of the Year, suddenly transformed into a geek hoodlum. Not whining for his nanny, as Preston had anticipated, but soliciting an assassin. That was a shapeshift worthy of a comic book hero, and it took Preston by surprise and made him wonder why.

"So we plug the risk hole with the feds. In case he's indicted. Is that your thinking?"

"Forget the *if*. My lawyers have contacts in the prosecutor's office. They're drawing up the paperwork as we speak. Nazar's got to know it's coming. Why else switch that last payment to diamonds?"

"So how do you see it working?"

"On the night of the party, I trade the diamonds for the go-live codes. You've already got the activator. So we'll be good to go at that point. He could have an accident, a drive shaft shearing on a chopper. It happens. Or something simpler. Yachts are dangerous. He could even fall down the stairs."

It all made sense. But then again, this was Nazar. Preston and Nazar had been partners in crime for over twenty years.

He was a friend.

Sort of...

Schilder was fidgeting. Usually, one-way conversations were his specialty, but this one was obviously troubling him. Nonetheless, he pressed ahead with his pitch. "I get the Domino. You get the diamonds..."

"And Nazar gets dead."

"I'd put it differently... he gets to solve his legal issues with the feds."

Preston eased back in his chair and looked across ten thousand miles into the other man's eyes. He was reassured. He'd been right. Fear and greed. And Schilder had maxed out on both, especially fear. He couldn't control Nazar, and he had to control everything in his world. Losing control was so frightening to him that he'd risk conspiracy to commit murder in the first degree—a capital offense—to duck it.

Preston leaned closer to the microphone to ensure that there was no misunderstanding.

"Deal," he said.

Nine

Before dawn, CJ was taking the tour he'd missed on arrival, padding around the villa, exploring its catacomb of rooms barefoot and in silence. No lights. He didn't need them. Outside, the aftermath of a full moon was hurrying through webs of wispy clouds and there was more than enough light left on the inside for man with turbocharged senses. The villa was vast—a movie set— and CJ logged its geography systematically. After days spent on that jagged itinerary from Texas to Marbella, he'd crashed into a deep sleep, but five hours later he was done with it, recharged, his veins coursing with adrenaline at the prospect of the day ahead. Besides, he needed a new plan. The Preston hit was off the table, and something else was sitting there in its place. Aidan. Until he was back with his mother, everything was second place.

He ended up outside on the terrace by the pool, standing at a wall looking out beyond the distant sea, marshaling his thoughts as the mountains of the Moroccan Rif edged out of the haze above the horizon.

"Alex." CJ snapped his head to the side. Surprised as ever. He hadn't seen him since Nevada—since before his arrest—and like every sighting of his dead friend, he'd wondered if that had been his last. The apparitions were hallucinations, his doctors had told him, a curious hybrid of survivor's guilt and scar tissue on the brain. Sooner or later those damaged cells would heal, guilt would loosen its grip, and the visits from the dead would cease. But evidently not yet. Alex was dressed in MCCUU, the Marine Corps Combat Utility Uniform, ready to get to work. CJ nodded towards it and raised his hand in a salute that never made it, turning into a lazy wave instead.

"Second to none," he said, smiling.

"Don't start that again." Alex jabbed an admonishing finger and they both chuckled. In the Korean War, the Corps had set up a basecamp with a sign outside saying:

US Marine Corps – Second to None

Shortly thereafter, the British Royal Marines had set up a camp next door, and they had a sign too. Theirs said:

Royal Marines – None

Alex and CJ stood side by side at the wall and stared out into the night. Two comrades, easy in each other's company, untroubled by the trivia of a death that had tried to separate them and failed.

"We can get him back," CJ said.

"No question."

CJ turned away from the vista with its infinite shades of dark and hitched his butt up on the wall, so he was facing Alex looking up at him.

"Tomorrow—while Paz is entertaining José—I'll nip over there in his van and…" He trailed off. He'd been mulling it over when Alex had shown up, but now the decision came to him easily… "instead of killing Preston, I'll take him hostage and trade him with himself—so to speak—for Aidan."

"Where are you going to keep him while you negotiate the release? This place won't work."

"Yeah… that's the tricky part. I'll have definitely outstayed my welcome here."

"I still like it."

"Me too."

"Don't forget to give Preston my kindest regards."

CJ hopped off the wall and turned to face Alex, but he was already gone, all except the feel of him in the air, that lingered, something beyond eyes and ears.

Back in the house, CJ fixed breakfast, and with the prospect of an eat-and-sleep-when-you-can mission ahead, he made it a big one, the full English, eggs, bacon, mushrooms, tomatoes, toast and *mermelada* and mugs of tea. He was on his second cup when Paz joined him. She looked like she'd had a sleepless night, her face flushed and wan at the same time, her eyes rubbed red.

"This place smells like a goddamn McDonald's," she said, jerking open the refrigerator door and taking out a yoghurt. "Aren't you supposed to piss off somewhere. He'll be here any minute."

"I'm on my way." CJ jumped up and glugged his brew. "I'll take a run." He patted his belly and grinned. "Burn off the Big Mac and fries." She poked a teaspoon in her yogurt and sucked on it, glaring at him like she was having trouble finding a rejoinder rude enough before giving up and sweeping out of the room, spooning her strawberry-flavored low-fat as she went.

With the morning greetings done, CJ headed outside. He needed to find a secluded spot to call Jeanine, and that turned out to be easy. Alcazada's villas were separated from each other by buffer zones of natural wilderness, and he soon found a hidey-hole where he could make the call and look out for José's arrival at the same time. He tried Jeanine several times, but there was no reply. Most likely, she was somewhere over the Arctic, five miles up. So he worked on the details of the hostage plan instead. He might even sweeten up the offer by walking away from the hit in perpetuity. He'd wind the clock back to that Nevada convenience store and take the philosopher's option. No more vigilante justice. He'd give Preston his word. It was the only way to guarantee Aidan's safety in the long term.

CJ was pondering all this when José's vehicle slowed at the entrance to the Icon Dreams villa, then disappeared into the driveway. He waited an appropriate time, long enough for José to have his cup of coffee and get on the job, before sneaking back onto the property. He already knew where the van would be and that the key would be in the lock. José was clearly a man comfortable with routines, and his were cut with deep grooves. Later, he'd find his vehicle was gone, and there'd be considerable screeching about that, mostly from Paz. But that was a jetsam he was going to have to dump on her. It was too bad about WWIII, and CJ was the last guy on the planet to vote for a war, but that was still just a threat buried in the greed of these men. Ashford and his cohorts on both sides of the Atlantic would have a plan

B, and they'd have to go with that. They might wreak vengeance on him, but that was a risk he had to live with.

CJ drove the winding road up the hill to Preston's villa.

Hallelujah!

The gate was open. All according to plan.

Only it wasn't. The gate was open, yes. But then the plan went off script. The security guard was not fiddling with his phone and he didn't wave CJ through. He was blocking the driveway with his palm held out like a traffic cop. CJ pulled up. No one likes plans going wrong, but realistically he was going to have to deal with this guy sooner or later. It just turned out to be sooner. The guy stepped around to the driver's side. The window was already down.

"*Buenos días,*" CJ said, exhausting much of his Spanish vocabulary in a single breath. He was wearing José's mirror shades and his baseball cap with the dead beetle logo, but he had no illusions about passing as a lookalike. The cap and shades, along with the whiskers he'd sprouted since his arrest, might at least delay any recognition of who he was. Preston would be anticipating a remote hit, a sniper's round or a car bomb. No one ever plans on a Trojan horse.

"Where's the usual guy?" the man said, hooking his shirt up over the gun butt sticking out of his belt.

"He's screwing his girlfriend. He said you wouldn't mind me coming in his place. I'm good. I used to do the gardens at Buckingham Palace."

"Really. I'm impressed." The man made a beckoning gesture with his fingers. "Out you get, wise guy."

So far, so good. The guard didn't recognize him, but that was sure to change the moment he stepped out of the van. Just in case, CJ had his Glock pistol on the seat next to him, tucked under José's Spanish-language edition of *Bikini Plus* magazine. That was very much a last resort. Even with its suppressor, the 9mm would knock out three digits of decibels—about the same as a thunderclap. In a leafy Mediterranean glade where bird songs trailed echoes through the trees, that was plenty enough to get noticed. In any case, the get-out-of-the-car scenario was playing out well. When they say that, they always take a step back, and as he did so, CJ jerked open the door, slamming its bottom edge into the man's shinbone. He staggered back with a muffled gasp, fumbling for his gun, but CJ was already out of the car. He kicked the man's arm as he drew his weapon, and the gun fell to the ground. Then he slotted a sidekick through his flailing arms with the same leg, his foot flowing from one kick to the next without touching the ground. The man folded up and keeled over, and CJ dropped into a low stance, cracking his jaw with a straight right. He picked up his gun, covering him and listening.

Nothing. No more bird songs.

They'd obviously noticed, but they appeared to be the only ones. CJ dragged the guy to the back of the van and secured him inside, using the gardener's tape to shut his mouth and tie his hands. Then he took a cordless hedge trimmer from the tool rack—an attempt to look gardenerish—and carried it into the trees, making his way up towards the house. The estate was landscaped with naturally wooded "wild" areas that gave way to terraces closer to the villa cultivated with fruit trees and decorative bushes. It all gave CJ plenty of cover as he approached the house, soon spotting a second guard from a ways off. This one was on his phone. He was standing on the pool terrace in the shade of the house.

Tricky.

Hard to approach without being seen and impossible without being spotted by one of the CCTV cameras. The motto of CJ's old military unit, the SBS, was *By strength and guile*, and this was clearly a guile moment. He was running options through his head when Preston appeared on the upper terrace directly above the man below. Having studied the house layout, CJ knew that it led off his office. Preston went to the rail and looked off into the distance, but then he noticed the guard below. His man was grinning and flicking his finger back and forth across a phone screen like he was fanning through photos. Preston stared at him awhile. Then he bent down by a small palm, one of many plants decorating the terrace, and when he straightened up, he was holding a rock. Not a big one, but not a small one either. Definitely more rock than stone. And after sizing up the shot, he tossed it overhand like someone shooting for a trash bin in their office. It bounced off the marble behind the guard and cracked against the wall. The phone spun out of his hand, its glass shattering at his feet. The man whipped out his gun and dropped into an unsteady combat stance, panning the empty terrace with his weapon. Preston cooed from above, waving his hand lazily.

"Hi, Tony," he said, as the man looked up at him and pieced it together. He holstered his weapon and picked up the phone.

"I was checking the forecast for our Majorca trip," he said, putting his smashed phone back in his pocket without looking at it. "It's good."

Same old Preston.

CJ remembered his old boss once confiding in him that no one ever gave the job one hundred percent unless they knew the deck was burning under their feet. So as the boss, his job was simple… *light the deck.*

Preston disappeared off the terrace, heading through sliding glass doors, and CJ made a wide loop and scouted the back of the property before his thoughts coalesced into a plan and he headed back to the van. He drove it up the driveway and stopped before reaching the top. It was a tactical location, close enough to be seen by Tony but only just. He got out of the van and stood on the far side, where he'd be hidden from view and took an extension ladder from the roof rack. He jacked it up so it would be easily visible, leaned it against a tree and slipped off the driveway, hiding behind an oleander whose white flowers shimmered in the sun.

CJ was setting a trap and relying on human nature to trigger it. After the humiliating dressing-down Tony had gotten from Preston, he'd be desperate to assert himself and recover his self-esteem. In this context, the gardener was an irresistible bait. Someone down the pecking order and eminently bullyable.

When he finally got there, he flipped his shirt up over the gun butt just like the other guy had. CJ had José's claw hammer ready to crack open his head, but at the last minute he changed his mind, and in a swish of white flowers he was standing next to the guy with one hand on the man's gun and the other sticking the silenced Glock under his throat.

"It's been a lousy day for me too," he said. "But let's not make it worse."

Tony tensed up, then relaxed, a realist accepting his fate. Lousy is bad, but it beats terminal. CJ stuffed him, bound and gagged, in the back of the van with the other guy. Then he put the ladder back on the roof and drove beyond the house and off the driveway into the trees.

There were no terraces in back. It was all manicured wildness. From this point on, success came down to luck. Not extreme, but calculated. If his intel was correct, he had now accounted for the rotation day's lone security guard and Preston's PA. So the big man was alone, and busy as he was throwing rocks at his employees, he was pretty sure not to be eyeballing the CCTV feed. That was the risk. The guile part was over. Now it was down to strength and a bit of luck.

CJ propped his ladder against the back of the house, climbed onto the roof and walked over to the front. The view was terrific, all the way to Africa, and much closer, a bird's-eye take on Preston's terrace directly below. He pulled the Glock and stepped off the edge, spinning en route and landing in a crouch with his gun aimed at Preston. There he was: the great man, sitting on the other side of a desk. He saw CJ and made a grab for something and CJ fired, a warning shot that whistled so close to his ear Preston stopped like someone had hit the pause button. CJ cleared the room and checked the desk drawers, finding a Browning 9mm with a fancy inlay on the butt. He stuck it under his belt, checked the other drawers and searched Preston but found no other weapons.

"They'll kill the Solo kid if you touch me," Preston said, raising his hands above his head.

"Right down to business, eh? Too bad. I was looking forward to beating that out of you."

"The kid is safe. He's here in Spain." He nodded at his phone on the desk. "One call is all it takes."

"So he comes here. You and me shake hands. And I walk out of here with Aidan, and we all live happily ever after."

"Why not?"

"You and I are going camping."

"Where?"

"No idea. But it's a big country. Plenty of forests and mountains. We'll find a cozy spot somewhere. And when Aidan's mother confirms that she has him back, our camping days will be over. And you'll be on your way back to all this with a big bonus… a pardon. That's right. You'll be off the hook for Alex. You have my word."

"It's not just Alex, though, is it? What did Colby give you to kill me?"

"I told her I'd do it for free."

"So who killed her?"

Whaam!

That knocked CJ sideways and Preston saw it. "You thought it was me?" he said. "I'm flattered. You think I'm that far on top of this. We followed your trail from Nevada, but we got there way too late."

"Who's we?"

"My team… you want to see?" He glanced at the computer. CJ gave him the nod, and he worked the keyboard while CJ held the gun to his head, following the Tratfors crew as they arrived at the Texas airstrip and started the search. It only took a few minutes. The sound was muted, but he didn't need it. The video was enough. Preston wasn't lying, and neither was the Uzi man with the dark web story.

So who else wanted CJ dead and Domino alive?

CJ wondered about that computer. What if he could find something incriminating on it? Something so valuable he could blackmail Preston into releasing Aidan? It might work. Preston was already logged in, and it was a lot more straightforward than a camping trip with his ex-boss.

"Stand up," CJ said, stepping back and switching his gun hand from right to left. Preston stood warily, his eyes following the gun as CJ dropped his right shoulder, locking his elbow down by his hip… *and snap*. His open hand whipped out, flipping horizontal at the last moment, the butt cracking Preston's jaw, sending his head spinning in a spit of teeth and blood. Preston reeled backwards, smashed into the wall and collapsed at its base. CJ checked him out. The jaw was dislocated and broken, and he was unconscious. CJ was now free to search that computer. His new plan was more hopeful than anything else, but it was worth a try. And if it failed, he could always revert to plan A and drag Preston to the van. With that broken jaw, when he came to, he'd be even more eager to get the swap done and get to a hospital.

CJ went to the computer and copied the Texas video to his phone. No special reason why, but no reason why not either. He hadn't seen it all, and it might come in useful. He was using search to check out the most recent files Preston had accessed when the man himself coughed up blood. CJ went to him and rolled him onto his side, so he'd dribble blood on the floor instead of choking on it. The last thing he needed now was for Preston to drown in his own blood. And as he sorted him out, he found the strangest thing…

A cross.

It was hanging from his neck on a chain.

CJ stared at it, incredulous.

Vance Preston had found God.

That was quite a conversion—from warmongering child-stealer to cross-toting believer—and one that stretched credulity to the breaking point. CJ took it off him and wiped off the blood. It was a Latin cross, a fancy one, copper red with ornate engravings. CJ examined it more closely, soon finding the memory stick. He stuck it in Preston's computer, expecting to find sensitive files. It had to be something precious to be hidden on his person like that. Surprise. What he got was a system command window with streaming lines of code, or something. He had no idea what because these weren't text characters. They were Chinese logograms, and since Chinese was a language CJ knew even less well than Spanish, he was stumped. The scrolling came to a halt, displaying what looked like a menu of options. CJ copied it and pasted it in Google Translate.

EM-88 ACTIVATOR MENU
1. Run system check
2. Enter target codes
3. Engineer login

CJ read it over and over as its implications spun through his head. This was pay dirt. He looked across at Preston, bleeding peacefully on the marble floor. Now he had no need to abduct him. This was it, the something he needed to trade for Aidan. The Domino was an EM-88, a weapon he'd never heard of, but that hardly mattered. This was Aidan's ticket out of captivity. He unplugged the activator and hung it around his own neck. Time to go. He ripped a sheet of paper from the scratchpad on the desk and rolled it up, fashioning a crude quill pen. He went to Preston, breathing evenly now, and daubed it in the pool of blood dribbling from his mouth. It was tough, writing on the wall with just a stick of bloodied paper. So he made it snappy, then headed downstairs. Back outside, the birds were back in tune, a cheery soundtrack as CJ returned to the van. He dumped the two men and headed back to Icon's villa, skidding to a halt in the driveway outside.

Where was the car?

The 4x4 Paz had picked him up with. It had been right there at the end of the drive. He was out of the van, moving, gun first, eyes and ears scanning.

Nothing.

Gingerly, he entered the house via the kitchen door.

"Paz," he called out as he made his way through the property clearing it room by room. Then upstairs, he went straight to the master bedroom that Paz had declared her own. José was lying naked on the bed, spread-eagled on his back, his wrists and ankles tied with silk scarves to the bedposts and a knife sticking out of his chest.

So that was Ashford's plan…

CJ had popped the cork on it by going against instructions and following through on the Preston hit. Or so they must have thought. And they'd reacted accordingly, hightailing it over the horizon, leaving CJ in the hot seat. He had no way off the urbanization except in the gardener's van, and that meant driving past the gatehouse cameras. The Spanish cops would hardly need a degree in forensic science to rank him as a prime suspect. The British government would no doubt be more than helpful, providing them with the broken hero dossier—the sad story of a damaged veteran who'd finally lost his battle with insanity. It was a hell of a plan: find a well-known psycho with a grudge against the victim, make him an offer he can't refuse, set up incriminating evidence, and maroon him at the scene of the crime surrounded by armed guards.

Nice.

Only he hadn't killed Preston, and he hadn't killed the gardener, and he wasn't going to take the fall for anyone.

Time… the elastic dimension.

Times were when it disappeared in a blink, good times, sucked into ether. Then there were taunting times, never-ending, stretching pain into eternity. Jeanine was lying on a bed in a Madrid hotel. She wasn't given much to philosophy unless it was the homespun kind, but time's predations were hard to miss, with each moment carving into her like the spikes on a medieval rack. It was nearly thirteen years since she'd birthed Aidan. Blink years, crammed with joy and struggle, hardship and loss. So many things had gone out of her life since then. That craziness that slops over from teens into twenties. There'd been parties, booze and a few pills here and there that didn't come with a doctor's scrip. Mistakes aplenty, including the big one. Her ex. But having to cope with Aidan alone had been a lifesaver. She'd gotten the badge that came with a real career. She'd turned her life around and set it on track to better.

Now everything was on the line.

Her son. Her job.

Reality hit her, the cold loneliness of the hotel room, some special sort of cold, way beyond the controls on that blasting aircon.

Aidan.

Would she ever see him again? She swerved away from that thought. Better to take a bullet in the head. It would hurt less. As for the career, she'd lied to get the leave, and now she was in some foreign hotel room on a mission to kill a man she'd never met.

Some cop… some mother!

She checked her phone yet again. That goddamn phone—the time taunter's ally—the phone that never rings. She put it on the nightstand and paced the room, stopping by the minibar and surveying its contents. Another yet-again habit she'd taken up. No American whiskeys. But that black label scotch looked promising. She shut the door, sat back on the bed and slugged her bottle of sparkling mineral water instead, staring at the phone. Even Ernald would be welcome. She could make promises and demands, say she'd spoken to Brink, that she had him on a line and was reeling him in. But she'd have to see Aidan first. The phone rang. She slopped the water, grabbing it off the nightstand.

"You arrived?"

CJ's voice hit her like a bolt of something. What? She couldn't say. Hope and strength? Maybe. Or was it desperation and despair, or worse yet, delusion?

"I'm at a hotel in Madrid," she said. "They didn't call me yet."

"No, they won't. They've had some setbacks."

"Some what?" she said, alarmed at the prospect of CJ interfering and endangering her son.

"These guys have no hearts. But that works for us. They're pragmatists. Aidan is a bargaining chip. Nothing else. So we need something to trade. And I've got something of theirs even more important to them than killing me. And the only way they're going to get it back is to hand over Aidan unharmed."

Jeanine leapt up, struggling to think straight. This was a turn so sharp she was skidding off the tracks.

"What thing?"

"It's too complicated to explain now. We need to meet. You okay with that?"

"You're in Madrid?"

"No, I'm in Marbella, but I'm on my way to the Costa Blanca."

"Why? Who are these people?"

"You remember Tratfors, or Ratforce as Alex used to call it, the outfit we worked for in Iraq? Your guy Ernald works for Preston, the Tratfors boss. And I'm using the words 'works for' loosely, as in—he's not on the payroll. So Preston has a deal going down in Majorca. His yacht is currently moored in Denia on the Spanish coast a few hours' sail from Majorca. So that's where he'll be heading. Right now, he's taking care of an unexpected dental emergency. So we have time to get there."

"So what do I say when Ernald calls?"

"You're going to have to be strong. It'll get rough. You're made of the same stuff as Alex. I'm counting on that. They'll threaten you. They'll threaten Aidan. I know what I'm asking…"

"This is my son we're talking about. Did you ever have a son? Do you even understand what you're asking me?"

"I never even had a mum or a dad, and Alex was the closest I ever got to family."

"Then what?"

"I'm asking you for blind faith."

"Is that all?"

"It'll work so long as they don't break you, but they'll try real hard."

"Aren't you afraid? What if I do a deal with them?"

"To kill me?" She didn't answer. "Blind faith," he said. "That works both ways."

"So what's your plan? You give back the mysterious and valuable object you stole in exchange for my son and they let us sail off into the sunset without killing us all?"

"You don't sound convinced."

"Well… my bad. I guess I'm running low on faith today, especially the blind variety."

A sob leaked out unexpectedly and she choked it back, wiping angrily at the tears. CJ didn't come back at first, and that was for the best. She took deep breaths as though more oxygen might dry those tears.

"Jeanine, this is going to sound crazy. But I'm not alone in this, and nor are you. Alex is here. He's here with me now. He's always with me. We're a team. Death didn't have the balls to take him. Not all of him anyway. This is not sentimental crap. This is real. I've planned this with Alex. We can do it. The three of us."

Jeanine held the phone away from her face and stared at it, the moment unreal and taking her by surprise. He was right. It wasn't sentimental. That's not how it sounded. Crazy, maybe. And from anyone else, that would have been the case. But this wasn't crazy either. It was creepy. Not Halloween creepy, but heaven creepy, feeling its way down from the back of her neck and into her chest, resonating with the glow of truth. Maybe those vat-grown brain cells they'd shot him up with did have something special after all. Either way, there was only one thing left and that was to call it. And what she felt was plenty enough for her to go with her gut.

"You got it. Blind faith… coming up."

"And that's not all we'll be running on. I've got you a gun too." Jeanine jumped on the spot, one of her preteen hops running twenty years late. That was great news. She'd felt so powerless since getting off that plane—the consummate victim. Her own gun, and a battle-hardened Marine and special forces veteran watching her back, and who knew—maybe someone extra-special looking down on her. She'd been forcing herself to believe, but now real hope kindled inside her. No more forcing it. "I'll message you all the info you need. It's quite a ways to Denia, so you'd better get moving. We'll meet up tomorrow."

Minutes later, Jeanine was hurrying out the door of that hotel and on her way.

Ten

As Jeanine hurried to Madrid Atocha Station to catch the AVE bullet train to Valencia, CJ sat on the bed in the Icon Dreams villa and stared at the dead gardener.

The José problem…

And that wasn't the only thing troubling him. Jeanine's tearful breakdown had hit him hard. Such a strong woman, but this was ripping her open. She was right. He had no idea what he was asking and no right to ask it. No way could he permit Preston and his goons to threaten and torment her. He had to put a stop to that right now. So there it was—Jeanine, José, and his urgent need for a new set of wheels—three problems looking for a solution. In any event, he couldn't leave José here like this. So he set to work, and as he was cutting him loose the answer hit him.

A tripartite solution. Risky. But perfect.

He carried José down to the van and propped him in the passenger seat. Then he took the wheel and drove back to Preston's villa. It was a bold move with echoes of that old detective trope about returning to the scene of the crime. But it made sense. It was less than an hour since he'd driven off the property. The only risk was that someone had come by in the interim, but that hadn't happened. Tony and his buddy were exactly where CJ had left them in the driveway. CJ bundled them both into the back of the van and continued to the house, approaching warily. But his caution was unnecessary as all was silent there. He'd expected as much. After taking a blow like that, Preston was sure to be out for a long count, and even when he came to, he'd be in no shape to rumble.

CJ parked the van in the driveway where it could easily be seen and cautiously made his way back into the house. Preston was still a crumpled heap on the floor of his office. CJ found a Post-it pad in a desk drawer and scribbled an addendum to the note he'd left on the wall earlier. He stuck the note below the graffiti message, then left the house and headed for the carport, a multivehicle metal structure sandwiched between walls of bougainvillea. He chose a Hyundai four-wheeler whose keys were on the front seat. Minutes later, he cruised out of the urbanization and was on his way. The car was trackable, but that hardly mattered. He'd told Preston where he was headed in the note and set a date. Preston was far too smart to risk losing that activator in some sort of botched ambush. Besides, he had plenty of other things to keep him busy. CJ had made sure of that.

It was a long journey back for Preston, and it was getting dark by the time the first images from the outside world tumbled into his troubled dreamscape. They were strange images too, bands of wrinkled white like crevasses in an ice field as far as the eye could see. But not for long. The dream segued abruptly into a terrifying reality. It wasn't an ice field. It was the Carrara marble, the expensive stuff he'd had specially imported from Italy. He could have gone with a Spanish option and saved thousands, but no. Only the best for our boy Preston, and now his face was ground into it, eyeballs millimeters from its chiaroscuro of whites.

He moved, barely lifting his cheek off the cold rock floor, but it was way too much. His jaw slid off its sockets and pain snapped through him like a bolt nailing him from brain to butt. His hand jerked up and he grabbed his jaw, easing it back into place. He couldn't even holler properly. So he made do with a hybrid sound, a growl-cum-gurgle that gave up on itself and dissolved into a whimper. He struggled to stand, levering himself off the floor with his free hand. But it slipped in the pool of blood, and he crashed down on his elbow with a yelp. He hadn't even seen the blood, but now his eyes followed its splattered trail all the way to his scarlet-smudged teeth, visible in the half-light of the computer screensaver.

Teeth!

He moaned as he pulled himself straight and marched on his knees to the desk where, with one hand on his jaw and the other on the desktop, he hauled himself up on his feet. He steadied himself a moment, looking around the room before flicking on some lights and pacing to his dressing room. He picked a tie at first, then tossed it aside in favor of a scarf, holding it under his chin and tying a knot with either end on top of his skull, making a sling to hold his jaw. But it was too tight, so he loosened it to give his mouth enough room to breathe and grunt. Turning on the vanity lights at his dressing table, he checked the results.

"Aaagh…" He stumbled back from the mirror.

That had to be someone else, that puffed-up face all black and blue and that ridiculous paisley scarf tied in a knot on his head, its silk tassels trailing to each side like a bow. He looked like a blowfish decked out as a gift under a Christmas tree. Rage swooned through him, curling his lips. But that only made it worse, showcasing his toothless gums.

He returned to the office and fetched a gun from the panic room, where everything appeared to be in order. The pain was excruciating still, but at least he felt better. The jaw sling, the gun. He was getting back control, but he was befuddled, and straight thinking was hard. He had to get to a hospital, get a shot to kill the pain, then get surgeons working on his jaw. There was no making sense of this until then. And before all that, he had to find his morons and hope at least one of them was still alive to make the emergency call as that was a conversation way beyond his current speech range. He shut the door of the panic room as he left it and turned on the main lights in the office. That was when he saw CJ's message. In the dim light from the desk earlier, he'd stumbled right past it, but now there was no missing it, scrawled on the wall in ugly graffiti with his own blood.

SWAP KID 4 ACTIVATOR
CU IN DENIA

Preston stiffened, pain gone, flushed aside by a wave of terror.

Activator?

His hand went to his throat.

No cross!

It was only then that he noticed the note stuck on the wall below the graffiti. He tried to read it, but there was something wrong with his vision and the print kept flipping in and out of focus like he was having an eye test with different lenses cycling through a phoropter. He took it to the desk and tried under a lamp. Eventually, he got it. *Don't call the mother, or the activator goes to the cops.* Preston's mind was racing trying to figure out some way to turn the tables on it all. But he knew it was just bluster. That harebrained scheme to blackmail the mother had backfired horribly. Now Brink was calling the shots. Preston had no illusions. All he could do was kill the kid, but that would sabotage the Domino deal and turn him into an outlaw living like a dog in some jungle hideout. He grabbed a flashlight from the desk drawer and walked out into the dusk unsteadily, his gun in one hand, the flashlight in the other, his jaw swinging side to side and pulsing pain through him with every step. But somehow, he managed to ignore it. The painkillers could wait. There were other priorities, like scouring the grounds for his morons. They were due a performance bonus.

When he reached the gardener's van, he stared through the window at an unknown man. *José, the gardener,* he realized at length. Of course it was… it was his van. But he looked so different with his genitals sitting in his lap and that knife poking out of his chest. Preston heard a noise and sprang into a gawky combat stance, panning the trees with his gun arm braced, his jaw swinging wildly and pumping squirts of pain through his eyeballs as he snapped his head this way and that.

No one.

The noise came from inside the van.

He didn't want to open it. He didn't want to find his stalwart crew hogtied in the back of a utility truck. He wanted to pump all fifteen rounds from his pistol through its cheap metal sides. Write a word in bullet holes like one of those old dot-matrix printers…

Sadly, not enough bullets to type *assholes*.

Rage and pain. They were mishmashing into a single thing. A new emotion, jagged and vindictive, and in eager pursuit of victims. He reined it in, a residue of common sense seizing control. He had no choice. He couldn't speak. He couldn't even call a doctor. He opened the back of the van. No surprises. The humiliation of Brink stealing the activator, then busting his jaw was beefed up by the spectacle of his overpaid security morons writhing on bags of horseshit. He surveyed them with his flashlight. Tony's bright eyes had the terrified look of trapped prey, but Bill's were glazed—concussed, probably. Preston stuck his gun in his belt and used pruning shears to clip the ropes tying Tony, making sure to nick plenty of flesh in the process. Then he stepped back and let Tony cut Bill loose, casually pulling his pistol. The two men clambered out of the van, spouting excuses until Preston shut them up by aiming the flashlight at his own busted and swollen face. They winced in unison, the penny dropping. CJ Brink's besting them was only the overture. This day was heading for a lot worse.

Preston showed them his gun and grunted a question mark. Tony shrugged a hopeless gesture. "He disarmed us. He must have taken our guns unless they're somewhere around here." Tony looked around as though scrambling through greenery at night in search of their missing arsenal might be a plausible option.

Preston was struggling with the urge to kill them both, but he restrained himself, stabbing his gun at Bill and saying, "…on."

Bill flashed a nervous look at his partner but then got it. "Phone? Sure. I got my phone." He whipped it out.

"…all octor." Preston hammered each syllable with his gun for emphasis.

"What?"

Preston shot him in the head and turned his gun on Tony so fast that Bill's bloody-brain mash was still sliding down José's van when he tried again.

"…all a ucking octor."

Tony blinked, terrified. Closing seconds in countdown mode.

"Doctor." He bawled it out like an evangelist seeing the light. "Sure." He snatched up Bill's phone, wiped the blood off it and hit the emergency call icon. "I'll have the paramedics here in…" He trailed off. Preston was already way up the drive, snarling his way back towards the villa.

VALENCIA

Eleven

CJ watched her from a backstreet bodega that gave him a line of sight to Denia port. Then he followed her as she crossed the parking lot and stood by a bollard down by the marina, looking out across the moored yachts and fishing boats towards the ferry terminal. As he approached, she whirled around and he stopped to take in the moment. This wasn't Jeanine Solo. This wasn't the girl in the photo Alex had showed him so many years before. This was a woman. The difference written on her face not so much by years carving lines as by emotion etching character in a thousand small ways. It was the face of a woman who had learned life's most important lesson and accepted its dictum without complaint.

Bad things happen to good people. So live with it.

CJ felt a kindred spirit the moment he saw her. Life had dealt him a few shit hands too. He didn't know much about her, but that face said a lot, those eyes especially—not jaded, but undefeated and indelibly hopeful. The rest he could imagine, the marriage exploding, coping with a child and making ends meet as a single parent, and succeeding in a notoriously male-dominated profession. No easy way for this lady, and now her life had gotten exponentially worse. Her son—that one blessing—had been abducted, and no way was she going to take that. Maybe she was a great-looking woman too. And, yes, she was. That didn't skip his attention either. But it was missing the point. To CJ Brink, she was perfect. He stepped closer, and she stared up into his eyes. He smiled and spread his arms wide, but she held up her hands as if to ward off the hug.

"They want me to kill you."

They were the first words that came out of her mouth.

CJ dropped his open arms. He shook his head and chuckled. This was Alex's sister alright. He reached out again and she took the hug this time, some bubble of tension bursting around them. He patted her back reassuringly, their faces cheek to cheek.

"It's going to be okay," he whispered. "We're going to get Aidan back. We can do this."

They broke apart and she nodded, adjusting her jacket, her arms trembling. CJ steered her away from the port. "Let's grab some food," he said. "Somewhere we can talk."

They walked in a palm-shaded pedestrian avenue across the road from the marina as CJ painted the big-picture view of his life since Nevada, explaining how he'd been spirited out of the US by Ashford and Colby and why Preston was accountable for her brother's death. His edited version was light on details, and she was peppering him with questions until he stopped and pointed out one of the superyachts moored there. "*True Grit*, that's Preston's yacht. He's heading to Majorca in it the day after tomorrow, and he needs something from us first. This way..." He led her off the walkway into a hotel restaurant, where they stopped at the bar and ordered tapas before taking a booth tucked away at the end of the bar.

"What's *the something he needs* that makes you so sure he'll play ball?" Jeanine said as soon as they were seated.

"It's called an activator."

"And what does it activate?"

"I'll get to that. Right now, you have to know that it's the most precious thing in Preston's world."

"That yacht. You think Aidan's on it?"

"No way. He'll be a thousand light years from anything connected to Preston."

"So what's the plan?"

"This afternoon I'll take you on a tour and explain everything. I have to prep some things too. I misspent some of my bad-boy years on this coast. So I know it well. I was into extreme sports back then and I still have some contacts here. So bright and early tomorrow, we're on. This time tomorrow, you and Aidan are going to be having lunch together." She went quiet at that, her eyes forlorn as though she didn't dare believe. CJ reached across the table and squeezed her hand. "I guarantee it."

As CJ and Jeanine set off on their tour, Preston was heading back to his Alcazada villa after a brief stay in the hospital, where surgeons had worked on him for hours, drilling and screwing for much of that time. His jaw had been dislocated and broken in two places, calling for an impressive array of hardware to patch it up—screws, plates, wires and some high-tech elastic invention that the surgeon was especially proud of. Preston could talk again and he was pain-free, although tripping major league on opioid painkillers and megadoses of antibiotics.

He had new security too, flown in from LA, and surprisingly, Tony had survived, recycled into the new team. He'd dodged a bullet by getting Preston prompt medical attention, then dumping those inconvenient bodies in a forested ravine where hungry boars would find them long before anyone else. So, with his jaw hinged by intermaxillary fixation screws, his safety guaranteed by his beefed-up security squad, and his spirit emboldened by enough narcotics to kill a large dog, Preston was on a roll.

At the villa, Tony helped him out of the car and escorted him inside. They went directly to the bar, where Preston planned on defying his doctors by topping up his meds with a shot of thirty-seven-year-old Islay malt.

"Here, Tony…," he said, sliding the first glass across to his stunned assistant before pouring a more generous measure for himself. They raised their glasses and intoned a solemn toast in union. "Domino." The burn was good, giving his heart a welcome thump. Preston took his scotch to the seating well under the atrium, where white leather sofas surrounded an art deco table in black Murano glass.

"They both called," Tony said. "Schilder three times."

"And you told him…?"

"You'd had an accident playing polo and were at the dentist."

"Good man." Preston owned a string of polo ponies, and he was well known on the circuit as the ringleader of a handful of aggressive players known as the Bruise Brothers. Tony had come up with a brilliant excuse, believable and pumping up his macho image at the same time.

"I'll get the room ready?" Tony was talking about the office annex where Preston made his secure calls. But as he turned to go, Preston called him back. He couldn't be bothered to head up there. The calls would be quick, with no critical exchanges, no details. They'd touch base and be done. Besides, he could just as easily use the encrypted app here as in the panic room.

"Take a seat." Preston waved to the sofas. "I want to go through some stuff with you after." And with that, he took out his phone and called Nazar… taking care of the easy one first.

Their conversation was short, but after a few jokes about Preston's slurred speech, it went straight to the point. According to Nazar, the Domino drop had gone as planned and he was already in Majorca and ready to rumble. Preston explained his schedule—how he would fly up to Denia, board his yacht and sail to the island. Everything was on track. As expected, Nazar whined on: the usual stuff, rants about Schilder. Preston let him whine away, sipping his Lagavulin meditatively and interjecting periodically with default platitudes before bringing the conversation to a close when he noticed his glass was empty. He gave it to Tony and signaled for him to fetch another, then called Schilder, who didn't waste a moment on small talk.

"What about our *special plan*?" he said.

This was exactly not the moment to get into this. *Our special plan* was what the creep was calling the hit on Nazar.

"Everything's in place. What about the diamonds?" Preston said, wanting to put him on the defensive and change the subject.

"Ditto."

"See you at the fiesta, then…"

"Hold on. I need details about the special plan, like—"

"The less you know the better. It's important to protect your deniability." That made sense, but Schilder was like a dog with a bone on this one and Preston was running out of patience. "Look, Mark, I'm not going to spell it out. Okay? Nazar will not be around to cause either of us any problems. That, I guarantee. Is that clear? Or are you saying that I don't have your trust?"

Ouch… that was a pinch point, and Schilder must have felt it because he backed off. More whining, of course. But that was okay. Just a few minutes' more handholding and Preston was off the phone.

He picked up the glass Tony had refreshed, noting that his PA had helped himself to another good slug in his own glass. He waved for him to sit down again. Tony had found Brink's messages and instructions and they had already discussed the activator's loss and the deal with Brink to get it back.

"Where's the kid?" Preston said.

"On the road… coming down from the mountains. They'll be at the rendezvous in time for the exchange tomorrow."

Preston nodded. "I want to talk to you about a *special plan* I've cooked up with Schilder."

"I think I got that from your call there… Mr. Nazar will be leaving the party early."

"Exactly. Let's work on the details on the flight later."

"Good enough."

"Tell me again how it went with Brink that day." He'd heard already, but that had been en route to the hospital with his attention crippled by pain. So Tony went through it all again, his nervous, sketchy account making one thing clear. Brink had made two trips that day, both in the gardener's vehicle, the first with no gardener, the second with the naked, dead gardener.

Why?

It troubled Preston. If Brink had bushwhacked the gardener to steal his vehicle, why wouldn't he just dump the guy in the woods? And why would he go fetch him later and bring him back? Compelling questions, and they were barely the warm-up for the biggie: *Why the hell was he naked?* The idea that Brink had abducted the gardener, stripped him, stabbed him, stashed him somewhere, then slipped into Preston's villa, neutralized the guards, interrogated and beaten Preston, stolen the activator, and gone to fetch the stashed naked gardener was completely preposterous.

So what, then?

The only answer that worked was *prior association*. Brink and the gardener had been part of a team and for some reason the gardener had run out of usefulness. Preston was staring as he thought this, his eyes parked on a *Rhapis excelsa*, better known as a lady palm. There were four of them, located at the corners of the seating well. He knew the name because it was written on a plastic tag stuck in the potting soil. A visitor had once asked him about the palms, and he'd felt like a fool for not knowing. So he'd had name tags put on every palm in the house, and that was plenty of tags. There were ten varieties of palms spread all over the house, and each one had its own requirements as to shade or light, moisture and acidity. So the name tag wasn't the only thing stuck in the pots. Each had a gizmo too. He wasn't sure exactly what it was, a thingy to check the pH, or take its pulse, or something. Palms are fussy beasts. That's why the naked gardener had to spend so much time in the house fussing with them.

Oh no… it couldn't be…

Preston leapt to his feet and stumbled to the closest palm. He ripped out the meter and gasped as it trailed wires, electrical wires, and plenty more gizmos. He held the bundle aloft and looked at Tony, his mouth agape, his silent scream all studs and screws.

"I'm on it, sir." Tony was on his feet, chugging his scotch like it might be his last.

Preston didn't move. He stood there like a mime holding the wires aloft as Tony disappeared upstairs, presumably fetching a scanner and retiring at a safe distance. Preston was sure to have a moment, and it was likely to be hazardous to the health of anyone within gunshot range. But that was not how it went. After a few minutes, Preston dropped the bug and lay on the sofa. He had a lot to think about. First there was an inventory to run. Not so difficult. Assuming there was a bug in each palm, all he had to do was count the palms, then check the last date the house had been swept and remember every call he'd taken from Nazar or Schilder in that vicinity and what they'd talked about. He gave up before starting. Even if he could remember it all, it would only be a fraction of what they'd heard. What about the conversations he'd had with Tony? But if they knew so much, why was he still a free man? They obviously didn't have enough. They didn't have the target and they didn't have the weapon. Thank God they'd given the EM-88 a code name. What they did have was enough to kill him, but not convict him. So all he had to do was see out these next few days.

He reached over and picked up his scotch. It was hard to drink it lying on his back with a busted jaw, and most of it dribbled down onto the white leather. He dropped the empty glass on the floor and closed his eyes. Moments later, none of it was an issue when the spirit of ancient stills and the science of synthetic opioids slammed together and knocked him out cold.

Jeanine looked at CJ, dumbfounded. She still didn't know the plan, but the first step was too weird already. She was standing next to him on Denia's main drag outside a high-end swimwear store. He was aiming his finger through the window at a one-piece in white.

"Or if you prefer—" He went to point out another option, but she cut him off.

"And this is the plan? We go to the beach?"

"Not the plan, the preplan. And you'll need some shorts and swim shoes."

"Why… may I ask?"

"Because you didn't bring any swimwear."

"No, I mean… why are we going to need them?"

He put his finger to his lips. "Blind faith. Remember. It's a lot easier to show you than tell you and a lot quicker too."

That at least made sense, and the sooner they got to that part the better. So Jeanine stopped protesting and followed him into the store, where she was appropriately outfitted, and they were soon on their way with CJ driving a tiny sedan. As he drove, he detailed his plan, the preparations he'd made and the bits that were still in the works. He'd rented a villa that came with the car they were driving, and he'd paid cash. So they were off everyone's radar. Bit by bit, he laid it out, and at every turn he'd scoot off into a sidebar about how Preston would push back or double-cross. His plan was both simple and detailed, brilliant and insane.

Ever the cop, Jeanine noted their route as they left the area. The N-323, it was a two-lane blacktop, winding south through rugged hills, squeezing between imposing bluffs of white-and-red rock and forested slopes of pine. They turned off that road in Benissa and cut down towards the sea, driving twisty canyon lanes bordered with white walls topped with bursts of bougainvillea. On switchback bends, she caught flashes of the Mediterranean and a coastline of craggy coves and sheer cliffs—more blond than white—and a distant city too, its high-rise skyline dwarfed between mountains. They drove into a narrow side road, a cul-de-sac, and CJ pulled up by the gate of a house at its end.

"Our base," he said, opening the gate with a fob on his key ring.

It was straight to business. No guided tour. So Jeanine shoveled it all in as she hurried behind CJ through the lush gardens, past the pool and the sea view to die for with none of it cracking her Kevlar-coated focus on one thing.

Aidan.

She changed while CJ made phone calls. She heard him arranging a taxi ride in execrable Spanish. That made her smile at least. With fifteen million Latinos in California, her fluent Spanish had proved to be a real asset in her career, and she could have helped him with that task. But she didn't offer. She might not know him so well, but she could sense his pride, and she didn't want to bruise it. Besides, his simple Spanish sounded cute, like a four-year-old kid. A much longer call followed in English, with CJ organizing a jet ski rental with Hans. He was evidently an old acquaintance who ran a sports equipment rental business in a nearby town, and CJ had a huge shopping list. He was still on that call when she was done with the dress code changes and joined him in the kitchen. She got them cold drinks as he talked, feeling his eyes checking her out as she stood at the fridge, then swerving away when she turned to face him and staring at that handsome Phoenix palm in the garden instead.

When he hung up, Jeanine passed him a glass of orange juice and said, "Speaking of equipment, where's my gun?"

CJ swigged his juice. "Later," he said, his eyes on her again and this time not flinching. He waved his hand at her like a conductor coaxing a mellow tone from the lead violin, a virtual caress of her beachwear body, all decked out in swimsuit and shorts. "That 9mm Glock would just kill your new look." She grinned despite it all. He was trying to cheer her up, and that was fine in her book.

"Okay, Romeo," she said, heading for the door. "Let's do it!"

They drove to a place called Cap Blanc. It wasn't Cabo Blanco, in Spanish, but Cap Blanc in French—it was that posh. Either way, it was a cape ending in a rocky point, the road to it lined with high-end homes, getting narrower until it dead-ended in a tiny parking area on a clifftop hundreds of feet above a rock-strewn beach. They got out of the car and stood by a rock wall, looking down the vertiginous drop to the beach.

"No sand." CJ pointed down at it and indicated how it stretched for miles. "So no tourists." There was a steep walkway of steps snaking down from the road to a slab of concrete with a metal ladder giving access to the sea, a crude swimming platform, but strictly for the brave and hearty fit enough to make the climb.

"With only a couple of parking spots," CJ said, "no beach and the triathletes-only stairway, no one comes here at this time of year. A few lovers maybe. But we'll be here at dawn, when they've got way better things to do, and the sunrise is on the other side of the cape, so nothing to see then either."

"You've thought of everything."

"Nobody ever does."

"And these villas?"

"Holiday rentals or second homes. Most are empty now."

So this was the place. Within twenty-four hours, she was going to get Aidan back, right here. It was so quiet except for the roll of waves on rocks hundreds of feet below, and the birds, the raucous caw of gulls soaring above the clifftop and the twitter of their land-bound cousins, hidden by bushes and trees.

Their taxi arrived, and they left their car and were soon heading down the coast towards Calpe, a tourist town of high-rise and beaches. They picked up their prearranged jet ski and were soon heading north, rounding a limestone outcrop sticking hundreds of meters out of the sea. Beyond the rock, the sea was choppy, but still benign compared to the Pacific waves that rolled up at Jeanine's closest beach in Venice. And CJ took it easy, no skimming wavetops on full throttle.

"We're saving gas," he explained, hollering over his shoulder.

It was her first time on a jet ski, and CJ had briefed her on riding double. So she started out with both hands on the rear grab handles. But that seemed awkward, or so she told herself, and after an intermediate hooking on the straps of his flotation device, her arms ended up wrapped around CJ's waist. And like that they cruised steadily, passing coves, rocky and empty for the most part, until they reached the long stretch of unbroken cliffs before Cap Blanc.

To Jeanine, it was surreal, a paradise in its way, but like the road to the pearly gates, scary. That bluff could turn into a heaven or a hell. Would she drive off with Aidan? Or would the worst thing happen? She refused to go there. To even think it. But she could feel it. She could hear it whispering to her from the other side of a thin wall of possibility. The only outcome that never occurred to her was that she might be killed herself. That wasn't something that even crossed her mind. The one taking all the risk was CJ. He'd be sitting in a bull's-eye, saying *try your luck, pal*, and his confidence was contagious with them both signed off on the bottom line. She was going to get Aidan back, or very bad things were going to happen to a lot of people.

About four hundred meters from Cap Blanc, CJ steered the jet ski towards the shore and dropped its speed to a crawl. "That's about as close as I can get with all those rocks," he said, choking the jet ski back to a halt.

Jeanine nodded and slipped off into the water. It wasn't so far, an easy swim. The hard part was getting out of the water. This wasn't a stone beach. These were rocks, and she was grateful for the swim shoes with their thick rubber soles. By the time she reached the beach, CJ had already pulled the jet ski further out. He was steering it back and forth, constantly glancing up at the cliffs, figuring out some logistics. When he finally cut the engine, he took out a foldaway anchor and opened the flukes. Then he put on a face mask and snorkel and dived the anchor. She didn't check her watch, but he had to be down there three or four minutes at least. When he came up, he checked the jet ski and swam to the shore, and together they navigated the field of rocks to the swim platform and made the long climb back to the car.

CJ took the wheel and they drove back to the villa. Jeanine's head was racing back and forth through the plan, her body stiffening up in anticipation, when CJ glanced across at her.

"Hey." He squeezed her hand. "It's time to get you that gun."

Twelve

It was always a possibility, floating at the edges of CJ's plan, and when they arrived the following morning a few hours before dawn, it turned into a reality. The cops were there, specifically, the Guardia Civil. Known as the *benemérita* or "reputables," Spain's oldest police force is half army and half cop and tasked with wide-ranging national security responsibilities, including coast guard and antismuggling operations. Although, all that being said, these two guys were just having a smoke. One was leaning against the squad car facing out to sea, the other sitting on the wall looking up at him. They were parked at the end of the road on Cap Blanc, right at the clifftop overlooking the rugged beach where CJ and Jeanine had swum ashore the night before after parking the jet ski.

CJ pulled up just a few feet away. Their presence at the fade of night was not unexpected. Maybe it was the jet ski that had caught their interest. Its sudden arrival on an empty stretch of coast that was so bather-unfriendly had piqued their curiosity. After all, it was an odd place to park an expensive toy like that when a kilometer down the coast there was a blue flag beach with safe moorings, lifeguards, and a gourmet's choice of lunch venues. Most likely, they patrolled that spot routinely a few times a night. It was a great observation post, a sea eagle's nest with a stupendous view of the coast all the way to the high-rise blocks of Calpe. But although it might have caught their attention, it was no biggie and certainly not a vessel of concern. No one was going to smuggle people or drugs on that.

CJ had encountered the *benemérita* on vacation trips in the distant past. They were nighttime ghosts, haunting highways and beaches, parking lots and alleyways, quiet places where the righteous do not end up at such times. So their presence was unwelcome, but not unexpected, and CJ had a plan. It was far from foolproof and called for a smidgen of luck, but it was workable, exploiting as it did cunning insights into the brains of cops, males and Spaniards.

"Oh dear…," Jeanine said, eying the cops furtively.

"*Viva España.*" CJ grinned and winked at her. "It's my lucky day." He got out of the car, buffoon's grin intact. "*Señores.*" He wiped the grin off his cheeks and snapped a curt US-style salute with the downturned palm, following it up with a warm smile. Both cops said, "*Señor,*" rather formally, and the younger one sitting on the wall with the best eyeshot of Jeanine getting out of the car added, "*Señora.*"

CJ stepped up to the wall a few feet away from the young cop. Jeanine stood beside him, and he draped his arm around her shoulders and pulled her close.

"There…" He pointed along the coast to the limestone plinth poking out of the sea at Calpe. "We're going to climb that later. It's three hundred and thirty-two meters. It's a natural park with hundreds of bird species and unique plants. The Phoenicians called it the Northern Rock to distinguish it from Gibraltar, its big brother, the Southern Rock."

"Really… that's so interesting."

And with that, they kicked off their scripted dialogue, looking down at the stone-strewn coast as they continued their banter for the benefit of the cops in case they spoke or understood English. And as they talked, they edged away from the wall and sauntered down the steep path to the sea, hand in hand, swaying apart, then back together. CJ heard a cop's whispered comment followed by his partner's gruff chortling, a locker room riposte, no doubt. Perfect. They were approaching a twist in the path, about to disappear from the cops' line of sight, when CJ cued Jeanine by squeezing her hand. She stopped, and for a moment, they stood staring at each other at arm's length, hands entwined.

Then Jeanine stepped into his arms. It had to come from her. They'd both agreed. She reached up and pulled his head down onto her face. CJ had jokingly told her to shoot for an Oscar if they had to put on a show, but this was no Hollywood kiss, no mealy-mouthed faking. This was the real thing. She pushed him back to the wall and rolled his head to the side, getting in so deep CJ lost track for a moment. He heard the cop car rumble into life, more laughter, and a macho hoot echoing off stone walls as it climbed back up the twisting road.

Jeanine stepped back, heaving a few breaths through her mouth, and they stared at each other. CJ felt giddy, reining it in. They both looked back up the road. No cops. CJ checked his watch. And not much time either. The love scene had been sketched out but unrehearsed. All the rest of the show was drilled down to a T and they went straight at it, racing back to the car and popping the trunk on their treasure trove of gear.

From now on, it was strictly business.

As CJ and Jeanine prepared the landing zone for Preston, the Tratfors CEO was on his way somewhere else, heading for the wrong place. He knew that. And he knew exactly what would happen when he got there. He'd get a message from Brink sending him on another leg of the goose chase, and maybe there'd be another message when he got there. Brink might even cancel and set it all up for another day. And why not? He had the upper hand. That son of a bitch could send them to the town square and have them sing "Ring Around the Rosie" if he wanted to and they'd be sure to comply.

Or would they?

What if Preston said *Screw it? To hell with you. To hell with Schilder, Nazar. All of you.*

To hell with Domino!

He looked out the window at mountains, bluffs, forests, all passing eerily in moonlight.

Why was he thinking this garbage?

He was becoming obsessed with Brink, a hunter so focused on his prey that he was melding with it. Brink was his white whale. Brink was crazy. That wasn't rhetoric. That was a fact. Now Preston was becoming crazy too, his world slipping out of focus. Brink believed he was immortal, his life cocooned in safety by his dead comrade, Saint Alex. Preston had read all this in Brink's misappropriated medical file. No one was immortal. That was a fact, but an irrelevant one. In the real world, believing was the key to transformation. American soldiers were the best in the world not because they were the best trained and equipped—although they were certainly both of those—but because they *believed* they were. Of all the lessons he'd learned at West Point, that was the most valuable. The awesome power of belief. And Brink had it stenciled into his guts.

Preston took a tissue from his pocket and wiped his brow.

The AC was blasting, but he was in a cold sweat.

Not good.

"You okay, boss?" Tony was sitting next to him in the back of a Mercedes SUV, eying him like a worried spouse. There were two armed men up front and three more in the people carrier traveling in the convoy. Ernald was in a third car, along with the kid and his babysitter, the psychopathic nurse Ernald had dug out of that socialist-medicine dung heap in the UK.

Preston nodded to Tony that he was okay. *What an asshole!* Of course he wasn't okay. He had more bolts in his head than Frankenstein, and if he didn't get that goddamn activator, he'd be twice as dead.

His phone signaled an incoming message.

Brink. New instructions.

They hadn't even gotten to their destination, and he'd peeled them off to a new one. Nice tactics. Keep the bastards guessing and always stay one step ahead. Dawn. That was his target window for sure. It would all come down in that crack beloved by military planners, the fateful seconds between the darkest hour and first glint of light when the world rolls over and comes back to life. The new place was Cap Blanc. He checked the map on his phone. It was a cape on the nearby coast, an exchange point at the end of a road to nowhere.

Interesting.

He showed Tony, who relayed instructions while he messaged his pilot on the *True Grit*. The yacht had left Denia Marina during the night and was loitering with intent a few miles offshore, hiding behind Cap d'Or, another craggy cape, a few minutes to the north by chopper. Brink would anticipate an aerial intervention, and he'd have a contingency. So Preston had made no particular plan other than to have the chopper ferry him out to his yacht after the exchange. But now he told the pilot to get ready. Just in case.

They left the main road at Teulada and cut down through narrow lanes to the coast. The first daylight was emerging as they wound through switchback bends between rock walls and sleepy villas, slowing to a crawl on the last few bends before running out of road at a stone wall on a cliff's edge.

And there he was…

Brink.

He'd anticipated an aerial intervention alright, and he'd figured out a defense. Not exactly high-tech. In fact, it was laughably analog. Only Preston didn't laugh. He gasped, his jammed-up jaws squeezing it into a grunt.

There it was.

The activator.

The cross was dangling from a string.

One end of the string was in Brink's hand, and at the other end was a kite jerking back and forth. The sun was up now, the winds switching from offshore to onshore and getting whipped up by canyons and cliffs. If Brink let go of that string, the kite would spiral hundreds of meters in seconds and get buffeted inland, ending up in some wasteland of rocks and scrub in the mountains.

Brink raised his other hand, the one holding the 9mm pistol, but he didn't aim it. He waved it above his head like he was some kind of goddamn tour guide waving a flag to assemble his group. Always the comedian. Him and that dickhead Solo.

Tony poked him with his elbow and nodded to the side.

Preston had almost missed it. The cop mom crouching behind some poky Eurotrash sedan. She was squeezed between the car and the rock wall of a driveway, effectively in a sniper hole, impossible to take out, and the angles were perfect. His team was in a crossfire at oblique angles.

Preston gave the word and the vehicle doors opened, and as soon as he stepped out, he checked the kite more closely. It was an eagle. One of those kites they use to frighten seagulls and stop them from crapping on their precious villas.

"Let's see the boy." Brink was pointing the gun now, and Preston had no illusions about who would get his first bullet. Preston nodded and the psycho nurse stepped out of the car with the kid. It was the first Preston had seen him. He'd been unconscious when they'd bundled him into the car, but now he was awake, if only barely. They must have given him a shot of something. The boy stumbled and the nurse jerked his hand, pulling him up onto his feet.

"You bastard." Jeanine's voice cut through the fake calm and cranked the tension up to stratospheric. CJ had told her to watch out. It'll hit you like a Mack truck, he'd said. And that was pretty much it. She'd thought she was ready. But that was thought. This was reality. This was her son getting abused right in front of her. She was a cop, trained to control her emotions. But all that cop stuff went right off the cliff, and the woman left behind holding the gun was pure mom. She could barely breathe, rage scorching her insides, the urge to splatter that bitch's brains all over that white rock wall overwhelming her.

"Preston," CJ barked out, more for her benefit than the others and she knew it. She snatched a breath, her teeth grinding, her gunsights beaded on the woman's face.

Just one twitch, please.

"I've got a plan," CJ said. "Everyone gets what they want and lives. Jeanine gets Aidan, you get the activator, and no one gets dead. But all that can go tits up in a heartbeat. The most dangerous thing around here is not me or any of your goons, but a mother with a gun who knows how to shoot. So I'd caution your madam there to avoid provocations. Or all bets are off."

Preston looked around. Jeanine felt his eyes on her, but she kept hers on her gunsights and the woman who was looking at her now, her face angling away like she might duck and cover at any moment. But that was not going to work. Jeanine was on this. The first bullet would blow her head off. The second would take out Preston while CJ targeted his henchmen. No need to call Aidan. He'd be on his way. Doped or not, he was smart. He'd be stumbling as best he could across the road to the driveway. It wasn't so far. No one would shoot him. They'd be aiming at her, but she was well covered. Preston would no doubt be figuring all this out, and as a former lieutenant colonel, he was sure not to miss the obvious. Although his team had the numbers, they were outmaneuvered. Behind them was a stone wall twelve feet high, so any bullets that missed them might very well catch them on the ricochet.

Preston looked at the big woman and she nodded compliantly, restraining Aidan with her hands on his shoulders more gently. Jeanine was glad of that. She was nowhere close to calm, but at least she wasn't going to lose it. Not unless that woman did one stupid thing.

"Send Ernald on over here to check the activator," CJ said. "When he gives you the okay, you release the boy to his mother. Ernald will get to hold the string and multitask as a bulletproof vest for me while mother and son drive out of here. So this is a good time for you to fess up if you have any guys waiting up the road. If so, you better tell them to get lost."

"No guys up there."

"That's great, because if I don't get an okay message from Jeanine, I put one bullet in Ernald's head and you can watch your activator fly up to heaven. But not for long, because I'll put a second bullet in that fancy lamp up there." He waved his gun and they all screwed their heads up to the period piece lamp stuck high up on the wall behind them. "You may have noticed that rock quarry up on the road from Denia. *Boom.* Someone broke into their operations center last night and nicked a few sticks of dynamite. So you'll get to join the activator after a messy but brief interval." Jeanine enjoyed a secret smile. CJ had stood on the car and stuffed the lamp with flour. But from where these guys were standing, it just could be. Besides, who'd take the chance with Crazy James Brink? Preston jerked his head at Ernald to get on with it, but Ernald had other ideas. He glared at CJ, then looked back at Preston, his face melting into a plea, begging for some alternative to his leading role as a Kevlar shield.

"Tony...," Preston said.

Ernald took the hint, reaching into the people carrier, then making his way to CJ—forlorn and cowed—with a tablet. Jeanine watched, a sense of justice brimming in her chest, her tormentor, the arrogant child thief, now just a whipped dog. As the woman stepped back to let him by, Jeanine got a better look at Aidan. They'd obviously doped him up. But his eyes were alert, picking her out and coming to life. He went to speak, but the tiniest flick of her head shut that down.

CJ pulled on the kite string, tugging it down a few feet so Ernald could grab the cross. He stuck it in the tablet and hit a few keys on the virtual keyboard. It only took a couple of minutes. He turned to Preston and nodded. CJ gave him the kite string to hold with its precious cargo hanging a few feet above his head. Then he jerked him around so he was facing his comrades and CJ was tucked behind him.

"Send the boy over to his mom," CJ said. "Your man's got what you want."

"But if you shoot him, I'll lose it," Preston said.

"Why would I do that?"

"To spite me."

"I'm beyond that, Preston. This is all about the boy."

"Then why not make me happy and tie the kite string to him? You never know—he might trip and fall on the way back here. Wouldn't that be a tragedy?"

CJ looked around like he was figuring something out, then dragged Ernald back towards the clifftop wall. "If I see a gun," he said, "he gets tossed down the cliff, and you guys have to dig me out from behind a stone wall."

Jeanine followed it with her peripheral vision, Ernald stiffening up as CJ tied the string around his throat. Hard not to enjoy that one. The sadistic bastard squealing as the kite tucked and tossed in the stiff breeze, yanking at his throat.

"And now, the boy goes to his mother," CJ said.

Preston looked at her. This was hurting him, reluctant even now, a man who hated to be beaten. She took her eyes off the woman for the first time and met his gaze, aiming her weapon at him in a show of force. They'd rehearsed this moment, so she knew that CJ was now covering the woman and if she pulled the trigger, both Preston and the woman would be dead. Even so, Preston played it out, the calculating son of a bitch. Then he smirked and waved his hand for the woman to release Aidan as though he was giving away nothing.

"Aidan," Jeanine called and he ran towards her. She scooped him up with one arm as he slipped between the car and the driveway wall, feeling his face against hers, his wet lips on her cheek… his touch, his smell. But her eyes and her gun were still on Preston as she kicked wide the half-open door and put Aidan on the back seat.

"Get down." He went to speak, but she quietened him. "You're safe now. We're going home."

They weren't safe and she knew it, but it felt safe. The Aidan effect. Having her son back in her arms was a shot of medicine that cured all ills. She was strong again, confident. She had her son and a gun to protect him and she had CJ Brink covering her back. The life she'd lost had been recovered.

She pulled out of the driveway and drove up the winding road. She'd made it. They'd made it. Aidan was shaking his head, clawing his way out of whatever they'd doped him up on. He'd be okay, she told herself. Beyond the coast road, she headed up steep, twisting lanes and pulled into the villa.

"Mom…," Aidan said, looking around as they pulled into its driveway. "Was that really CJ? Is this his HQ?"

Jeanine jumped out of the car. Aidan was born after Alex had been taken hostage. So what could he know about CJ? Even his uncle was just photos, videos, and family memories. The answer was everything. Her son lived on the internet, and he'd always been fascinated by his hero uncle Alex. He was sure to have hunted down every bit of information out there about CJ too. She opened the back door to help him out, but he didn't need it.

"We've got a plane to catch," she said, ignoring his question. "There was supposed to be a taxi waiting for us. But guess what? This is Spain, so it's late."

She pulled out her phone and called the local taxi company, repeating the address twice and the word *rápido* three times just to make sure the message got through. Aidan looked up at her, smiling as she spoke, and she noticed it and ruffled his hair. Satisfied that the cab was just minutes away, she hung up and took his hand, and together they walked to the gate.

"Where are we going?" Aidan said.

"Home… we're heading to Alicante Airport."

"What about CJ? Shouldn't we help him?"

"Honey… CJ Brink does not need a lifesaver from the likes of us. Believe me, that man can take care of himself. He's pretty darn self-sufficient as far as survival goes."

Minutes later, they were huddled in the back of the cab, speeding up steep lanes to the *autopista*.

Next stop—USA.

At least, that was the plan.

Thirteen

CJ was doing fine.

So far…

He was nestled behind Ernald, his bullet stopper, his face creepily close as he whispered in Ernald's ear, "I hear you're quite a lad…"

"What d'you mean?" Ernald squeezed it out staccato, his delivery punctuated by kite-cord throttling.

"Torturing a mother by stealing her kid. Takes a big man to do that."

CJ was waiting for the all clear from Jeanine, and what better way to spend the time than to settle an outstanding account on her behalf? There was another reason too. He needed to distract Ernald and keep his mind on other things. That explained the noose. That wasn't all fun. It was designed to keep his eyes from wandering and looking down at the ground, where he might notice that the tail end of the kite string was not an end. It was a beginning. It was tied to a transparent fishing line that snaked backwards under CJ's foot and over the wall. Beyond that, it found its way down the cliff and out over the water where it was tethered to the jet ski. *To spite me,* Preston had speculated earlier, but this wasn't about spite. This was about Domino. Nazar, Schilder and Preston were not going to cash in on a new war that would cost hundreds of thousands of lives. CJ had seen way too much war for that to happen.

"No, that's all wrong," Ernald said. "Harriet would have killed him and said it was an accident. She gets off on it."

"You like the young ones? Easy to pick on. Vulnerable. Is that your type?"

"No, no…"

"I remember creeps like you."

"I was sick. I got treatment."

CJ leaned in closer, his lips trailing against Ernald's throat.

"Well… just in case you have a relapse, I'm going to give you a memento of our encounter, something to refresh your memory every time you look in the mirror."

He scooped up Ernald's ear, sucking it in between his teeth and slamming his jaws together lock tight. Ernald whimpered and Preston and his team jolted as one, mouths opening in disbelief, eyes in wonder. But no one moved, they all watched mesmerized as CJ snapped his head to the side, twisting his neck like a pit bull and ripping Ernald's ear clean off his head. Ernald screamed, trailing it off into a whinny when CJ spat the ear in front of him and his eyes fell on it. There it was lying on the sun-bleached asphalt with a river of his own piss steaming towards it.

Silence.

It was an impressive show, but not the type that gets a round of applause. Besides, the silence was broken by a ringing phone.

CJ's.

He let it ring and ring again. Ernald sniveled. And Preston's team eked back to life, some exchanging glances although most were still preoccupied with that ear.

CJ waited.

This was the hairy moment.

Two calls meant safe. Three meant unsafe. Two meant that they were clean away. Three meant that they'd been waylaid and someone was forcing Jeanine to send an *okay* message.

But the third ring never came.

CJ took the moment and let a wave of gratitude wash over him. Aidan was safe. Jeanine and her son were on the way to Alicante Airport. Soon they'd be inside the wall of airport security, and within hours they'd be on their way back to California. In a perfect world, the rest of the plan would go tick-tock. But ultimately, it didn't matter. Duty was done. Must-do was taken care of. Now it was all down to his want list, and that was short. Survival was number one, with sabotaging Preston's war plans a close second. No need to kill him. Killing his dream was enough. His partners in crime would take care of him after that.

CJ waved his gun at Preston's troops. "I'm going to let this guy go and step back over this wall. So take it easy and make nice."

They all nodded agreement in unison like choreographed marionettes, but their body language called it out as a lie, arms edging out, getting ready for a gun draw. Not unexpected. Preston had lost his hostage, and even if he got the activator, it still wouldn't be enough. Ending up even was not an acceptable scorecard for him.

"Say, CJ...," Preston said as CJ dragged Ernald backwards, getting closer to the wall with each step. "You remember that time I visited you guys in Iraq. We drank a few beers and played a few hands of hold'em." He made it sound like he'd been one of the boys. But CJ remembered it differently, the boss in a fleeting visit delivering a pep talk in a fresh-out-of-the-box camouflage outfit, then getting the hell out before any angry Iraqis with guns showed up. Preston's hand emerged above the SUV holding a pistol, but he wasn't threatening with it. He was doing it nice and slow, pointing the gun up in the air. "You're one hell of a poker player," he said before shooting out the booby-trapped lamp on the wall. Glass tinkled against rocks and clouds of flour swirled in the wind.

That was the starter pistol, and all eight of them went for their guns. CJ jerked the string, releasing the slip knot that tethered the kite to Ernald's throat, as he shot him in the shoulder and pushed him into the line of fire. Ernald stumbled, releasing the kite, and it blasted skyward, shrinking to a speck in an instant. CJ leapt back, smashing his foot down in wind-withered shrubs and bursting smoke grenades before rolling over the wall. He bounced off a narrow ledge and tumbled down the cliff face until a gnarly old pine broke his fall. That wasn't by chance but by choice, the tree carefully chosen. It was stunted and tough, a tree seeded on the edge of doom and made strong by it, the ultimate survivor tree saving the ultimate survivor man from a four-hundred-foot drop to oblivion.

CJ opened the knapsack he'd tied to it and took out more smokers. He'd bought an assorted box, the kind skydivers and stunt pilots use. He broke them open and the wind was soon whipping clouds of red, white and blue up the cliff to the parking lot. It gave him no visibility, but that didn't matter. He knew his way around the kit, and within minutes he was in the rig of his favorite ram-air chute.

There were no shots from above. No random shooting into clouds of smoke. CJ had called that one right. Preston was military, and any decision he made now would be tactical. Killing CJ would delight him, but he'd lost the activator and the boy. Killing a man lurking somewhere on a cliff hidden by clouds of billowing smoke was a major undertaking with plenty of downside. There'd already been too much gunfire. A couple of shots might get written off as fiesta firecrackers out of time. More than that was too risky. Preston would already be looking for an escape route back to the safety of his yacht.

CJ jumped off the ledge, and the static line he'd tied to the pine tree triggered the canopy. He was free, emerging from the smoke on an eight-second glide before hitting the water fifty feet from the jet ski. Weighted down with kit, he went under and stayed there several minutes, uncoupling himself before kicking up back to the surface in the cover of the jet ski.

Checkpoint one. He looked back at the clifftop. Just a few wisps of smoke left now and no one visible at the wall, no spotter with binoculars and a buddy with a sniper's rifle.

Checkpoint two. The sky. And there it was, his eagle dancing way above the jet ski. That eighty-pound monofilament line had held, and so had the knots he'd used to tie the spools together.

He double-checked the clifftop before climbing on board the jet ski, a smile itching to break out, his personal mantra buzzing in his ears.

When faced with the impossible… bold is best.

As CJ was pulling himself out of the water, Preston was calling his pilot and tasking him with an urgent mission.

"A kite?" the pilot said. "You're kidding me. A kite flying somewhere over these mountains? You want me to catch it?"

"And get yourself a nice bonus. Either that or get yourself a new job. Something more sedentary. Better suited to a man with broken arms and legs."

"Sir."

"After you get it, pick me up. You know where."

Preston hung up, and he was bemoaning his troubles when he heard a distant siren.

"Move it," he said as they sneaked up the winding lanes.

He'd been foolish. That cocky wild west show, shooting out Brink's lamp, calling his bluff. Sheer bravado. What was he thinking? This was not gunshot country. In a sleepy town like this, law enforcement was bound to be on the way, and a convoy of inordinately well-armed men in big black vehicles was not going to pass as a bunch of beachgoers out for an early-morning swim.

When they hit the coast road, the cars split up. The first vehicle had the psycho nurse at the wheel, Ernald bleeding on the back seat, and a trunk stuffed with all their guns. So if there were any cops up the road, they'd stop them first and have plenty of paperwork to keep them busy. The rest of the team was split between the other two vehicles, leaving Preston alone to call a taxi. He insisted on an English-speaking driver, and he was soon winding up narrow lanes to the N332, his eyes sweeping the vista of stony terraces strewn with vines and olive and almond trees. It was time to lick wounds and regroup, an empty moment of cool and quiet before the sun came up.

He'd been bested. No argument about that.

Goddamn Brink.

That slip knot… how slick was that?

But it wasn't just the losing that troubled him. Shooting Ernald had put Brink at risk, making it more likely he'd get shot himself. He'd risked his life, so the activator would fly off into nowhere. Why would he risk his life to stop Preston from getting that activator? Brink was crazy, not stupid. He was smart and calculating. That was what made him so dangerous. So why had he done it? The taxi had reached the N332 and they were wending their way through the rugged, rocky landscape when the answer came to him. The breeze was onshore. There was no doubt about that. He'd seen the flour, clouds of it bursting above their heads, and all of it whipped away up the hill, not out to sea. But as they'd made their speedy getaway, he'd spotted the kite through the pines and palms of the villas, and it had been in the wrong place. Out to sea, dodging around like it was tethered to a jet ski.

Some transparent thread… a fishing line.

It had to be.

So Brink still had the activator. The cunning bastard had staged that ear thing to look like madness, but it was a roadshow to keep them all distracted. And by God it had worked. He'd bitten off the whole goddamn ear. Unforgettable. And Ernald's face when Brink had spat it out like a plug of chewed tobacco. *Who's going to be looking anywhere else at a moment like that?*

Preston whipped out his phone. His pilot was already on the way and the sound of the rotors in the background reassured him. *Power.* That's what he had, oodles of the juice that ran the world.

"It's not over the mountains," he said.

"What?"

"The kite. The eagle kite. It'll be with Brink on a jet ski. He'll be heading for Calpe. So you've got time. Who's with you?"

"Jimmy."

Preston took a second to pull Jimmy's service file out of his head.

Good enough.

"You've got the usual kit?"

"Sir."

"Then get me that eagle. If possible… clean up. No traces. No *nada*. No Brink. But the priority is the eagle and the cross hanging off it. Don't risk anything for that."

He hung up, his mood brightening. Pain was oozing back into his jaw, but somehow it was less bothersome now.

This could turn out to be a great day.

Thirty minutes into the taxi ride to Alicante Airport, it all caught up with Jeanine—the sleepless night, the predawn call to battle and those waves of adrenaline coursing through her trigger finger. Her head lolled to the side before she snapped it back, her eyes flashing. It wasn't much of a siesta by Spanish standards, more of a marble-drop nap, a millisecond of unconsciousness, but it left her disoriented.

"*Dónde estámos?*" she said, eying a city bristling with high-rise towers, a city squeezed between jagged mountains and the sea.

The driver looked at her in the rear-view mirror. "Benidorm," he said.

Aidan was peering down at the city too.

"You okay?" she said.

He nodded. "But we have to go back, Mom."

"We are going back. We're getting on a plane to LA. Or we will be soon. We'll have an hour between flights in Madrid, but then it's homeward bound for us."

"We have to go back and help CJ. I need to tell him something."

"He doesn't need our help. He's got a plan. This is part of it. Our part. Getting to safety. And whatever you want to say, you can tell him later."

"I heard something in the car this morning."

Jeanine swiveled her head down to get a closer look at her son.

"So tell me what you heard and I'll call him." Aidan looked up warily and nodded his head at the driver but said nothing. "The driver's not James Bond, Aidan, and neither are you. What is it?"

"It's not like that. It's the context, the way they said it. I've got to explain the whole thing. It's important."

"And so is getting back to LA. Believe me, after what we've been through to get you out, there's no way we're going back. Now get some rest."

Aidan checked the driver again and reached up to whisper in her ear. "Thousands of people are going to die."

Jeanine put her arm around him. He'd heard something all right. Her son wasn't the type to make stuff up, and that jibed with what CJ had told her. But they'd doped him up. Anything he remembered could hardly be relied on.

"Maybe they were talking about a movie or some video game."

"Mom… please."

"It doesn't make sense. They wouldn't talk about their plans in front of you."

"Why not? They were going to kill me anyway." Jeanine's face blanked over, his words hammering her with the frightening reality of what he'd been through.

Jeanine hugged him, reassuring herself as much as him. The horror was over. They were minutes away from safety. Jeanine spoke to the driver in Spanish, and he confirmed that they were less than thirty minutes out from the airport. She checked her watch.

"We'll get some coffee at the airport. You can tell me about it then."

"You mean we're not going back?"

"We're going home, Aidan. And that's final. Whatever's going on back there—it's not our battle."

Aidan was quiet after that, turning his head away and staring out the window. She took his hand and gave it a little shake.

"At the airport, I'll call him," she said. "I promise. You can talk to him then. Okay?"

CJ was never going to pick up that phone. He'd be way too busy for a farewell chat, and Jeanine knew it, but the promise was enough to appease Aidan.

"Thanks, Mom," he said, but he kept his eyes on the window.

Fourteen

Jeanine was right. CJ was way too busy, and about to get even busier. He was holding an even course, far enough offshore to skirt the capes and not so far as to pick up the swell further out. He was making good time too, but not good enough—a fact rammed home by a distant sound…

Rotor blades.

Beyond the din of the jet ski and the sloshing waves it left in its wake, he could make out a new sound echoing across the water. Choppers on the French Riviera might be routine, but not here. On this stretch of coast, a helicopter fly-by was a rare event and it was most likely to be official business, cops or firefighters. He looked over his shoulder. No second-guessing required—it was heading his way. Only he didn't call the cops or the fire brigade.

The kite?

It was still buffeting in the wind above the jet ski. CJ had sped from the scene in case Preston had deployed a sniper. Winding in a few hundred meters of fishing line on a stationary jet ski, he'd have made a great target. But he'd gambled on Preston not figuring out the ruse. The Tratfors CEO was supposed to think that the kite had blown free. But evidently, he'd found his way to the truth.

CJ weaved back and forth as the chopper approached, his options few and all of them ugly. Running to the shore was doom. He'd never make it, and there was nothing there but exposed beaches and cliffs. The jet ski was fast and maneuverable, but against the chopper it was a sitting duck. They'd cruise up, get real close, then take him out. He could cut the engine and hide under it. The jet ski was made of fiberglass, but it had plenty enough metal components to stop a bullet. But these guys were pros. Most likely they'd have grenades, or divers they could drop into the water.

The chopper swooped in low behind him. He swerved, kicking up as much spray as he could. It was a Band-Aid. Nothing more. They didn't have to go for a single shot. They were offshore with screaming engines to drown the sound of gunfire and deep waters to swallow the spent rounds. They could afford to be generous with lead. Automatic gunfire was the order of the day, and no amount of fancy driving was going to save him from that. The first burst almost did the job, with a round punching through the fiber at his feet. All he had was his 9mm pistol and a knife. Never bring a knife to a gunfight. Wasn't that what they said? But CJ suddenly realized that the knife was his only hope. The kite was the target. He was the bonus. He whipped out his knife, slashed the kite string and rolled off the back of the jet ski a split second before the next burst pocked it with holes. He tucked himself under the now silent engine compartment and waited, tracking events by the water whipped up in the downdraft of rotors. The chopper was idling, taking a closer look before heading off to snag that kite. Professional pride would demand it. But how long could they afford to risk losing that kite as it spiraled skyward? CJ's working time underwater on a single breath had been four minutes back in his days with the Special Boat Service. But this wasn't working time, this was static apnea, holding your breath while doing nothing, and the answer was six minutes. He timed it, his eyes flicking from his watch to the shifting patches of frenzied water above. But in the end, it was kite need to have, Brink nice to have. So the chopper went on its way. CJ surfaced, sucking in long breaths and watching the helicopter as it became a dot. He couldn't see the kite, but he had no doubts that they could. In any event, he had to assume the worst—they had the activator. That part of his mission had failed. Domino was go. It wasn't his war. But that didn't mean he wasn't going to fight it.

EM-88?

He still had no idea, but the acronym was somehow familiar. Theoretically, he could walk away, but that wasn't even on his option list. Some wars you get signed up for, and some you get to choose. And Domino was one of them. He was going to stop it.

But how?

He had a few ideas about that, most of them crazy, and all of them starting with the same first step, although it was not so much a step as a stroke. He checked his watch. Jeanine and Aidan would be at the airport. That comforted him as he set off for the shore.

Arriving at Alicante Airport, Jeanine scanned the scene with her cop's eyes—scurrying travelers, some with faces bright with expectation, others dark and anxious. It was the same show playing out simultaneously at airports around the planet. Tender moments with no stage to play them out on and never enough time. The taxi edged around vehicles vying for a spot to offload their passengers before cutting into the curb. She'd never been to this airport before, but it all looked as it should have. It had a comforting familiarity, and blessedly nothing and nobody seemed out of place, most especially the uniformed officers cradling submachine guns and parsing the comings and goings with watchful eyes.

"I need a bathroom," Aidan said as they hurried into the departure building. "They drove me down from the mountains. It took like hours."

No problem there. Jeanine needed a bathroom too. She had to dump her pistol in the trash before hitting the security gate. And with that done, she waited outside the *Caballeros*, grabbing Aidan's hand when he exited and steering him towards a check-in counter.

"You said you'd call CJ."

"And I will. We'll have plenty of time for that when we get through security."

"That'll take forever." Aidan waved at the waiting throng funneling into the security gates. "And I'm hungry."

That was a good sign. He was bouncing back to his old self. She checked her watch and looked around, thinking about the cops she'd seen on the forecourt. They were already safe. They'd made it. And they had plenty of time before the flight. So they found a kiosk selling coffee and sandwiches and ate hungrily at a table nearby, the air rich with the smell of coffee as an endless stream of travelers fueled their journeys with shots of caffeine.

"So now you can call CJ," Aidan began, lifting his sandwich above his mouth and scooping down a trailing morsel of ham. "What you can say is—"

"I'm not sure it's so smart."

"You said you'd call."

"I think it's better I send a message. We don't know what's happening on his end. A call could come at the wrong time, and if he misses it, he might think we're in danger. It's risky. I don't want to endanger him." She didn't add "do you?" but that was the subtext, and Aidan was way smart enough to get it.

"Okay," he said, stringing out the word and lacing it with disappointment.

Jeanine put down her sandwich, wiped her hands on a napkin and took out her phone. "So what do you want me to say?"

"Important… that's got to be the first word." Aidan dictated the message between mouthfuls of sandwich. But Jeanine soon stopped him. "You're spinning it. *Demonic plot?* Come on, Aidan, give me a break. Stick to the facts and make it short."

"Okay…" Aidan made a face. "So just write… USS *Abe*."

"That's it?"

"I'll betcha he knows what it means."

Jeanine eyed her son thoughtfully, then tapped his message into the phone and sent it.

"Thanks, Mom." Aidan was all smiles now.

Jeanine picked up her sandwich.

"While you finish that, I'm going to get that soccer shirt." He waved at the window of a store adjoining the coffee kiosk.

"Oh, really? And what are you going to use for money?"

"Come on, Mom. It's Real Madrid, Ronaldo, number 7. This is a real find. He moved to Juventus. It must be old stock. It's a collector's item."

Jeanine shook her head. It was not just a no to his request. It was wonderment at his prodigious memory for trivia. He was a sporting almanac and he'd evidently added European soccer to his voluminous knowledge of US sports.

"Please, Mom, it'll be like a souvenir."

"Are you pulling my leg? That word means to bring something to mind. You want to bring all this back."

Aidan sat back, his face angling away from her and looking down at the floor. "Thanks for the French lesson."

"You've got no phone," she said. "And I'm not letting you out of my sight until you get one."

"I won't be out of your sight. I'll be right there." He pointed at the store, and Jeanine looked it over again. She could see through the display window. There was a young woman sales assistant, tidying shelves of folded sports shirts. No one else. No customers. "C'mon, Mom. There are cops outside with machine guns. No one's going to mess with me."

"Five minutes," Jeanine said, taking a credit card out of a leather billfold. "And if it's more than fifty euros, don't get it. These airport stores are a rip-off."

Aidan stood up, took the card, and went to go. But then he turned back. "You were incredible this morning. I wasn't so out of it that I couldn't see what was going down. *Incredible*. That's the only word. I'm never going to forget that. And when you're an old lady, I'm going to remind you… how you were once this incredible warrior who fought for her son."

All that was so sudden, his words so unexpected, it triggered an emotional gear shift she couldn't handle, and she teared up, sniffing it back, and mouthing a silent thank-you. Aidan smiled and walked off to the store. Jeanine pulled it together, chiding herself. This wasn't like her. Nothing like her. She'd held it together so long, but now she was turning into an emotional train wreck.

She watched Aidan, snatches of him between the mannequins in the store windows. She drank her coffee. Her sandwich was almost done and she set it aside, sneaking the ham out of it as an afterthought and chewing it slowly as her thoughts ranged over the morning's events before getting snagged on CJ. She was secretly pleased that Aidan had cajoled her into sending that text. She wanted to hear from CJ. She wanted to know he was okay. She picked up her bag and was heading for the store when it hit her. The shop assistant was alone at the cash register. Aidan had disappeared.

She raced inside.

The girl behind the counter looked up with alarm.

"The young boy," Jeanine said, forgetting her Spanish. "Where is he?"

The girl made a sound like *poof* and waved at the sports shirts before going back to her cash register. "He said they were fake," she went on. "But they're official replicas and—"

"Where is he?" Jeanine boomed it out and the girl shrank back, pointing to the doors at the front of the building.

Jeanine sprinted to the exit, bursting through its doors in time to catch sight of him, his head, just enough to know it was him. He was sitting in the back seat of a taxi.

Alone.

So at least one fear was allayed. This was no abduction. This was a getaway, and there was only one place he could be headed. *Damn that late taxi.* She remembered Aidan looking up at her as she berated the dispatcher and barked out the address repeatedly. She stamped her foot and threw her bag down on the concrete.

"You little—"

She cut it short. This was no place to throw a tantrum. She'd already caught the attention of a young cop standing only feet away. She smiled at him and picked up her bag, and she was about to grab a cab when she remembered something. Yet another thing she'd have to thank her son for later, the pleasure of fishing in a trash can of wet towels and God only knows what else looking for that gun. She went back into the terminal and headed directly to *Mujeres*, praying it was still there.

As requested, Preston's taxi driver was a proficient English speaker. But better yet, he was flexible, especially in the presence of Osama bin Laden. They shared a laugh about the world's most famous terrorist as Preston fanned himself with a five-hundred-euro note and explained that OBL had died with a bunch of them sewn into his jacket. So the bin Laden bill was the go-between, the lure, the piece of meat trailed in the dirt for the taxi driver to sniff after. Preston needed flexibility as he had a few unusual requests. The first was getting the driver to go off-road and drop him on a hunter's trail back in the hills.

No problem about that.

And there they waited, windows closed, engine running, and AC blasting, while Preston shifted their conversation from polite to purposeful. One way or another, his chopper was en route, and either it had the kite on board or it didn't. As for Brink, he'd either be dead or not. So what Preston was looking for here was insurance, a policy he could cash in the event that they didn't recover the activator or couldn't terminate Brink. If Brink survived, he'd surely do everything in his power to stop D-Day. So one way or another, he'd need to find Brink urgently.

"Long time driving a taxi?" Preston sounded casual, eyes scouring the blue skies above the rocky crests of a rugged, empty landscape.

"Twenty-four years."

"You must know every driver in the—" His phone rang and he answered it.

"Talk." He listened in silence his face brightening, then said, "I'm there already. How long?" He hung up, beaming a kite smile and sharing it with the driver.

"Good news, *señor*?"

"Oh yes." The smile was the least of it. He'd got the activator back. Disaster had been averted. But it was too bad Brink had escaped. "How would you like to make a few more bin Ladens?" The driver's eyes lit up, but then his face darkened, so Preston reassured him. "Nothing illegal. It's Pablo, isn't it?" The driver nodded, still wary. "I can see you're an honest man, Pablo. I wouldn't insult you by asking you to do anything illegal. In fact, the opposite. You'll be helping a family get back together."

"What do I have to do?"

"I bet you know all the local drivers."

"Of course, twenty-four years. And my sister is a dispatcher."

"That must come in handy." It was more than handy. It was perfect. "She must give you all the long rides."

"Shhh…" Pablo raised his finger to his lips and winked.

Preston held up his phone. "Ever seen this man?" He showed him a photo of Brink. The driver shook his head. That was okay. That was a long shot. "Or this woman?" He showed him the photo and waited. The driver shook his head. "Or this kid." Once again it was a negative. "So here's the deal. I'm going to send you these photos, and I want you to check with your buddies. They must have taken a taxi at some point." He held up another OBL and waved it. "This one is just for asking your buddies. Now you could take it and do nothing. But I trust you, Pablo. I know you'll try at least." Preston passed him the bill. "Anything you find out, I want you to tell to this man." He held up a photo of Ernald. "He'll contact you." Preston had second thoughts, remembering the bleeding pimp who'd driven off with the nurse. Maybe Ernald wouldn't make it. "Or this woman." He flashed him a photo of the nurse.

The sound of clattering rotors drifted in from beyond a nearby ridge. Preston broke off and scanned the sky. Nothing visible yet. He still had a few minutes to clinch this. It might even work. This guy was local, a clannish Valenciano, plugged into its milquetoast mafia of good old boys. For him, negotiating special favors wasn't a vice, it was a job skill.

Preston fanned the bills. Four of them.

"Two thousand euros, my friend. Come up with something and they are yours." He worked his phone. "Okay. I sent you a link to those photos. Share it with your buddies, and these bills"—they disappeared into his pocket—"could be yours." He offered his hand. "Deal?"

Pablo's answer was lost in the roar of rotors, but his hand shot over the seat and a firm shake sealed it.

Fifteen

CJ had a lot to be cheerful about. He was still breathing, and Aidan and Jeanine were on the plane home. But there was a blot on the day's diary page and it was nagging at him all the way back to Moraira. He picked up a Nepalese takeout when he got there and threaded his way on foot through steep streets back to the villa. With no lights or traffic, it was a dark trek, but the darkness was a comfort, shielding him like a cocoon, and he needed that. Thinking time. There was so much going on, writhing and squirming under a blanket of normal. He started with the big blot. He'd lost the activator and had to assume that Preston had recovered it. He mulled it over as he made his customary circumspect approach to the villa, distracted only by a growling stomach and the smell of tandoori chicken and vegetable curry. An hour later, sitting at the kitchen table behind a pile of empty tinfoil containers, the answer came to him. He picked up his burner phone, noticing a message from Jeanine.

USS Abe… Aidan says you'll know.

Really?

CJ had no idea.

He knew what it was, of course. He'd seen the aircraft carrier in the Persian Gulf during Operation Enduring Freedom. But what an enigmatic message. Aidan? Something he'd heard during his captivity, perhaps. But surely not the target. That warship and its escort had more firepower than the entire military of virtually any other country on the planet. He set it aside, resolving to call her later and dig into it. But first, he had an important call to make. He looked up the phone number, then dialed a hotel in Valencia and inquired about a room. The hotel was central and he'd stayed there before. Yes, they had one, and all they needed was his name and a card number to hold it for him. So that was it—the nuke button he was looking for—and CJ pressed it.

"Calan Jake Flynn," he said, following up with his new Visa card number, not so much treading on thin ice as crashing through it headfirst. This was a gut call, but it made sense too. He had to stop Domino. A plan to start WWIII might seem farfetched, but rattling sabers can cut deep, and when big militaries and big egos coalesce, it's always a risk. Archduke Franz Ferdinand was just one man, but his assassination had sparked WWI, with close to forty million casualties. Besides, everything that had happened to him since Nevada was linked to Preston and Domino. That made it personal. Whoever had killed Colby wanted him dead too. It doesn't get more personal than that. So the hotel booking was a solid boot kicking a hornet's nest. He was plugging himself back into the game by giving Ashford notice he wanted to meet.

A sound caught his attention... a car, voices.

Aidan?

He leapt up and ran outside.

So where was Jeanine?

That was a question that took some explaining, ten minutes' worth in fact. That's how long it took with Aidan's stuttering account constantly interrupted by CJ with yelps of incredulity that left the boy trembling. CJ caught himself, reining it back. This wasn't like him, but Aidan's parachuting himself back into the firing line was a nightmare turn of events.

"It's okay, mate." CJ softened his tone, forcing a feeble smile. "Come on in. I'll make you a cup of tea, and we can talk about it."

CJ waited. But Aidan didn't move, except for the shaking. There was a pale light from the house on him, and he suddenly seemed so small and weak. CJ's own boyhood rushed up to him, moments alone with no mother or father in a terrifyingly big world. "Then you can tell me all about it. I'm dying to hear." He reached out his hand, doing a better job with that smile. "We'll sort it all out together."

Aidan took the offered hand and CJ led him into the villa, locking the doors behind them. The boy took a seat at the kitchen table while CJ made the tea.

"There you go, sport." CJ sat opposite him and put down the mugs of tea. Aidan sipped, and CJ nodded appreciatively. "The great British cure-all," he explained. "Mine's got no sugar, just milk. Builder's tea, they call it. No idea why. I made yours the same. Is it okay? Or you want sugar?"

"We don't have much time," Aidan said.

"Why's that?"

"Mom's going to be here and she'll be mad as hell. I better tell you before she gets here."

"Did you send her a message telling her where you were going?"

"I don't have a phone."

Of course he didn't. Preston's goons were hardly likely to have given it back to him.

CJ pulled out his phone…

"Please, don't call her," Aidan said. "She can chew me out later. I need to tell you something first. She's already on the way… I promise."

"Okay, let's talk. But I'm going to send her a message first." Aidan went to speak, but CJ was already tapping at his phone, and when he was done, he said, "So what have you got for me?"

"You heard about Domino?"

"Bits and pieces. What did you hear?"

"The same. Just enough to make me curious and listen harder."

"To Ernald?"

"He didn't know jack. It was the other guys, the big guys with guns. They kept me at someplace in the mountains, like a hunting lodge. No cars, no roads, no Wi-Fi, no cell signal. So they got bored, I guess. In the day they'd shoot off their guns in the forest, and at night they'd get liquored up and talk. So I'd pretend to be asleep and listen. I'd pretty much perfected that by the time they doped me up for the trip today. So as it wore off, I stayed dopey with my head lolling around in the car."

"Where does the USS *Abraham Lincoln* come into this?"

"That's the target. That's how they'll kick off this war."

"They said that?"

"One guy says, *There it is… the ship, it's on CNN.* And he shows the other guy his phone and says, *Do you think it's possible?* So the other guy looks and shakes his head, and he says, *Holy shit*—I'm quoting here—*that's one awesome motherfucker.*"

CJ waited. "That's it?"

Aidan pointed at CJ's phone and said, "CNN."

CJ picked it up and checked their site. It was May 6, 2019, and the headline read:

US deploying carrier and bomber task force in response to 'troubling' Iran actions

Washington (CNN) The United States is deploying the USS Abraham Lincoln Carrier Strike Group and a bomber task force to the Middle East in response to a "number of troubling and escalatory indications and warnings" from Iran, US national security adviser John Bolton said Sunday...

CJ read through the article without looking up until a key sentence stopped him dead, a direct quote from John Bolton, saying that the actions were meant *"to send a clear and unmistakable message to the Iranian regime that any attack on United States interests or on those of our allies will be met with unrelenting force."*

CJ had gotten this all wrong. He'd been thinking along the lines of a terrorist attack on a soft target. 9/11, the sequel. But this was the hardest target in the world, a target way beyond the dreams of terrorists, and the capabilities of all but a few states. He continued reading, finding an oddly prophetic quote from Javad Zarif, the Iranian foreign minister, at the bottom of the page. *"It is not a crisis yet, but it is a dangerous situation. Accidents, plotted accidents, are possible. I wouldn't discount the B-Team plotting an accident anywhere in the region particularly as we get closer to the election."*

The B-Team was a reference to Bolton, Benjamin Netanyahu, and Saudi and UAE Crown Princes bin Salman and bin Zayed. How ironic that he'd gotten it so right and so wrong in the same sentence. A plotted *accident* authored by the B-Team was about to happen all right, but the plotters were not Zarif's politicos, but Paz's bandidos.

CJ patted Aidan on the shoulder. "Good work, mate."

"So what are we going to do?" Aidan said.

CJ couldn't help but notice the *we*.

"I'm working on a plan. But… and while I appreciate your telling me all this, the plan doesn't involve you or your mum. Other than you both getting on a plane back to LA."

"She's going to be real mad. She's got an awesome temper."

"Don't worry. I'll calm her down."

"Really? Good luck with that, pal. She can be terrifying. Believe me."

"Your mum?"

"You don't know her like I do. My advice is don't get on the wrong side of her. Even you'd regret that."

"Am I likely to?"

"You like her well enough, don't you?"

"Of course, she's Alex's sister. He was my buddy. You're his nephew. I've got a—"

"That's not what I mean. She's Uncle Alex's sister, not his wife."

"Oh…"

"Now you're getting it. So do you like her or not?"

"Hold on… how old are you?"

"I think she's got a crush on you."

"What makes you say that?"

"When I was telling her we had to go back… *to help CJ*, she said, *He doesn't need our help. He's pretty darn self-sufficient.*"

CJ waited for more.

"That's it?" he said finally. "Self-sufficient."

"It was the way she said it. Some sort of pride in her voice. It was like Lois Lane telling Clark Kent about Superman."

"Blimey."

CJ enjoyed the moment, but it came to an abrupt end when he heard something outside. He snapped his head around and leapt up.

"You hear something?" Aidan said, perking up. "That's incredible. I didn't hear anything."

CJ was at the door already, reaching for the gun in the small of his back. He slipped through the kitchen, opened the door and crouched in the darkness, peeking his gun out between the steel bars of its *reja*. But he was soon back on his feet.

Muffled voices, a car idling, then hurried steps.

By the time Jeanine reached the gate, CJ was already there, holding it open.

She nodded curtly, her face a flash of white in the half light as she hurried towards the house.

"Where is he?"

"Jeanine." CJ caught up with her, a firm hand on her shoulder. There was better light here. He stepped in close, his hand still on her shoulder.

"Aidan's doing great. We've had a fantastic talk. He's cheery and well, and although it wasn't my place, I already chewed him out about running out on you like that. He's super sorry. He thought it was the right thing to do, and he's a bit of a hard head like his mum."

She looked up at him, the flicker of a smile soon swept aside by a tangle of emotions. CJ hugged her, cradling her head and kissing her. "I'm okay," she said, breaking away.

They turned towards the house, where Aidan was standing in the doorway, watching them. He ran to his mother, his arms outstretched.

Preston looked across the waves as his chopper zoomed towards the *True Grit*, his early-morning arrival staging a spectacular show with the sun on the horizon ahead laying down a shimmering carpet of silver and gold all around it.

Confirmation.

According to Preston, it was a fundamental human need, like air and water. Everyone needed it. And every time he touched down on *his* superyacht in *his* helicopter, he got it in spades.

I made it… I'm somebody.

And on this day, he was swooning on it. He could smell triumph. It was that close. He had the activator. Domino was go. The venue was set and all the players were en route. Soon the good old days would be back, the glory days of Iraq when billions flowed from Uncle Sam's coffers into the bottomless maw of his greed. There'd be no more sucking up to corporate types and digital worms like Schilder. The only blemish spoiling this perfect picture was Brink's survival along with that cop. But they weren't so important. More a matter of pride than necessity. And in any event, they still might get theirs, served up at the end where sweet things belong.

"Mine," he whispered, his skin tingling as if stroked by some mystical lover.

On landing, he took his private elevator from the helicopter pad to the top deck, the Owner's Deck. This part of the vessel was every bit the rich man's toy, housing his accommodation suite, his office, his personal gym, and a luxurious lounge with a fully stocked wet bar and wine cellar. But the *True Grit* was much more than a flashy toy. A once-upon-a-time icebreaker, it had been stripped to the hull and rebuilt as an exploration vessel, giving it extraordinary range and operational capabilities. It was, in effect, a personal warship. The perfect venue to launch WWIII. He ordered breakfast and stood at the bay window waiting for its delivery, looking down over the bow of the yacht at the shimmering golden river that snaked off to the rising sun.

CJ's qualifications as a family counselor were nil. So he stepped aside for an hour or so, letting mom and son sort it out and supporting their efforts with plenty of mugs of tea, in Jeanine's case fortified with Spanish brandy. When the normal mom-son service appeared to have resumed, he joined them. Jeanine was swiping pages on her tablet computer, a frown here, half a smile there. CJ tried to read her signals while giving Aidan one of his own, a stout thumbs-up.

"So… all on the same page again," he said, more hopeful than certain.

"We got there eventually," Jeanine said, her eyes still on the screen.

Aidan nodded glumly, there having been some scolding in the resolution process.

"So how's the flights look?" CJ said.

"Not good. Booked for days. Our best shot is to try for a standby in the morning. What about you?"

"I'm off to Valencia right now. I booked a hotel for this evening already."

"Why? What's in Valencia?"

"Answers, I hope. I need to connect with people who can stop this. Or help me stop it."

"Let's stay and help him, Mom." Aidan grabbed his mother with both hands.

"Whoa…" CJ leapt to his feet. "I'm on my way, guys. And so are you. Next stop for you is LA."

That was a priority. CJ was determined to protect them, and tagging along with him was certainly not a step in that direction.

"This place is off the grid. You should be okay here. Do you still have your pistol?"

She nodded, glaring at Aidan and notching up the volume as she said, "Luckily, the trash can I dumped it in hadn't been emptied. So I got to fish it out from under a foot and a half of paper soaked in gunk."

CJ followed her lead, glaring at Aidan, but it was hard to keep the smile off his face. The boy was staring at the floor, lost in concentration on some anonymous spot of nothing. How many times had CJ been there and done that as a kid?

After that, CJ fetched his bag, and Jeanine walked him to the gate in silence, a walk heavy with so much unsaid. When they got to the street, she stopped him, pulling him around by his arm.

"You could still come with us," she said.

CJ put his hand on her shoulder, then slipped it behind her neck and pulled her closer. She reached her arms around him and they kissed in the street, sliding into the cover of a bougainvillea whose spiky branches and flaming blossoms hid them from prying eyes.

Sixteen

The hotel was in a pedestrian zone at the edge of the city center. CJ cast his eyes left and right as he made his way to the reception desk. To the left was a cafeteria and breakfast room, its doors closed till morning. To the right was a lounge with seating around low tables, and beyond it, a bar with a mirrored wall of shelves stocked with bottles of various shades. A barman was shaking a cocktail, and a lone woman sat at the bar waiting for it and no doubt spying on CJ in the mirror. He stopped and looked at her. She didn't turn around, but she did signal, raising her arm and wafting her hand in the sort of low-energy wave perfected by British royals. But she was distinctly unroyal. She was Paz. CJ checked in. Then he went to the bar and perched on the stool next to her. She was drinking from a tall glass, something transparent with ice and lemon.

"Mine's a gin and tonic," she said, sipping it through a straw.

"And this?" CJ nodded as the barman placed a martini glass in front of him.

"Martini, you peasant. What else? Shaken, not stirred, à la you-know-who."

CJ pushed it away. "You got a beer, pal?" he said to the barman, jerking his thumb at the taps. "*Caña.*" The barman grinned slyly and poured him a glass, clearing its frothing head with a scraper while CJ looked on approvingly. "Why did you kill the gardener?" he said after sampling his brew and sweeping a foamy mustache from his lips with the back of his hand.

She leaned closer as if to whisper. But she pecked him on the cheek instead.

"He was a pathetic screw."

"And you're a pathetic comedian." CJ eyeballed her, faces real close. "Why?"

She edged away, pulling his martini over and lining it up behind her gin and tonic.

"No choice after you cocked everything up."

"How's that? He didn't know anything."

"Like hell he didn't. He planted the bugs?"

What bugs?

CJ didn't ask the question, but evidently it was written on his face.

She shrugged. "It wasn't just a simple honeytrap to get you access. I had to get him on the team. We were in love and we were going to get married. He'd already promised to leave his wife. It was all bullshit, of course. Mutual, I'm sure."

CJ thought back to Preston's villa. There were plants everywhere, all over the terraces and most of the rooms, even the office, although that panic room was plant-free. Preston was sure to have restricted sensitive conversations to his bug-proof annex. But over time, bits and pieces would slip out into routine conversations elsewhere.

"How long?" he said.

"Months. But it felt like years."

"Did you have access to the recordings, or just Ashford?"

"Sometimes. When Ashford wasn't around. But he had eyes on everything. He used to upload them to London. He kept me in the loop."

"So you heard what happened when I confronted Preston? You know why I went against orders and why I couldn't kill him."

She rolled her eyes.

"Let me think… was that the time I was screwing José and Ashford stormed in, yanked me off him, and stuck a knife in him? Yeah, I think I remember that."

"What did he say?"

"With or without expletives? Cleaning up the syntax, it was something like… we should leave now. What did you expect? Our cover was blown. Poor old José. Then you dumped him back there. That wasn't helpful either. Needless to say, the bugs are gone and so we're totally in the dark again."

"Did Ashford play you the recording of my conversation with Preston?"

"He said you wanted to take Preston hostage to trade for the cop's kid. But then you whacked him and found something else to trade. We knew he had the activator, so that was our guess. And we assume he's got it back now."

"Your assumption is correct," CJ said, noting an important omission in her account. *Texas.* They'd been quick to judge Preston as Colby's killer, but they'd been wrong. CJ had watched the video of Preston's team with the sound muted. So Ashford hadn't gotten any of that. But he'd heard Preston's denial and knew that CJ had seen the evidence. And yet none of that had filtered through to Paz. There might be a plausible reason for that. On hearing the bad news about Colby, she'd been angry and lost focus, blaming CJ in no uncertain terms. Maybe Ashford hadn't told her because it wasn't operationally necessary for her to know and he wanted her to keep her eye on the ball. Nonetheless, it was a curious omission.

"So where's Ashford?" he said.

"Waiting."

"For?"

"A message from me to let him know if you're homicidal or not."

"And what's your judgment?"

"No more than normal. It's part of your charm."

"You wouldn't be here if you didn't want Preston dead."

"True enough… but after that Alcazada fiasco, can we trust you?"

"I had an agenda. I don't now."

"So are you up for it?"

"What's the deal?"

She finished her drink, picked up his abandoned martini and drank it in two drafts with her eyes fixed on his bottle-framed image in the mirror behind the bar. She took out a phone and tapped in a message, then slid off her stool and leaned in close. He was expecting a whisper, something confidential, maybe personal. But no whisper came. She licked his throat instead, trailing the tip of her tongue up into the bristles on his chin.

"See ya," she said and was gone.

CJ was huddled over his second beer when he caught sight of Ashford striding into the bar. CJ followed his progress in a series of clips in the mirror as his image navigated the bottles. Ashford put his hand on CJ's shoulder and gave it a squeeze. "Good to see you, old chap." Then he levered himself up onto Paz's barstool.

The bartender arrived and Ashford scanned the bottles behind the bar before ordering a Highland single malt. He offered CJ one as a chaser, but CJ declined. When Ashford's drink arrived, he sniffed it, then shot it straight back in one go and ordered another.

"Rough day?" CJ said.

Ashford winked. "Not yet," he said. "But sitting next to you, that's always a possibility." The barman delivered his scotch and Ashford took his time with this one, flicking a spot of water in from a pitcher and sipping it daintily before getting to the point. "Why did you reach out? Use that card? What do you want from us?" he said.

"Domino?"

Ashford took his time with that too, his eyes going back and forth between their reflections in the mirror, rubbery lips caressing the rim of his glass and savoring his drink.

"What happened with Preston?"

There was no point in lying since he'd heard most of it. So CJ told him how he'd taken the activator and swapped it for Aidan. He left out the weapon identification code he'd learned from the activator's menu, as well as the Texas video. Ashford nodded, and that was it. Not a single question. According to Paz, neither of them knew what kind of weapon they were dealing with. But if that was true, surely he'd wonder about the activator. What kind of device was it? How big? Stuff like that.

CJ was tempted to say, *EM-88 mean anything to you?* But instead, he said, "Do you have any idea what it activates?"

"Plenty of ideas. But that's all they are. A suitcase nuke would be the ultimate… every terrorist's wet dream."

"But these guys aren't terrorists."

"No… but their goal is to start a war, and that would guarantee one."

"How did they get hold of it in China?"

"Nazar's contacts, most likely. He's done plenty of favors for Pakistani intelligence, and you know what those boys are like. They might cozy up to the Chinese government, but they surely have links with TIM as well." The Turkestan Islamic Movement was a terrorist group linked to Al Qaeda, fighting for an independent state for the Uighurs, Chinese Muslims. Ashford was right about ISI. Pakistan's Inter-Services Intelligence Agency had plenty of form playing both sides against the middle. They'd been a bridge between the CIA and the Mujahideen during the Russian invasion of Afghanistan, but they'd somehow failed to notice Osama bin Laden living in a fortified compound under their noses only a few years later.

"If terrorists got hold of it, why wouldn't they use it themselves?"

"Maybe it's too complicated, too difficult to deploy, or maybe they got offered a shitload of money."

"So where does that leave us?"

"With the same problem we had in Marbella."

"You want me to kill Preston? To stop it?"

"That's what you agreed, and it's in your best interests, if you plan on keeping that shiny new EU passport. And don't forget that murder charge. It could always come back to life."

"So that's my end of the deal. What's yours?"

"The three principals will meet on Preston's yacht on the night of the fiesta. Schilder will make the final payment and get the activator from Preston and the go-live codes from Nazar."

"And I shoot Preston in front of them?"

"The mission objective is to terminate Preston, recover the activator, and stop Domino. Try to minimize casualties, especially partygoers. But the objective must be achieved, and you're expected to remove all obstacles. I can give you intel support, logistics, and whatever kit you need, plus a sultry and talented assistant."

"You can skip the hired help."

"And trust you after what you did in Marbella?"

"So Paz is what? Big Sister, keeping her eye on me?"

"Don't sell her short. That bimbo act is a front. She's put men in the ground. She was a bloody hero in Afghanistan, and she's got the medals to prove it." That was quite a defense, and a bit of a surprise too. Ashford turned back to the bar, picking up his drink and holding it in both hands like a comfort toy. "Either that… or you can spend the rest of your life looking over your shoulder."

"I'm the perfect guy for the job. I get that. But all this trouble to sign me up—passports, etc.—wouldn't it have been easier to get a guy from Wetslope?"

Ashford was sipping his scotch when CJ's troll bait hit him and he paused with the glass halfway to his mouth. Not exactly a bite. But close. And that was followed by the world's longest sip, almost chewing on the whisky before saying, "What's that, some rent-a-gun outfit? A poor man's Tratfors?"

"It's an online chat room, according to the guy who killed Colby."

Ashford put down his scotch and swiveled around to face CJ.

"You cannot seriously think I killed her. Is that where you're going with this?"

Serious was too big a word. It was more of a whim. But Ashford knew about the location, and that was reason enough for CJ to chum the waters.

"Preston didn't, so—"

"I know. I heard all that—his denial and then he showed you something convincing. But how do you get from that to me? Do you know how important this is to me? How success is going to perk up my otherwise wilting career? You think I'd rig a cowboy stunt like that to sabotage my own operation? For God's sake, why?"

"If not, then who?"

Ashford leaned closer, lowering his voice.

"And if none of that makes sense to you, even your Swiss-cheese brain can surely figure out that what I'm trying to do now is persuade you to kill Preston. So pray enlighten me… why would I kill my partner to stop you killing Preston, then hire you to do just that?" He snatched his scotch off the counter and downed it, chasing it up with a sharp intake of breath. "You're an idiot, Brink. Certifiable. And do I really look like the sort of chap who knows his way around the dark web? I'm a Luddite… a technophobe. I can barely keep up with the apps on my iPhone."

Ashford had been doing so well until then, his logic infallible. CJ's speculations made no sense.

But who'd said anything about the dark web?

That could have been a wild guess. Even a technophobe would know that assassins were not for sale on the regular web. So maybe he'd just made a deduction. It was hard to tell. Ashford was a class act, a spy so practiced at lying he was impossible to read. But no one could piss people off like CJ Brink, and maybe he'd flushed out a mistake. Either way, he was rolling with it.

"Why didn't you tell Paz about Preston?"

"Come on. You saw how she was that night. There was no point in telling her. Right now, she's just where I need her to be, focused on the job. She's a great asset. Too bad you're not on the team, or you'd see that."

"I didn't say so."

"Then what?"

CJ finished his scotch and dropped off the stool.

"I'll do it," he said, offering his hand to seal the deal like a real gentleman. Ashford hesitated. Life-or-death decision here. Despite that new passport, this was still Crazy James Brink. In the end, he manned up, chubby paw tentatively extended. CJ shook it solemnly, laying it on thick. Ashford wasn't the only one who knew how to shovel it.

There were only so many times you could check a lock before you had to accept…

It's locked!

Jeanine was keyed up, her heart-pumping. In cop speak, this was her operational buzz, a ready-for-anything surge of strength, a sharpening that made all the difference at the crucial moment of arrival and assessment. Domestic violence, a break-in, a routine call could be nothing at all, or it could be everything. So Jeanine was ready. Too bad ready wasn't called for. What she needed was calm. Tomorrow was a long day and it was getting late. Aidan was already sleeping on the king-sized bed in the master bedroom. The streets were silent, the locks triple-checked. The house was officially secure.

She'd even tested the burglar bars that protected the windows and doors. Called *rejas* and common on traditional villas in Spain, they were ornate, curvy steel bars set in the wall around each window. But despite their presence, she had locked all the windows and adjusted the AC to accommodate the warmer-than-usual weather. So there was nothing more to do but sleep.

If only she could…

She sat instead with a glass of milk in the kitchen, one hand on the glass, the other resting on the table inches from her pistol. CJ had said he would call.

If he didn't, something had gone wrong, and she'd have to…

Do what?

A big something, that was for sure.

Before CJ had left, there had been a moment of trust, a man-woman moment she wasn't likely to forget. Huddling by a wall in the street, shaded from the moonlight by a whatever-tree. An exchange. No words of bargaining necessary, a truth for a truth, and a deal was done.

The phone rang. She was expecting it, hoping for it, waiting for it, but it hit her with a jolt nonetheless.

"How'd it go?" she said.

She could feel his breath through the phone. Intense. That didn't even begin to describe this man. A sniff. He'd do that. A thoughtful moment, a sniff of air as though there was quite a speech coming and then one or two words at most. Brief was his thing. It was like he was getting billed by the word. Minimum effort, maximum effect. He was tuned right into that.

"I bought in."

"Majorca?"

"That's where the man is."

"You'll do it alone?"

"Most likely. That's still a question mark. But I've got support. Intel, kit, a plan. How's Aidan?"

"Sleeping."

"You should get some rest too."

"Like that's easy."

"I'll be fine."

Lots of silence then, but with plenty still going on between them, a moment of comfort that meant more than any of the words that might have filled it.

"I'll text you," she said finally and hung up.

She put the phone down next to her gun and stared at it, idly picking up the milk and sipping it. When she was done, she washed the glass and wandered along the corridor that ran through the single-story house, checking all the rooms as she went. In the master bedroom, Aidan was sleeping under a sheet. The AC unit was up on the wall. She adjusted it with the remote and sat on the bed. She slid the 9mm under the pillow and lay down, nestling her head on it, suddenly tired, and in moments, she was asleep.

Dreams have baggage. Sometimes, most times, it gets lost in darkness, fading away as the sleeper wakes up like a body falling from a sky-high jet. It gets smaller and smaller until it scopes into a dot and is gone. But sometimes baggage lingers, straddling worlds as images and feelings intertwine. Images can enthrall or frighten, but it's feelings that carry the weight.

Terror.

Was it a dream or real?

Fear ripped through her. Something terrible happening.

But what?

Voices. Strange voices. Muffled, distorted, otherworldly, yet somehow familiar. Suffocating. She was trying to breathe, her mouth open, gasping.

But where was the air?

Her throat was closing down, clawed to shreds by scraping nails. Pain slammed into her chest and her body fell with a crashing sound, and she was awakened. This was no dream. Or not one that was God-given. This was a man-made nightmare and it was happening now.

"I'll get the kid. Take care of her." A man's voice, tinny, unreal.

Jeanine struggled up on all fours.

The gun?

Was it still there? Could she even pull the trigger?

Something hit her in the ribs and knocked her on her side. The pain was worthy of a scream, but she had no air to make it. A kick. That's what it was. She didn't need a video to figure it out. That's what happens when you're on the floor in a street fight. Instinctively, her arms folded around her, protecting her chest and neck.

"Bitch…" A woman's voice, closer, the kicker, now stamper, her foot crashing Jeanine's head into the floor. Her eyes were useless. She tried opening them, but all she got was scorching pain and floods of tears, a world out of shape. She grabbed that stamping foot and twisted it, setting the woman off balance. A moment was all it gave her. She had to make it work.

"Do it," the man's voice again. "I'll take this little bugger out to the car."

Ernald and Harriet. They were going to take him, and they were going to make it. That hit Jeanine like a shot of amphetamine, and her eyes popped open, shrugging off tears, her brain switching on and turning off the pain.

Somehow, she was on her feet, surging upward with a primordial scream.

"Mom." Aidan's voice was faint, anguished. He was struggling in the doorway with Ernald, holding on to the door, doing his best not to get taken. She went to go to him, but Harriet slammed her back over the nightstand, her head cracking the wall. Jeanine grabbed at her attacker's gas mask, but Harriet was too strong. She was taller, had a longer reach and outweighed her by fifty pounds or more.

In the doorway, Aidan was still holding on to that door and Ernald was striking him into compliance.

"You little bastard…"

Jeanine's hands were all over the nightstand. Harriet had one hand on her throat and the other on her hair, pumping her head against the wall. Jeanine found something. A book. She whipped it around and hit the woman full in the face, and she flinched and for an instant her grip faded. It was enough. Jeanine wriggled free and dropped belly first onto the bed, her hand shooting under the pillow and finding the gun. Harriet landed on top of her, and they bounced, the mattress yielding to the big woman's weight. But Jeanine still had the shot. Ernald was feet away, and in choosing to strike Aidan, he had set it up by moving away from the boy. She fired and Ernald's head snapped back, blood and brain spraying the door.

"Run, hide." Jeanine got the words out, but the cost was heavy. Harriet was on top of her with both her hands on Jeanine's gun arm, controlling her aim, pointing the gun at Aidan. "Run." She got the words out again. "Hide." But Aidan just stood there, his eyes widening, his body shaking.

One chance…

Jeanine angled the gun as far from Aidan as she could and fired. The bullet punched through the door, frighteningly close to her son, but it worked. It scared him back to life and he disappeared into the hallway. The shot seemed to jolt the woman too, and Jeanine broke her grip and whipped the gun around. But the big woman struck it away and it went skidding off the bed onto the floor. Then she clambered up on Jeanine's back and sat astride her, pinning her arms with her legs. She yanked Jeanine's head back by a handful of hair, her thick arm snaking under her throat and folding into a submission lock. Struggle was a vanity now. There was no way out of this. So she thought about Aidan, praying for that smart brain of his to figure out the right place to hide. The tourniquet on her throat tightened. This woman was a nurse. She knew exactly what she was doing. A soft darkness closed in on Jeanine and she framed Aidan in her mind's eye to flush away the obscenity of dying in this woman's embrace, the feel of her, the stink of her sweat.

When the explosion came, it might have been from another planet, an intrusion into Jeanine's lost world. But then, the tourniquet on her throat slackened, the weight on her back shifted, and oxygen enough to sustain life found its way into her lungs.

That wasn't an explosion. It was a gunshot.

"Get off my mom." Aidan's screech reeked of tears.

Jeanine wriggled to get out from under the woman, but Aidan wasn't done. More shots. She froze, unable to speak, to stop him. Any one of those bullets could go wrong, could ricochet and kill either of them.

Please, God…

The gun clicked on empty and clattered to the stone floor. Jeanine wriggled free and tossed the heap of dead flesh on her back to the side.

Aidan was bawling, shaking.

She ran to him, swept him up in her arms and took him outside. It was still night with a hint of day in the sky above the pine trees to the east. She huddled with Aidan on a bench carved from white stone. She knew enough about trauma to understand that he wasn't the only one who was in trouble here. No one gets that close to dying without changing, and she took it as a given that her compass bearings would be shot out for the foreseeable future. *Stay focused*, she told herself over and over as she waited for the fresh air to clean that putrid toxin out of their lungs. As the first light came, she could make out a gas bottle leaning against the wall with a hose running up to the AC unit, and nearby a smashed window with its burglar bars missing. So much for those fancy *rejas*. They were attached to the wall with struts and cemented in place. They'd used a car jack to lever them off the wall.

How easy was that?

Just stick a pipe in the AC, turn on the gas, then lever the bars off. But they'd made a mistake. They'd taken a shortcut. Instead of forcing a window, then closing it after entering the house, they'd smashed one. It had saved them time but also allowed the breeze to suck out the gas.

Aidan had mercifully fallen asleep in her arms and she laid him out on the bench and went back to the house. It looked like a war zone, and two bodies. She got her bag and collected the gun and her phone. Back in the garden, she called CJ. She'd been determined not to. He'd be operational. The last thing he'd need was this. She paced back and forth by the bench glancing down at Aidan as she listened to the call ring out and go to voicemail. Once, twice. That was enough. The text message would have to do, but better sent from the airport when she could give him some peace of mind by telling him they were getting on the plane. She squeezed onto the end of the bench next to Aidan, loneliness overwhelming her and catching her by surprise. She so wanted to cry, to let it all out, but she sucked it up. She stroked Aidan's hair, waking him gently.

"Come on, honey. We've got things to do."

Seventeen

It was early, barely dawn, but CJ was already way into his new day when the phone in his pocket vibrated.

"Let me guess," Paz said. "The cop mom calling to coo *hasta la vista, bebé.*"

CJ checked the phone.

"Pretty much," he said, ignoring her snarky comment as well as the call. Jeanine would be on her way to Alicante already. He'd have time to catch up with her later. He was in Paz's hotel room, sitting at a table loaded with breads and pastries and a pot of coffee. Breakfast for two. Paz was taking hers sitting at the end of the bed, a pile of sheets and blankets in a tangle of colors behind her. She was wearing a hotel bathrobe and nothing else, a tidbit of info she had shared with CJ by lounging back across the bed to reach the phone and order breakfast, her body twisting at the waist, legs askew, fleecy-white toweling riding all the way up lean brown thighs. She'd called him after his meeting with Ashford and invited him to join her, but he'd declined, spending the night alone with his thoughts. She'd tried again at dawn and reluctantly he'd agreed to join her—for breakfast, that was. After all, she was part of the deal. Ashford had made that clear. She dunked a sweet pastry in her coffee, angled it above her open mouth and let it drip for a moment before gobbling it in mushy bites that smeared her lips with wetness. She licked them clean afterwards and emptied her coffee cup in three gulps, putting on a real show.

CJ watched and waited. He'd had his coffee—his eggs too—before she'd even called him.

"When's the flight to Majorca?" he said.

"Ten o'clock. We've got time."

"For what?"

Paz got up off the bed and stood in front of him, untying the belt of her bathrobe so it fell open wide enough for him to check her out and shroud her in mystery at the same time. The sweep of her cleavage, her long legs losing themselves in shadows, CJ took it all in— a woman supremely confident of her body and the effect it had on men. CJ rose up out of the chair, taking his time, not coy, not shy, and letting her know it. He slipped his hand behind her neck and drew her against him, kissing her hard, edgy and savage. Then he pushed her off, his breath a rasp, shaking his head.

"This is not going to work."

"Why not? We'll be playing Mr. and Mrs. in Majorca."

"Says who?"

"What are you so uptight about anyway?"

"I don't do fake. I'm not an undercover guy. I'm not a spy."

Paz laughed. "Ashford said you were old-school, but I had no idea you went that far back. We could hold hands first if you want." She laughed again, hosing him with derision.

CJ let it all wash over him. "My sultry assistant," he said.

"Sultry?"

"It's what Ashford called you."

"That's a weird word. A bit sexist. I'm not a slut. I'm sex-positive. This is 2019 last I heard."

"None of this is a comment on you." He faked a sigh of regret as he ran his eyes over her, trying to be nice. They had to work together. Besides, if things had been different… but they weren't. "We've got a lot on our plates. Let's keep it simple."

"As in?"

"You're my QM…"

"Quartermaster? Like in the army, taking care of supplies and billeting?"

"You were in the army?"

She nodded, "Believe it or not."

"In the Royal Navy, the quartermaster steers the ship. Big job. And to make this work I'm going to need a QM who's a bit army and a bit navy. Are you up to it?"

"You saw my Majorca plan. You tell me."

CJ took out his phone. She'd already sent him a bullet-point plan that had them both boarding Preston's yacht on the night of the Es Firó fiesta. She'd also attached the marine architect's drawings of Preston's yacht, and he'd spent the night studying them.

"I need to work on this, make changes."

Paz tied her robe, moving on. "Okay," she said. "Get on it." She headed to the bathroom but stopped halfway, spinning around and aiming an accusing finger at him. "You don't know what you're missing."

CJ smiled as she disappeared and closed the door.

She was wrong about that. He knew exactly what he was missing—a complication. But even so, it took him a while to get back to his notes. He sat there instead, staring at the bathroom door, his thoughts struggling their way back to Jeanine with the image of Paz half-in, half-out of a bathrobe still sizzling on his retinas.

"Only one?" Jeanine said.

"And we're about to close it." The ticket agent at the standby desk at Alicante Airport nodded past Jeanine at the people waiting behind her. The obvious didn't need to be said. That's how standby works. Take it or leave it. Jeanine looked over her shoulder. There were plenty of other takers, a line of them, shuffling impatiently.

"I'll take it."

"Okay." The ticket agent looked at Aidan warily and back at her. "Who's the passenger?"

Jeanine slid Aidan's passport over the counter. The agent checked it, referred to the booking screen and went back to the passport.

"He's nearly thirteen," Jeanine said. "And an experienced traveler." It was baloney and, as it turned out, irrelevant.

"The local flight's okay, although you'll need to sign a parental consent form. The connection in Madrid is an issue. You'll need to pay an escort charge of one hundred euros and a staff member will meet him and make sure he gets on the right plane."

"What am I? Stupid?" Aidan said. "I can do that myself. Don't pay it, Mom. It's a rip-off." Jeanine ruffled his hair and smiled an apology to the agent who took it in good humor.

"I'm sure you can, sir," she said. "But you've got a two-hour wait there, so you'll have someone to talk to."

"You can practice your Spanish," Jeanine said. "It'll be fun." She pulled out her credit card, carefully selecting the only one that wasn't maxed out. A hundred euros was pretty steep, but she was delighted to pay it. Knowing Aidan would be shepherded from one flight to the next on that crucial link in Madrid was a great comfort. Separation was hard enough, but having Aidan wandering unsupervised around a major European airport was a worry too far. With this settled, he'd be in a pipe with no holes, funneled all the way to Los Angeles. This possibility—only one standby available—had been on her mind all the way to the airport, and she'd called Eileen to make sure she was available to meet Aidan on his arrival. Eileen was her best friend, a former cop turned full-time mom whose husband was still on the force. She couldn't bring herself to lie to Eileen, but she could hardly tell her the truth either. Luckily, Eileen was the sort of friend who didn't need excuses. Jeanine needed her. That was enough.

When the ticket agent had processed the paperwork, Jeanine said, "Do I have a shot at another standby today?"

The agent checked the screen and shook her head. "You'll have to try tomorrow."

"So what's the next day you could get me a seat for sure?"

"Five days is the soonest. Do you want me to book that?"

Jeanine was figuring out her options and spending day after day hanging around the airport hoping to get lucky was not high up the list. She checked with Aidan. A glance was enough.

"Do it, Mom. I'll be okay. Jimmie's got a new PlayStation." Jimmie was Eileen's youngest and Aidan's video game nemesis. "You can go to Majorca." Jeanine smiled, wondering at her son's uncanny ability to read her thoughts. That's exactly what was on her mind. With Aidan safely back in the US, she could lock in the next flight and spend a few days in Majorca. She liked to think of it as watching CJ's back although she was smart enough to know she was fooling herself.

"What about Majorca?" she asked the agent.

"Majorca?"

Aidan yanked her arm. "The ferry!"

The agent frowned, looking from one to the other. Aidan had barked it out, and it took Jeanine a moment to figure out why. The pistol in her purse. She'd planned on dumping it prior to heading through security on the flight back to the US. But if she took the ferry, that could wait.

"Forget Majorca," she said. "I'll take that flight in five days."

Ticketing done, they used the few minutes they had left together to stockpile provisions in Aidan's carry-on, trail mix and granola bars. Just in case. One last hug and her son was on his way into the security line, heading for a world of people all of whom seemed so much bigger than him, but somehow not. She watched him, a future moment touching her, the day when her son would be fully grown and walk alone into the world, his own man at last. She shuddered. It was a beautiful image, but framed in sadness.

"Aidan," she called after him, and he turned around. "Don't forget to buy some water. And go to the bathroom on the way to the gate."

MAJORCA

Eighteen

On arrival in Palma, CJ and Paz were still putting on a brave show of teamwork. On the face of it, they were united by a common goal, but like some awkward couple on a blind date, all they shared was suspicion. They picked up a Toyota with all-wheel drive and headed to their operations center, a vacation rental on Majorca's mountainous west coast. Film companies splash big bucks on locations, often choosing exotic resorts and glamorous homes. But Icon Dreams had its own set of priorities, with privacy and access to Preston's operations at the top of the list. So they had rented a secluded stone farmhouse, or *finca*, set in olive groves at the end of a winding drive a few miles outside Sóller, the site of Es Firó. Paz dropped CJ off there and went to Sóller to pick up provisions for their brief stay, giving him welcome space to take stock. He'd already missed another call from Jeanine on the plane and, checking his phone as he explored the house, he saw he'd missed a message too while they were on the drive up from Palma. It was her update, and the opening line was a comfort—Aidan was on his way to California—but the next stopped him in his tracks. *Our clifftop friends dropped by. All OK. But short 2 HRPs.*

HRPs?

Human Remains Pouches!

She's left dead bodies?

With his head spinning, CJ moved on to her closing line… *On ferry TO MAJORCA. Losing signal. Hasta luego!*

CJ grunted like he'd stopped a shotgun load with his gut, his finger frantically stabbing the screen, dialing her number, excuses lining up on his tongue, solid reasons why she had to get off that ferry.

No reply.

He tried again, but both times it rang through to voicemail. Too late. She was on her way. He found a bottle of brandy in a drinks cupboard and poured himself a shot. He wasn't much of a shot man, but this was clearly a *bon moment* to become one. It was a fine brandy too, aged in oak casks seasoned by years of nurturing sweet sherries. Not that he noticed any of that. He slugged it back, emptying the glass as he strode out onto the terrace. He had to think fast.

Kit list. Tons of kit.

That was the first thing that came to mind. Not that he needed it, necessarily. It was always good to have. But the real purpose of a kit-heavy approach was that sourcing it would keep Paz busy for forty-eight hours and give him time to regroup, as in deal with Jeanine and figure out what the hell was going on. Ashford's switcheroo, for example, his off-then-on-again hit on Preston. Calling it off had been explained away by the Texas ambush with the finger of suspicion pointing at Preston. But that was a red herring. Homicide detectives always stick the person closest to the victim at the top of their suspect list, and following that paradigm would make Ashford the prime suspect. But he had no obvious motive. Besides, his performance that first night in Alcazada when Paz had blown a fuse and they'd both accused him of the killing had been utterly convincing.

So who?

As for Paz, the U-turn in her affections was a whiplash event. She'd gone from dropping him with a 9mm bullet to dropping her pants in a matter of days. What was driving that? All those teasy pouts and flirty stares, not to mention the slideshow of bare flesh. There was something phony about it all. CJ was a rugged and clean-looking man, but he had no illusions about his pin-up status. No woman with both oars in the water was ever going to tack his photo up on her bathroom wall. What he needed was a set of plans. Not the usual plan A and plan B stuff, but a Russian doll set where one plan sits hidden inside the other. One doll for Paz and another for Ashford, cute ones with a full set of colors. Show plans, with the real plans hidden inside, and for the moment that hidden plan had to be a plain doll, no colors yet, still a work in progress.

When Paz rolled back into the driveway, CJ went to meet her and help her with the provisions. He'd been busy, and as soon as they were done, he sat her at the table on the terrace and went straight to it.

"I put together a kit list." He sent it to her phone and waited as she read through it.

"Willie Pete?" she said.

"White phosphorus. It's an incendiary. We used it in Iraq."

"And M183?"

"Demolition charge assembly. Sixteen strips of C-4 and primers."

"Where is he supposed to get this stuff? You think they keep kit like this in the British Consulate in Palma?"

"I would if I was in charge."

"They repatriate drunken Brits and scrape up pill poppers who jump off hotel balconies thinking they can fly. This is Spain, not Yemen."

"If he wants the job done, he'll get it."

"SDV?"

"Swimmer delivery vehicles."

"You mean those SEAL things?"

"Something recreational will do."

"What about jet boots? I've used them for fun diving, and they're easy to get here."

CJ was showing his vintage. Jet boots had been little more than a wish list item when he'd been in the service, propulsion units strapped to the calves that left hands free for tactical operations. But for this operation, strapping them on and off would be a timewaster.

"Great idea," he said. "Something recreational… but a sled would be better."

His verbal pat on the back got a smile out of her and she made the amendment. "I'm sending it to Ashford," she said. They ate lunch after that and were halfway through it when her phone rang. It was Ashford following up on the kit list. CJ followed her side of the call as he munched away at a chunk of bread topped with the local soft sausage.

"CJ wrote the list… don't blame me," Paz said.

After a long silence, she broke away from the phone and said, "Why do you need the Willie Pete?"

"Burn holes in the network. Knock out the CCTV. It's built on two interconnected fiberoptic rings like a warship's. It self-repairs. But in the time it takes, we'll slip through the blind spots."

She nodded and went back to Ashford. "Screw up the cameras," she said, then to CJ. "What about the M183?"

"Controlled explosions to block access for their security guys."

She relayed it, then went quiet, her eyes downcast, her face furrowed with concentration.

"If you say so," she said finally. "You're the boss." She hung up, looking up at CJ, her phone dangling in her hand as it dropped at her side. "It looks like Mr. and Mrs. Smith are not going to be doing their love island thing after all."

"What's going on?"

"He says I have to go back to the mainland to get this. So you're going to be on your lonesome."

CJ shrugged, like *what can a guy do?* Then he went back to his sausage.

"This wasn't supposed to be like this," she said.

"It never is."

"No, I mean…" she waved her hand between them, "us."

"So how was it supposed to be."

She pushed her plate aside and sipped her beer. "Shagarama."

CJ chuckled, "You have a definite way with words." He sipped more beer too, then said, "I don't usually have that effect on women. Regrettably. Are you going to let me in on the *why* of it all?"

"I guess so… if my vagina's of no interest to you, how about diamonds?" CJ stopped sipping. *The switcheroos?* He'd been looking for answers, and diamonds sounded just about perfect. "Schilder's making the final payment in diamonds. It was a last-minute change. Nazar insisted."

"And you heard all this courtesy of José's bugs?"

"Not directly. Ashford told me."

"When?"

"After you booked the hotel in Valencia and the Visa was flagged up. He called me. He told me then. He metes out information on a need-to-know basis."

"He didn't share it with me."

"That's the point. You don't need to know about the diamonds and neither does London."

"So he offered you a deal?"

She nodded. "Did they tell you about my war record? My heroism?"

"Yeah… medals and all. Well done!"

"It's all bullshit. I turned tail. The real heroes all died there. I was just the last man standing. Only I wasn't a man. I was a woman. That made it even better. All our guys were dead. The insurgents were all dead too. So I picked up a gun and rewrote history. What do you think of that?"

"I think you're not so proud of it now."

"I didn't plan on being a hero. I just lied to cover up my cowardice. But the brass went crazy. These days, all combat roles are open to women. But back then it was different—the big debate, for and against. They needed a poster girl, and there I was. I could hardly say I'd lied and shit on the dreams of all those young women with guts who'd have done a better job than me. In fact, I've never told anyone until right now."

"So why are you telling me?"

"Because I'm not going to shoot you in the back of the head on D-Day."

"Ashford's plan?"

She nodded. "It turns out that I'm a make-love-not-war type, not the stone-cold killer I'm billed as."

"Don't sweat it. Being a stone-cold killer is not what it's cracked up to be." CJ finished his beer, penciling a list of questions in his head.

"So you rejigged Ashford's plan… you seduce me, then what?"

"We make off with the diamonds and live happily ever after."

"I take it that Ashford is not one of your conquests?"

"You're kidding. I said I was sex-positive, not a sex pervert. Besides, there's no way he'll split those diamonds with me anyway. I'm not an idiot."

"So in Ashford's crystal ball, you and me, we're unfortunate casualties. Preston is dead. Domino is stopped. London gets the activator, and he gets the diamonds that don't exist and a pat on the back for pulling off a government-sanctioned, but unofficial and deniable, illegal operation to stop WWIII."

"When he pitched it to me, I kept thinking about Alcazada… the way he stuck that knife in José. It was like he was picking his nose, he was that casual. Forty million in diamonds… split down the middle. What was I supposed to say? *No, thank you.* He knows my war record… my official record. I'm a lethal bitch. I had to play along, or I'd be dead."

"What about me? Maybe I'll kill you for the diamonds."

"I know what happened to Alex Solo, and I know what you did to the creeps who put him through that. Preston's the last link in that chain and here you are so many years later still hunting him. What drives you? *Honor?* Maybe that's not the right word, but it's as close as I can get. I don't know if it's misplaced, stupid even, but I understand it. You're not going to shoot me in the back of the head, and that's something I'm ready to bet my life on."

CJ had heard enough. He took her hand and squeezed it gently.

"You don't have to shag me to get me on your side. All you have to do is play it straight. You made the right call here today. Was there anything else that came through on those bugs before they got ripped out?"

She shook her head. "Not that I remember… Nazar was the last biggie. Ashford told you about the hit?"

"On Nazar?"

"They call it their *special plan.*"

CJ nodded. Killing Nazar made sense. He knew where Preston had buried bodies and he was likely to be a guest of the FBI sometime soon, an intolerable risk. And the more CJ thought about it, the more it explained.

"I better get going," she said, standing up. "I'd feel a lot better knowing where I am with you on this. You know I won't get back until D-Day, early in the morning."

"I'll have everything ready, and we'll have time to go through it. It'll all be good." He stood up. "You're not going to have to shoot anyone, and no one's going to be shooting at you either." He held his arms open, a hug invitation, and she took it. He held her against him, patting her back, his head against hers. "Thanks," he whispered. "I owe you."

Preston was on the *True Grit,* sitting on its aft deck at a table with a laptop and a glass of juice. He was working the keys, looking up from time to time, his eyes panning the marina, idly following the yachts coming and going and the foot traffic on the quay checking out the goods in its luxury stores. This was Port Adriano in the southwest of Majorca, one of the few marinas on the island that a fifty-five-meter yacht could call home.

"Sir." It was Tony, disturbing the day's calm, interrupting Preston's reveries with a look that augured bad news. Even so, the question had to be asked.

"Any word?"

Tony shook his head.

"Worthless son of a bitch…" Preston jerked himself up onto his feet. The SOB in question was Ernald. "Belgians!" Preston spat the word.

"And the boy's gone back to America. The cop's kid."

"So they got away?"

"No, the kid was alone. He flew out of Alicante."

"And the mom?"

"The kid got a standby. She's probably still there trying to get a flight. Do you want me to—"

"No, forget it. It'll be too late now. Too late to stop Brink. That dumb Belgian must have screwed up. Find him and take care of him, and that monster woman of his. Let's do the world a favor at least."

"I'll take care of it, sir."

Preston dragged his chair back to the table and sat down, stretching his legs under it.

"Preparations on track?" he said, moving on to Domino, a word that didn't need to be said.

"Everything's in place."

"And the party?"

"We'll ship out tomorrow as usual, same route as last year. Catering is on track. Weather forecast good."

Preston nodded, letting his mind dawdle on the mundane. The subtleties of entertaining twenty-eight VIPs—some with their own girl or boy toys in tow, but most alone—was a relaxing diversion after the tumult of the recent past, and gourmet catering and weather forecasts were the least of it.

"The companionship team?" he said, his euphemism prompting a wry smile from Tony.

"Arriving in Palma today. They'll board in the morning."

"The extras on the beach?"

"They're setting it all up today."

The beach party was a sidebar to the onboard festivities, a security hole that couldn't be ducked. After sunset, the *True Grit* would anchor off an isolated beach with an open bar, a roaring fire, and precooked suckling pigs getting finished off over the flames. It was an optional trip by tender with guests often sliding off into the shadows with newfound friends, offering a feast of infrared video opportunities. Guests were looking for a fantasy island adventure and Preston was happy to supply it. Who knew when those X-rated videos might come in handy? The chosen beach was inaccessible from the shore, but a yacht might arrive by chance and gate-crash the scene. There were ways of discouraging that. But it was an uncomfortable risk, which brought him inevitably to...

"Brink?"

"Nothing yet."

Preston nodded. Not unexpected. Anyone who could set up a stunt like that gardener fiasco could certainly get him new documents.

"That party beach. Brink could be sitting behind a bush there already."

"But you're not going ashore, and neither are the principals."

Too true. His plan was to schmooze on board until sunset, then sneak off to clinch the deal as the party spilled over onto the beach. Schilder and Nazar would be late arrivals, hustled down in his private elevator.

"Put more men on it," he said. "And get a drone to scout the cliffs."

"There are no roads. We don't—"

Preston banged his fist on the table.

"He'll be in a cave, or a goddamn grave. He's been in one before and come out of it. Do not underestimate him. That's the weak spot. The beach. I want eyes all over it."

He waved Tony away with a sweep of his arm, then shut the lid on his laptop, his eyes wandering back across the marina to those designer-label stores. They were troubling him now. Those rooftops? Were they accessible from the back? They were only a few hundred yards away. An easy shot for a guy like Brink. He headed for the door, his movements slow, not hurried. No panic. But when he stepped inside and shut the door, he leaned back against it and took a long breath, its cold steel a mighty comfort.

Never in her life...

Sitting in the lounge of the fast-ferry skimming to Majorca, Jeanine had to wonder. She was nursing a cocktail and gobbling everything down with gusto—the experience, the excitement, the relief. Her wildest dreams and craziest fantasies could never have reached this far. Yes. It was deadly serious. And, yes, there was a pistol in her bag, a concealed weapon, and here in Europe her cop badge was worth zilch. So that put her in the same category as a terrorist or an arch felon. But Aidan was safe. And she was free. Alone in a foreign country aboard a catamaran ferry hurtling towards an island celebrated in song as the Isle of Love. There was a shadow of guilt at one point. Or was it responsibility? But it flicked on by, lost like the frothy wake in the deep blue water. CJ? How important he'd become. And so unexpectedly, with no contrivance, and none of the usual posing and faking. She'd been sent to kill him, and now this.

The five-hour trip took her to Palma, Majorca's capital, and a much bigger city than she'd anticipated. It was late evening, the city a sea of lights with hills silhouetted against a starry sky. She took a cab from the port area to a downtown hotel. It was just a stopover. Arriving at nightfall, she had to regroup and she was exhausted. She put off calling CJ until the morning, and after a shower, she crashed on the bed and was asleep within minutes.

The phone woke her. A text from Eileen. She was at the airport and Aidan's flight had touched down. Jeanine took a moment of relief, then eased off back to sleep. But not for long; Aidan's call soon had her wide awake and listening as her son recounted the trivia of his long flight, reeling it all off against a background of traffic noise, interrupted now and again by Eileen with snippets of local news. Jeanine was picturing it all, enjoying their company as if she was sitting in the car alongside them. It was a long call and it was only when Eileen was pulling into her driveway and they were about to hang up that Aidan said, "Mom, I found an empty memory card in the tablet, so I copied some game files on it for Jimmie. Just so you know."

What memory card?

The words were almost on her lips when she remembered it. She'd dropped the frame with Alex's photo and found an SD card taped to the cardboard backplate. That empty memory card. She'd been so preoccupied with getting Aidan back, she'd completely forgotten it. She hadn't even mentioned it to CJ.

"Oh, that…," she said. "Sure. That's fine."

She heard Eileen announce their arrival, so she signed off with love and a reminder that he was to be on his best behavior while he was a guest of her best friend. Sleep was difficult after that. So much going on. And the memory card? How strange was that? Now that she knew CJ better, she had to wonder. He was deliberate and thoughtful. Why would he hide an empty memory card behind her brother's photo? She dozed until the sun was up, then sent him a message.

Nineteen

Dawn.

CJ was already out of the shower and toweling off when his phone signaled a message from Jeanine. He was delighted to hear from her, but troubled too with the conundrum of what role she had to play in this—if any—still unsolved. With her training and experience, she could be a tremendous asset. But what a worry. What if something bad happened to her? Even setting aside his personal feelings, Jeanine was a mother. He'd had a childhood without one, and taking any risk that might endanger her and cause her son to share the same fate was out of the question. Aidan might survive such a loss, but CJ knew that he never would. Outside, the first light was a glow on a landscape softened with dew. He stood on the terrace, eyes scanning the green that fell away into the valley, ears combing the muffled sounds of an awakening world. Bells. They weren't ringing, but tinkling somewhere down there beyond the olive grove. It took him a while to place the sound. Not a church. Sheep, or maybe goats, foraging a breakfast. Something peaceful about it, a poignant counterpoint to all that was about to unfold. He sat down on the table and made the call.

"Jeanine. Is Aidan okay?"

"He's fine. Arrived safely."

"So what happened back at the villa there?"

"That's a conversation best had when we're sitting comfortably with a stiff drink. Where are you?"

"I'm on the west of the island."

"How do I get there?"

So there it was. Decision time. And the awkward moment turned easy. Jeanine was in. He was never going to call it any other way. He just had to keep her safe, her and Paz.

"Where are you now?"

"Palma."

CJ talked her through the options and she settled on a taxi. They exchanged details, and CJ was about to ring off when Jeanine said, "Before I forget… why did you put that memory card behind the photo you sent me?"

That wrong-footed him. She wasn't the only one who'd forgotten.

"That's a story for another time too," he said finally. "And maybe we'd better make those drinks doubles. But the soundbite version is that it's what got your brother killed."

"But it was empty?"

"*Was?*"

"Wasn't it?"

"It was tricked to look empty, but there was a hidden key on it."

"A key to what?"

"Secrets. Preston's dirty deeds. Names, dates, places."

"Why did you put it there and not tell me?"

"I didn't expect you to find it. I wanted to keep it safe, and it wasn't safe on me. So I…" He lost track, feelings swamping his thoughts.

"So you what…? Are you okay?"

"I gave it to Alex to look after."

There was silence for a while, then Jeanine said, "I understand. I miss him, too. Every day."

"So what happened to it?"

"Would you kill me if I told you I copied a bunch of files onto it? I'm sorry, I thought it was empty."

He could hear the trepidation in her voice. But he wasn't angry. It was the oddest thing. He was happy, a great weight lifted that he'd never known he was carrying. That key had opened a door of truth to a rogue's gallery of CEOs, spooks, politicians and other crooks. They all merited a settlement of accounts, and while he'd had no particular plans to call in their markers, he'd had a few daydreams. On sunny days, he'd wanted to out them publicly by sharing the dirt with investigative journalists. On dark days, he'd yearned for a more hands-on approach—hands on their throats, that is, making it personal on behalf of those who no longer had that option.

"Alex called it right," he said, thinking back to the Nevada convenience store where he'd tried to reboot his life on a different track, reaching for a different future that wasn't built on the past. "Alex has set me free now. It's what a buddy would do, and I'll never get one like him. I'm going to end it here. Just one more mission. This one."

Jeanine said nothing until CJ went to sign off, then she said, "Buddies come in all shapes and sizes. Genders too. Did you know that? And sometimes, they're in the oddest places. Sometimes even right in front of your eyes."

Now that was telling him, and he got the message. Chuckling, he said, "Your taxi's waiting, ma'am."

After the call, he went back into the house and made some coffee. Jeanine was on the way. He felt good about that, stronger—inside and out—batteries fully charged. He had hours before her arrival too, and that was just what he needed. Space and time. He had to think. He sat in the living room in an armchair by a stone fireplace with iron trimmings. The room was furnished in weathered wood and half-lit by a sunbeam angling in through the blinds. It was a still-life artwork of traditional Spain, right down to the crucifix on the wall. Silence. Just a few birds singing in the bushes outside and the tinkling bells in the valley. He sipped his coffee and set his mind free to wander, looking for a connection.

Domino?

Ashford's speculation was a suitcase nuke, but CJ dismissed that. Now he knew the target, it made no sense. The USS *Abraham Lincoln* was at sea, and the EM-88 was en route on a freighter. How could they get it onboard, or otherwise target it? Besides, other than a few oddball experimental weapons like the US W-54 and the Russian RA-115s, suitcase nukes had been a bigger threat in Cold War spy novels than reality. It didn't fit the players either. Terrorists might dream about decimating such a warship and turning it into a metal coffin for five thousand souls. But it didn't fit the bandidos, especially not Preston. Once upon a time, he'd been US Army. That had to mean something. Prodding America into a war was one thing, but having a direct hand in the wholesale slaughter of US servicemen would be far beyond even his jaundiced ethical code.

EM-88?

EM had a faint whiff of familiarity. He'd definitely come across the acronym as a weapon somewhere before. He sat back and waited, shuffling back and forth through all the weapons he'd come across in his military career. And that's how it came to him, served up like a history page.

The Persian Gulf War. An incident.

In February 1991, the USS *Princeton*, a billion-dollar Aegis cruiser, was knocked out of action by an Italian Manta mine that the Iraqis had picked up for twenty-five thousand dollars.

How's that for value?

At a stroke, the new age of smart mines had been ushered in. The Manta sat on the ocean floor and listened and sniffed. Ships make unique sounds, especially warships, and they're big chunks of steel, so they make minute changes in the earth's magnetic field. Combine the two and you have an ID document, a unique signature identifying the ship. That attack was a message that echoed in corridors of power from Beijing to Tehran. Smart mines leveled the playing field. They were asymmetrical warfare's dream weapon. A billion dollars versus twenty-five thousand, with the budget player coming out on top. And for slow learners, the lesson was rammed home repeatedly during the Iraq Wars with fourteen US warships damaged by Iraqi mines. In the end, it wasn't their Russian tanks or Scud missiles that hurt the allies most. It was their mines. After the *Princeton* attack, alarm bells had gone hypersonic in Washington when the Chinese had sold the Iranians a rocket-propelled smart mine—their starter model—the EM-52. So what if they sold them their top model, an EM-57, a virtually undetectable underwater cruise missile with a range of 730 kilometers? Logically, the EM-88 had to be an even more advanced weapon, the latest generation, China's silver bullet able to neutralize the mighty US Navy.

CJ fetched his laptop and searched for the location of the USS *Abe*. For obvious reasons, warships tend not to advertise their comings and goings. Some navies—like the Chinese—never turn on their AIS to identify their location. Others, like the US and British navies, turn on their systems in peacetime while navigating crowded waterways to ensure the safety of other vessels. So that's how he found it. With the Suez Canal on one end and the Straits of Gibraltar on the other, the Mediterranean is a busy highway of maritime traffic that gets squeezed into tight sea lanes in places. CJ soon found the *Abe*'s blinking icon in the Eastern Mediterranean, heading for the Suez Canal. Most likely, that freighter had dumped the Domino container in the approaches to the canal. Hundreds of ships pass that way, but they'd be ignored. Nazar's go-live codes would give the EM-88 ears for one ship only, a *Nimitz*-class nuclear-powered aircraft carrier.

"You see this, Alex?" CJ barked it out to the empty room. "Those bastards are going to take out your warship." He stood up abruptly, his fists clenching. "Like hell they are."

Jeanine's taxi dropped her in Sóller and CJ picked her up, an easier option than trying to find the remote finca, and a more secure one too. On the drive to the house, Jeanine told CJ about the fate of Ernald and Harriet. CJ listened in silence, but the wide-eyed looks he gave her said it all—shocked that they'd tried a stunt like that and delighted that she'd handled it with consummate accomplishment.

When they pulled up in front of the finca, she was removing her seat belt when he pulled her close and kissed her, whispering in her ear, "Nice one." Jeanine wasn't sure if he was talking about the bodies at the villa or the kiss. Either way, she liked it.

Out on the terrace with a pot of coffee and CJ's laptop filling in blanks, it was straight down to business, and when CJ had finally laid it all out, the scale of it left her speechless.

The USS *Abraham Lincoln*!

She was staring at a recent news story describing its deployment from the Mediterranean to the Persian Gulf.

"Could one of these smart mines really take out a ship this big?" she said.

"It won't sink it. Maybe there won't even be fatalities, but they'll be plenty of casualties. Either way, it'll be disabled. Imagine that, the pride of the US Navy stuck in the Eastern Med, crippled within reach of Iranian missiles. The propaganda triumph would be epic."

"And there'll be a false trail pointing the finger at Iran."

"With all the mistrust between the US and Iran, that would be the easy part. Iran has military proxies all over the region. One of them will get fingered."

"So the Domino falls and war drags in country after country…"

"There's no business like war business. Cruise missiles cost a million bucks and they're single-use, with the added bonus that you have to rebuild the stuff you blow up. War is a money-printing business, only the bills are inked in blood."

"But how could the Chinese let something this important get stolen?"

"Maybe they turned a blind eye."

"C'mon… and risk war with the US?"

"There's no risk to them. It's a Chinese mine, but Beijing can wash its hands of it. They'll blame Muslim terrorists. They stole it and sneaked it out through Pakistan. The bandidos' trail will lead to Iran. The Chinese will arrest a few hundred scapegoats, parade them in a kangaroo court, then line them up in front of a wall and shoot them. Case closed."

"But what would they get out of it?"

"A risk-free live-fire exercise. Smart mines are part of their String of Pearls strategy."

"Which is?"

"Oil is China's strategic vulnerability. It comes from the Persian Gulf by sea around Southeast Asia. The US Navy could block that route in a day. So the Chinese have invested billions turning Southeast Asian nations into client states and creating a soft military footprint under the guise of port installations. If this weapon works, they can protect their String of Pearls."

It all made sense. But Jeanine was still troubled, with the hard reflexes of a cop giving her no peace. Where was the hard evidence? Police officers ended up making a call. Was this person arrestable? Down the road, there'd be a judge and jury to contend with and a reasonable doubt barrier to climb.

"None of this adds up to a smoking gun, though, does it?" she said.

"Guns only smoke when it's too late," CJ said. "Actionable intelligence is not about judicial thresholds. It's about justice. Prevention, disruption, elimination."

"So what's your plan?"

"It's better I show you," he said. "We're driving up the coast, but we've got some time. Do you want to get some rest before we head out?" He jerked his thumb back towards the house like she might be prime for a nap.

"Not exactly," she said, looping her arm around his neck and dragging him into a kiss. Her plan was simple: that kiss would start here and last all the way to some unknown bedroom, unknown because she hadn't yet had the tour of the house. But it never made it off the terrace, with CJ heaving her off her feet and carrying her, mouths fully engaged, to the nearby rattan sofa.

Later that day, when their private party had segued into a warm, fuzzy afterlude, they drove off, heading north and breezing past Sóller with CJ at the wheel, explaining the crucial role he wanted her to play and why he needed the 250cc dirt bike hitched to the back of the Toyota. Some miles north of Sóller, they headed off-road, cutting cross-country to the cliffs and coves near to where Preston's happening was scheduled to unfold. Jeanine was sitting at CJ's side, peppering him with questions, her feet on the hamper carrying a picnic, a last supper of sorts that they planned to enjoy on the beach at the end of this recon trip before going their separate ways. They wouldn't meet again until it was all over.

Tomorrow was Monday, May 13, 2019—Firó, the Battle of the Moors and the Christians, was about to take place. And that wasn't the only one. It was D-Day. Paz would be back with his kit and Preston would be sailing north, his party in full swing. It was game on for World War III.

As CJ and Jeanine passed Sóller, the *True Grit* was anchored close by, and the party's booze and food preparations were going like clockwork. Even the always-tricky sushi platters were promising nothing but the best, with a longline-caught bluefin tuna flown in directly from Hawaii. The chefs were hard at work, the posh hookers were on their way, and the DJs were setting up. It might have all looked like chaos, but it was far from that with all the staff feeling the burn of Preston's drill sergeant eyeballs as he wandered around querying this and that.

Detail.

That was Preston's major, and nobody did it better. It was one of the things he admired about CJ Brink too, an understanding that greatness was nothing but a thousand perfect details. Not that Brink was on his mind as the afternoon wore on into evening. There were far more important issues at hand, more important even than the party prep. After all, this was D-Day minus one. From this point on—to paraphrase Nazar—the die would be cast. Schilder would have the EM-88, now sitting in a sealed container in the Eastern Med, awaiting the underwater technicians who would pop open its tin can and expose its sleek, bulbous lethality. He would also have the activator and go-live codes. Days later, when the domino fell, all hell would break loose, and Tratfors' war business dividend would get paid in full.

D for domino, details and dependencies.

That last one was an issue. Any plan with so many dependencies was sure to have a few hiccups, and although Preston was no psychic, he did have anxiety antennas synced to reality. So when something got stuck in his head, it was typically a signal that a bucketload of crap was coming down the pipe. And that's how it played out on D-Day minus one. He was in the lounge on the Owner's Deck with the blinds down and the sunlight filtering through them as a comforting glow. He was alone, his elbows propped on the table and his broken chin sitting on his fists. He was hard at work worrying when the door buzzed and Tony entered.

"Schilder!" he said with the door still open and just one foot in the room.

"What!"

"He's here. I mean he's on board. He showed up on a launch with a bunch of security. I had no choice."

"Where are they now?"

"Waiting downstairs. I put that on me. I said no one comes up here without your say-so. I told him, but he's pissed. He's threatening to walk, so—"

"Get him up here. But just him. His security waits at the elevator. Go."

"Got it." Tony headed out the door, snapping orders through his comms button.

Preston paced. Schilder had been scheduled to arrive by helicopter when they were anchored up the coast and the party was in full swing. Nazar too. The pair of them would board the yacht after dark. They'd do the deal, then tidy up the loose ends. It was all agreed. Schilder had signed off on it. So why the hell was he here now?

The door opened and Tony ushered Schilder through it.

"This is not good..." Preston whirled around as Tony closed the door, leaving them alone.

"Indictments never are."

"Nazar? Already?"

"Within twenty-four hours. He's looking at thirty years in jail. Can you see him doing time? That pomade pansy! He'll sell us up the river. So screw deniability. What's happening? I have to know you'll take care of him."

The men were facing each other, barely a yard apart, but Schilder was hollering. Preston reached out a fatherly hand and held the younger man's shoulder.

"Mark. I understand your concerns and I share them. Nothing is going to go wrong."

"Here…" Schilder looked around the luxurious salon. "You're not going to do him here, are you?"

"No way. Down on the Explorer Deck. It's totally secure—away from the party. It's got direct access to the sea through the hangar doors."

"What about his guards?"

"No guards."

"He's never going to go for that."

"Yes, he is. And so are you." Schilder gave him a look, but Preston ignored it. He was calling the shots on this. "Just the three of us. Tony will be at the entrance. I'll allow up to two guards for each of you. But they wait with Tony. It has to look fair." Schilder said nothing, his brow furrowing with suspicion. That was not unexpected. Schilder went everywhere with a dozen armed men.

"So who takes care of Nazar if there's just the three of us?"

"I do."

Schilder nodded, furrows easing off his brow. "It makes sense," he said. "With the indictment pending. You could make it look like a suicide."

"There'll be plenty of speculation like that. But his body will never be found, so that's all it'll ever be."

Schilder snickered. "You're a smart one, Preston. Thank God you're on my side." He seemed pretty confident about that, although his eyes did flash up a question mark.

Preston chuckled too, but his was no snicker, more of a warm gurgle. That was pretty funny, after all.

Twenty

Their boat was a bowrider, a good day sailor, well equipped and a handy size, big enough to be useful and small enough to be inconspicuous on a coast busy with boaters. It also had plenty of power, not that CJ was shooting for any speed records, especially not as he passed the *True Grit* anchored at the mouth of Sóller's horseshoe bay. He was standing at the wheel, dressed in swim shorts with Paz busying herself to his rear. She was wearing a white bikini under a T-shirt and taking a video of the picturesque town, its iconic bay and the Tramuntana Mountains that surrounded it before zooming in on the superyacht. They made a good-looking pair, a lucky couple out for a day of fun.

A few miles up the coast—a quiet stretch—CJ cut back the power and edged into a bay. Time to fish and time to talk. Time to drop the bombshell on Paz. The plan was that they were a team. That they'd fake a bit of fishing here and wait for the *True Grit* to sail past offshore en route to its party beach. They'd follow discreetly as it got dark and make the last leg underwater and complete the mission. But that wasn't going to happen. CJ was doing this alone, and before Paz would agree to that, she'd need more than a change of mind. She'd need a change of heart. With fishing poles set like props, they ate a light meal and sipped energy drinks while CJ looked for words.

There were no easy ones.

"Do you ever wonder," he said, "what turns a zig into a zag?"

"Is this one of those Zen things?"

"Something's heading east, then, *boom*… it goes west. Why?"

She shrugged. "Something stops it."

"An obstruction. And Texas was the first one. Only it didn't zag like it was supposed to. I lived. That wasn't supposed to happen. So the hit was called off. Then it was back on…"

"I'm lost."

"Tell me about you and Colby?"

"What?" She looked up at him sharply. "She recruited me." That was true, but it was only half the truth. Colby was much more than that.

"No, I mean about *you* and Colby?"

"What's it to you?"

That sore spot was another confirmation. Not that he needed it. This was the only way it added up. When he'd arrived at the Texas airstrip, Colby had been on the phone. That call had started out professionally before changing tone to familiar and planning a rendezvous, a romantic one. So who was on the other end of that call? Ashford had been his first thought, albeit one that had taken considerable imagination. But he'd ruled that out in Marbella when Ashford had confronted him. The MI6 man had been angry alright, accusing CJ of being Colby's killer, but Paz was the one who was hurting. She'd been apoplectic, pulsing with emotional overload, like she'd lost a lover.

"It'll hurt forever," CJ said.

Her face softened, animosity fading and puzzlement taking its place.

"Why are you asking me this? Why now?"

It was a mess. He had to tell her the truth. It was the only way. He had to hurt her, and he was going to hate himself for it.

"Preston didn't kill Alicia. I know that for a fact. Ashford did. He hired the killers on a dark web site called Wetslope. I could never figure out why. But now I know the motive, thanks to you."

"Ashford? That's ridiculous. Why?"

"Diamonds."

"But how would killing Alicia get him the diamonds?"

"I was the target, not Alicia. The goal was to stop me killing Preston, to keep Domino alive. But they had to shoot her first because she had a weapon."

"How would killing you get Ashford the diamonds?"

"He did a deal with Nazar."

"Oh… like split the diamonds and I'll kill my colleague."

"My new ID, the Texas setup, the hit on Preston… all that was in motion when Nazar's brother was indicted, and that was when Nazar switched the last payment to diamonds." He waited, but he was pretty confident about that timeline and she didn't challenge it. "Ashford listened in on that, but he didn't pass it on to you or London. He cut a deal with Nazar instead. It's the only way to explain the zig becoming a zag."

"If that's true, why is he sending you to stop it now?"

"Nazar's not going to survive the night. Isn't that what you told me? The last bit of info from José's bugs. When Ashford heard that, he saw his diamond dream disappear. But then he got lucky. I used the VISA card and played myself back in the game. So Ashford switched the zag back to a zig. He knew I was good for killing Preston, but I'd never sign up to thieving. What did he say to get you on board? *If we don't take the diamonds, the Spanish cops will anyway...*"

"It sounds good, but you're retrofitting it. I get that Ashford's making a play for the diamonds now. So it makes sense that he's been after them all along. But a deal with Nazar? I don't buy that. How could Ashford enforce payment? What if Nazar welched? What would Ashford do? File a bad credit report?"

CJ was impressed. She'd zoomed right in on the gaping hole in his thesis.

"That's exactly what I'm going to find out tonight. There must have been more to that deal. Something on the back end to make sure Ashford got his diamonds."

"And that dark web thing," she said. "Did you find anything on the killers linking them to Ashford?"

"It was just talk."

"I can't see Ashford doing that... not even him, his own partner. You said you knew for a fact it wasn't Preston. How's that?"

CJ had been hoping to avoid it, but with words not working, he had no choice. He took out his phone and played the video he'd copied from Preston's computer. Texas, the aftermath. Paz watched and listened, and as the exchange between Preston and his men continued her face paled and her body drooped as if all the life was getting drained from it. CJ figured she'd seen enough at that point and he stopped it.

"No," she said. "I want to see it… I want to see her."

That was exactly where he didn't want to take her, but there was no denying her. He shifted around to sit at her side as he played it. When the team found Colby, she snatched the phone from him and froze the image, zooming in on her face. No big reaction. No shriek of pain, just eyes softening with wet. Some deep sadness screaming inside her. CJ took the phone off of her, strong arms smothering her weak effort to resist and folding her against his chest. Her face hidden, she sobbed and CJ held her, his eyes on the white cliffs, transformed into a tapestry of colors by the sun setting at his back. The beach below it was a tumble of huge rocks and patches of sand. Jeanine would be waiting there on the beach where they'd picnicked less than twenty-four hours before, where they'd made love as though it were the last time and had to be the best time.

Paz put herself back together bit by bit, extricating her body from CJ's arms and sniffling her way back under control.

"I get it," she said finally. "The timing fits."

CJ snapped his head around, eyes scanning the open seas. Motors and music. But still no sign of the *True Grit*.

"In about five minutes, we'll see the yacht rounding the point there," he said, nodding towards the headland to the south.

"So what now?" she said.

CJ pointed to the rigid inflatable dinghy on a towline behind the bowrider. "You get to take the RIB and head to that beach. My friend is waiting there for you."

"The cop?" He nodded. "So that worked out. You're an old romantic. I should have guessed."

"Just like you, eh?"

She got to her feet. "Maybe."

She went to the stern of the bowrider and hauled in the RIB.

"I'll message her," CJ said, taking out his phone. "Where do you want her to take you?"

Paz turned back towards him, her hand still on the RIB's towline. "Puerto d'Andratx."

That was Ashford's place. He was expecting her there to deliver the activator and divvy up the diamonds.

CJ held off on the encrypted message relay. "Didn't you tell me he was sure to bushwhack you?"

"Two can play at that game."

This was all wrong. She wanted vengeance, and how could he—of all people—deny her that? Wanting payback was always going to be the risk of telling her the truth. That still shot she'd frozen with Colby wide-eyed, her throat shot out—Paz was never going to let that lie. CJ shook his head warily. Finding the heart to deny her this was tough, but he had to do it. He'd be the first to agree that Ashford deserved it, but this was sure to end up badly.

"Don't do it," he said. "You're not a killer. You're a lover. They're your words."

"You weren't a killer once. Besides, I'm a fast learner."

"Go with Jeanine, disappear. I'll kill him. Then I'll get the activator to the right people in London and I'll out Ashford for the crook he was."

"Don't"—she threw up her hand defensively—"try to talk me out of it. I don't give a damn about the activator or the diamonds. I owe Alicia. I'm going to kill that bastard."

She jerked the RIB closer and stepped aboard.

CJ nodded, throwing in the towel. This was a battle he was never going to win. "Okay," he said. "I'll tell

Jeanine." And he tapped in the message as Paz started the outboard.

Jeanine was not on the beach, as CJ had supposed, but up on the clifftop above it, sitting in a knot of Aleppo pines bonsaied into bushes by a frugal rock diet and rigorous coastal winds. It was an odd spot for a bivouac and one she'd chosen for its ability to maintain a 3G signal. She'd been following CJ's revelations through binoculars, and although he'd already told her their contents, she found herself wishing she could lip-read, especially after Paz ended up in a huddle with her new beau shortly thereafter.

She read his message.

She's all yours now. Suggest kid gloves. She's fragile. BTW She wants to go to Port d'Andratx. Tried but failed to talk her out of it. You'll do a much better job (smiley face). xxx

Port d'Andratx?

That was too bad, and keeping her away from Ashford was not going to be easy.

Thanks, CJ….

Jeanine made her way to the stony path that snaked down the cliff to a jumble of giant rocks she had to navigate on all fours. By the time she was on the sand, Paz had nearly reached the beach. Jeanine looked beyond her dinghy at CJ's bowrider cutting a line of white foam as it turned around the north point of the bay. He would anchor it up the coast, a mile or so from Preston's superyacht and make the last leg underwater on some kind of sled. It would be night by then, a terrifying prospect. CJ's explanation had been matter-of-fact and she'd swallowed it whole. Now it seemed like total madness. She cleared her head by reminding herself that he and Alex had made amphibious assaults on heavily guarded installations at wartime. He was trained for this. He'd done it before, and from what she'd heard from Alex, nobody did it better.

The RIB ran up onto the sand as Paz cut the engine. She hopped out and looked at Jeanine but said nothing, reaching back into the boat for a rucksack. She took out some jeans and pulled them on, sliding them up snug and belting them while studying Jeanine. According to CJ, her dad was a Brit and her mom was local, and she'd certainly gotten her mother's Spanish eyes, big brown saucers, scanning Jeanine head to toe. She was taller than Jeanine had expected, slim but strong, a natural athlete, the sort of girl who would have cleaned up awards in high school athletics without even trying. After putting on sneakers, she slung her bag over her shoulder and stepped up to Jeanine, eye to eye, not so much with attitude as interest.

"We're up there," Jeanine said, pointing to the clifftop. "You're going to need your hands to make it."

They reached the clifftop and scrambled over rocky ground to the hollow where the truck was hidden in scrub. Next to it was the mountain bike they'd ferried out on the back of the Toyota.

"For CJ." Jeanine nodded at the bike as they boarded the all-wheeler, and when they were strapped in, she said, "CJ tells me you're local. So you'll know that this is country meant for helicopters and smart horses. Not trucks. Plus, I only drove it twice, and it's complicated, like right at the third tree and left at the fourth rock. Get that backwards and you're sailing down a thousand-foot ravine. That sort of complicated. Luckily, CJ had me film the route. So here's the plan. You're the navigator keeping your eyes on the video and the road, and I'm the driver keeping our asses out of the ravine. Got it?"

She gave Paz the phone, and Paz gave her a nod and the start of a smile. The drive was only a few kilometers point to point, but because of the fading light and the difficult terrain, Jeanine had to shift it. Even so, it was more than an hour later when they bounced onto the narrow mountain road, called "the snake" by locals. There'd been hairy moments en route, and one scary *Thelma and Louise* moment when they'd slid, howling, to the edge of a canyon and been saved by a last-minute wheelspin that piled them into a rock instead. So by the time they made it to the road, they were oddly lighthearted. Danger, survival and teamwork had bonded them, and the vibe had changed. But when they left the snake, picked up the M-10 and turned south, Jeanine had to get back to business.

"So I get to take you to Sóller to that villa there." She tried to make it sound matter of fact in the hope of getting a like response, but not really believing she would.

Paz said nothing, looking away and staring out into darkness. They soon hit a tunnel whose chiseled rock walls made eerie shadows in the mix of headlights and overhead streetlights. Even then, Paz kept her eyes averted, hiding her face, leaving Jeanine to guess what was going on in her world. Beyond the tunnel, the road fronted a ribbon lake, squeezed between mountains, with a crescent moon reflected in its still waters.

"It's beautiful," Jeanine said. It was not going to lighten the mood, but what the heck—it was true.

"Fake," Paz said. "It only looks natural. It's a reservoir, filling all those pools in those fake-people villas."

So that was their conversation done, and a few miles down the road, when Jeanine was thinking she might be off the hook, Paz said, "You couldn't run me to Puerto d'Andratx, could you? It's just a ways down the road here." Jeanine was articulating a response in her head, essentially rehearsing the word *no*, when Paz said, "He told you, of course. Why didn't I see that coming?"

"I'm a cop," Jeanine said. "Maybe not over here, but I'm still a cop."

"I just want a ride. I'm not asking you to do anything."

"Except be an accessory to murder."

There was more quiet after that until they were approaching the turnoff to Sóller.

"I heard about Aidan," Paz said. "Those bastards. I'm so glad he's safe. I really am. Especially now I've met you. And I know it's not the same. But I saw her with her throat shot out. I'm never going to walk away from that."

The road was straight approaching the junction, and Jeanine took her eyes off of it long enough to check her out. Paz wasn't looking off into space anymore. She was turned towards Jeanine, headlights of oncoming vehicles strobe-lighting a face gritted with passion.

So what if it had ended like that?

Aidan with his throat hanging out.

Paz eased back in her seat. "It's okay. I understand. I'll find a cab in Sóller."

So that was solved.

Or was it?

Something about Paz struck a chord with Jeanine. She was no killer. CJ was right. She was trained and tough, and bursting with the confidence that comes from never having known failure, the confidence of the young. She was in her twenties and reminded Jeanine of herself when she'd been that age and fresh out of the police academy, battling to get a fair shake in a man's world. She must have had those battles too in the army and it had made her strong. But none of that was going to help. She was going to die tonight. Ashford would be waiting. Older, smarter, and seasoned in killing with a PhD in treachery. If she got lucky, it'd go wrong and she'd end up in jail instead. But that was the best she was looking at.

Signage, streetlights, houses, and up ahead, the Ma-10 feeding into a traffic circle.

The right went to Sóller. The left continued, heading on south.

Son of a bitch.

Jeanine was willing herself…

Turn those arms. Don't be stupid. Take her to Sóller, help her get a taxi. But her arms weren't listening, and neither was her heart. So they stayed on that circle and headed on down the road together.

Covert or overt? That was the choice. Sneak in through the back, or smash open the front door? CJ was treading water, fine-tuning the plan as he surveyed the scene. The *True Grit* was throbbing with sound and pulsing with light. CJ was a ways off, weaving back and forth on the seaward side. *Plan* was a clumsy word for what he had in mind, too rigid and inflexible. His plan was more like the water he was bobbing in, versatile, and capable of penetrating the tiniest crack. The goal was to get to the bandidos and stop Domino. Most likely, they would be holed up on the private top deck, the Owner's Deck. Somehow, CJ had to get to that deck, preferably without a gunfight en route. A tough ask, but CJ had plenty of assets, an intimate knowledge of the ship's architecture and systems for starters, plus the best training in the world. Amphibious assault was his office, and like any martial confrontation, this one boiled down to the basics. No one fights with no eyes, no one hurts with no arms, and no one moves with no legs. Scaled up to a military conflict, that translated into intelligence, weapons, and mobility. Take out one of them and you're on the road to victory. Preston's eyes were the CCTV cameras. Taking them out was a challenge, but that's what he planned to do, timing the outage with tactical explosions before sneaking through the melee dressed as a partying drunken loon. It was elaborate, bold and crazy, and CJ loved it. But first, he had to get on the yacht. So step one was…

How to?

He went through the options, starting with *easy, but ugly*. That was walking up the accommodation ladder running down the side of the yacht facing the beach. There were two large men in aloha shirts at the top of it, assisting partygoers who were stumbling down to the tender that would ferry them to the beach. Those aloha shirts doubtless concealed pistols on their hips. So that was the front door, more of a last resort than a solid option. Another possibility was the ninja option. CJ planned to tether his sled and scuba to the anchor chain in any case. So why not climb up it, Mission-Impossible style, and hop over the railings onto the deck?

You must be joking.

That was worse than the front door. It was more like coming down the chimney à la Father Christmas. The best choice was literally the back door, the stern, where a hydraulic swim platform folded out of the transom and down to the water. CJ had noted the transom lift in the plans and figured that it would be in use. But it wasn't. There was a crew member close by ready to operate it, but no one wanted a swim. Or else they were in the pool, or heading to the beach.

No swimmers!

Pulling himself out of the water in his swimming shorts and onto the dive platform would have looked natural, and he could have retrieved his kit afterwards. But now, he'd have to heave himself up on to the transom, act drunk, and pretend he'd fallen overboard. It was doable, but hardly ideal. He checked his options again, watching the launch pull away from the accommodation ladder and head towards a beach dotted with flaming torches. There was a bonfire on the beach too and dozens of extras, hired for the Moors versus Christians battle Preston was staging, an exclusive private event to celebrate the Es Firó fiesta. The tender's departure meant that the ladder was an option, but the aloha shirts were still at the top of it and so were the cameras. In fact, there were even more people on the beach side of the yacht now than before. They were lining up at the railings, looking towards the beach, preoccupied with the show. That left no one on the seaward side and got CJ wondering about that anchor chain.

But before he could move on that, a roar went up from the beach and fireworks exploded above it in multicolored clusters. The whole beach was floodlit, and the rat-a-tat of firecrackers was peppered with screeches and howls as the attacking Saracens emerged from the water and the Christians fell on them cutting them down. Swords and scimitars, crucifixes and crescents, the battle raged. But CJ skipped it. He knew the end. The Christians won. Then all the dead, Christians and Muslims alike, came back to life and got drunk together.

If only…

He cruised along the seaward side. And with all eyes transfixed on the beach, he risked the surface, taking it slow. That was when opportunity knocked and hydraulic doors on the side of the hull slowly opened. CJ knew about the doors. They opened onto the Explorer Deck, where scientists worked when the yacht was leased by universities and foundations. Beyond the doors was a hangar where research equipment and specialist vehicles were stored, including a submarine. The hangar led through to labs and conference rooms. CJ had not anticipated these doors opening in the middle of a party. It was a puzzle. Who'd be down in the science labs in the middle of a blowout like this?

As the doors slid open, he hurried to the anchor chain, tethered his underwater kit to it and swam back to the open doors with his operational kit in a waterproof bag. He tucked himself against the hull, close to the doors, and listened, filtering out the raging beach battle and its pyrotechnics.

Nothing.

No voices. No winches preparing a vessel for launch.

He took out his pistol, reached up and looked inside the hangar. At first he thought there was no one there. But then he saw a man in a room behind the cavernous storage area. No aloha shirt, this one. He looked geeky and was studying a computer screen with laser-like concentration. CJ hauled himself out of the water. There were no cameras in this part of the ship as confidential research projects were undertaken there. But he crept off to the side anyway and hid behind a winch while he kitted up. Five minutes later, he was all dolled up as a Saracen warrior, a choice determined not so much by their ideology as their minimal wardrobe requirements, basically bedsheets and a headscarf. He'd rehearsed it in front of a mirror, and with a few smudges of makeup paint on his cheeks and a wooden saber in his sash, he was transformed. The grumble of hydraulic gates closing caught his attention. That was even more puzzling. Why open the gates, then close them without launching anything?

"You're not supposed to be in here." It was the techie, the sound of his approach hidden by the grinding steel doors.

CJ wobbled and acted surprised.

"I got lost." He grinned and drew his saber. "Where's the party?"

"How'd you get down here?"

CJ waved his saber at the doors in a wild drunken gesture.

"Walked in."

The man looked at the doors and back at CJ, a rush of authority straightening his back.

"That's bull. It was locked."

CJ straightened up too. Evidently, his *Pirates of the Caribbean* act was not going to wash.

"Can you hold my saber?" he said, offering the man his silver-painted prop.

Amazingly, the man took it.

CJ noted his polite cooperation and, digging into the folds of his bedsheets, he whipped out his Glock pistol. "I'm a New Age Saracen," he said. "We've upgraded the gear."

The man stared at the gun. His jaw dropped. The saber clattered to the floor, and his hands pinged up over his head like he was trying to reach the ceiling.

"Take it easy, mate." CJ waved him to lower his arms. "What's your name?"

"Craig."

"Hello, Craig. I'm CJ… American, eh?"

Craig nodded.

"This is a bit awkward. Your finding me."

"Are you going to kill me?"

"That's the awkward part. You could say it's negotiable."

"Wait…" The man sprang back. "You're CJ Brink." His eyes flashed with excitement. "You're here to kill the boss."

"Why'd you say that?"

"About time someone did. I don't blame you. After what you went through."

"You know about me?"

"Everybody does. At Tratfors, I mean. Rumors. Watercooler stuff."

"So what do you do here?"

"Operate the winches. I'm a grunt."

"A happy grunt?"

"Oh sure… I got a master's in computer science so I could spend all day oiling winches. I'm supposed to be in the lab with the scientists. That's what I signed up for."

"Why'd you open the doors?"

"He told me to."

"Preston?"

"Tony. He says, *Open up the hangar and the labs. Preston's heading down later.* So I figured he was taking the sub out. He likes to show off."

"So why'd you close them?"

"I told Tony I'd opened them and he balled me out. He said, *I didn't tell you to open the goddamn doors. Just the deck.* He told me to set up a laptop in the conference room, then *get lost.*"

"Why?"

"Preston's coming down with two *big shots.* That's what Tony called them. It's Schilder and Nazar. Like I'm too stupid to figure that out."

As CJ listened to Craig's account, he was playing it out in his head, running it parallel with his mission objectives.

His plan was built to tailor on the fly, but clearly not enough. This new information called for a total rethink. For starters, he no longer needed to dress up as a sixteenth-century Moorish warrior to blend in. So what used to be a cunning disguise was now a pantomime costume. He didn't need to burn out the network and take down the CCTV either, and he'd have extra tactical explosives too as he'd only need to block access to this deck.

"Did you set up the laptop?"

"Not yet."

"So let's go."

CJ followed Craig into the office. Then they went through a side door into a conference room with a long table and a wall screen.

"Computer science degree. That's impressive," CJ said as he watched Craig set up the laptop. "You must have great network access."

"Pretty much."

Craig's phone rang, he glanced at CJ, who gave him a nod and he pulled it out.

"Tony again?" CJ said.

Craig shook his head and showed him the phone as the caller's photo appeared, a woman in her twenties with dark blond hair and striking green eyes.

"Sophia, my girlfriend," Craig said. "She's Italian."

"Lucky boy." CJ waved him into the office. So Craig put the phone back in his pocket with the call unanswered and went into his office and sat at his workstation.

"Here's the takeaway," CJ said. "You need to find a new job."

"Holy crap, you *are* going to kill him."

"If that option doesn't appeal, I could shoot you and dump you through those doors, or else I could tie you up and stuff you in a closet. But then, one of Preston's goons would blow your brains out for screwing up. So that would be a waste of time."

"A new job is fine with me. I could take one of those RIBs." He pointed to the rigid inflatable boats by the hull doors.

"And maybe help me get into the CCTV system before you go."

Craig grabbed a pencil and scribbled on a notepad.

"Here's my admin login," he said. "I can show you how to operate this whole deck too. It's menu-driven. Super easy."

CJ tucked his pistol into his sash and pulled up a chair.

"You'll need to leave your phone with me. But I'll let you message Sophia first. Okay?"

Twenty-One

With Craig on his way to a new job in a purloined
dinghy, CJ checked out the Explorer Deck and planted
an explosive charge at its entrance, while keeping a
watchful eye on the CCTV feed on the technician's
phone. Preparations done, he hid in a storeroom off the
conference room where the bandidos were scheduled to
meet. Its shelves were stocked with connectors and
cables, and there were extra chairs too. He pulled one
close to the door, so he could listen in on the goings-on
beyond it. He was still clad in his Moorish pirates outfit.
Not much choice about that, since the only other option
was his swim briefs and no way was he going to burst out
of a closet in budgie smugglers brandishing a pistol. He
couldn't see Preston anywhere on CCTV, most likely
because he was still on the Owner's Deck and there
weren't any cameras there. Preston's gofer-in-chief was a
different matter. Tony was everywhere, one moment
hassling the aloha shirts into vigilance, the next up on the
helipad jawing with a landing technician.

By the time Preston did appear, CJ had spent so much time navigating the system that he was comfortable with it. He watched Preston emerge from his private elevator onto the helipad and chat to Tony. Some minutes later, a big chopper touched down, a twin-engined Leonardo and a tight fit on the helipad. Schilder emerged with two men wearing identical suits, all battleship gray with chalky stripes. One of them carried a metal briefcase cuffed to his wrist, his shoulder sagging under its weight despite his bulk. Both the men were larger than life with gym physiques puffed up with bulletproof underwear. Schilder was puffed up too. He was dressed to party and overdoing it big-time with a floral shirt under a pink suede bomber jacket embroidered with a peacock. The helicopter departed as greetings were exchanged. Then they all walked off-screen. CJ checked his inventory of cameras, but he couldn't find them. Most likely they were waiting in the helipad foyer, and the reason why was soon obvious. Another arrival.

Preston's chopper, a nippy Bell, swooped down on the pad. Nazar emerged with two men in tuxedos and bow ties. Nazar was carrying a briefcase, but his bodyguards weren't carrying anything except lots of muscle and plenty of attitude. They might have been twins too. Same height and weight. Same slick black hair and dainty mustaches. Turkish prison governors on a big night out was CJ's first thought, the sort of governors who wandered down to the basement after dark with a billy club and a dribble of anticipation. Once again, Preston and Tony emerged into view and greeted them before stepping out of range of the CCTV.

CJ jigged back and forth between screens until he found Preston and Tony emerging from the private elevator at the entrance to the Explorer Deck along with

Schilder and Nazar and their men. Schilder took the metal case from his man, clutching it to his chest with both arms as Preston unlocked the door with a thumbprint. Then they disappeared into the camera-free zone, leaving their bodyguards outside with Tony. CJ listened intently, finally picking up their approach as they entered the conference room. From that point, it was all down to feeding streams of sound into the video player in his head and building a moving picture. There was not much talk at first, but plenty of shuffling with the clink and thump of briefcases getting popped open. It was as though this part had been finely planned and nothing needed saying.

"Shall we begin?" Preston's voice was almost chummy, as if they were sipping gin and about to deal a hand of bridge. More clicks and scrapes and an electronic beep, but still no chat. CJ imagined them kicking the tires. For Nazar, that meant checking the diamonds and their digital certificates and doing a few random tests on the stones with some electronic device. For Schilder, it meant jacking into the activator and verifying the codes. CJ was following it all with his ears while his eyes monitored their security teams in the lobby, where a waiter emerged from the elevator pushing a refreshments trolley. He went to serve his wares, but Tony shooed him away and he disappeared in the elevator, leaving the men to help themselves to coffee. As time passed, the bandidos stirred into life, tension melting. It was all working out. The diamonds were good, and so were the codes. Preston talked about the aftermath and how they would disperse and maintain security. No longer mistrustful bandidos, but brothers bonded by crime.

But then…

Two shots. CJ heard them, distant and faint. He saw them too. Tony was the shooter, his pistol so small it was all but invisible in his hand, some kind of vest gun, firing tiny slugs that were now bouncing around inside the skulls of Nazar's governors. Both men went reeling, and Schilder's pinstripes finished them off with 9mm pistols equipped with stubby silencers, pumping shots into their heads at point-blank range. No reaction from the bandidos, those faint gunshots muffled by steel walls and lost in the background pulse of music and beachside pyrotechnics. In seconds, all was silent, coffee and broken cups everywhere, squished cakes and sandwiches soaking up blood with the mustachioed governors lying in the middle of it. That was the cue CJ had been waiting for. He opened the door and joined the meeting.

Preston was standing at the head of the table with his back to the storeroom. So CJ gave him a moment to catch up by reading the news on the faces of Schilder and Nazar. They might have said something about the new arrival too, but they didn't. They simply stopped and stared, their eyes and mouths inching wide. Preston whirled around, then followed suit. Silence all round. The Moorish pirate's getup surely had a lot to do with that, a big pirate even, with a blackface, a grin and a pistol. If only there'd been a bunch of kids in the room, they'd have applauded, but all the bandidos could do was stare as if waiting for a formal introduction. Preston was the first back to life. He clutched his chest and collapsed onto the desk, feigning a heart attack, or beaten-man act. CJ wasn't sure which. He knew what he was really doing. He was making a grab for the holstered Beretta taped under the table, but CJ was already shaking his head and waving the gun.

"I did a little recon," he said.

"What the hell is going on?" Schilder said, leaping to his feet.

CJ ignored him. "Part of your *special plan* for Nazar, I assume," he said, nodding at Preston's Beretta.

"Special what?" Nazar jumped to his feet too, attention fully engaged.

"Ignore him," Preston said. "He's here to kill me. He's here to stop Domino."

"You dumb assholes." Schilder's face glowed red as he flicked it back and forth between them. "You let it get out." He settled his rage on Preston. "What now?"

Before he could answer, Nazar said to CJ. "Kill them both, and get me out of here. You can have the diamonds."

CJ nodded, like he was thinking about it, then said, "Ashford never told you that these buggers were going to kill you, did he?" Nazar's face went limp, his eyes flicking around the table. Preston went to speak, but his protest was short-lived. CJ was already holding up his phone, playing the video, the elevator lobby massacre. It wasn't just cinema, either. It had a purpose, like those dogs hunters use to flush game. There was one last zig in this puzzle, and divide and conquer was the way to uncover it. CJ's Ashford-Nazar thesis had one flaw, and Paz had spotted it. *What if Nazar welched on the deal and ran off with the diamonds?* The trade had to be for much more than the Texas hit. There had to be a payoff right at the end, something worth more to Nazar than forty million in diamonds.

Nazar watched the killings with bug-eyed intensity, his fists and shoulders bunching, and when Schilder's men delivered the *coup de grâce*, he whirled on their boss and hit him so hard in the face his wrist buckled and he hollered like he was taking a beating instead of giving one. Schilder stumbled back, grabbing at Nazar's throat, and with fists flailing, they hit the floor. Preston glanced at CJ, but he let them get on with it. Schilder came out on top of the tumble, and he was thumping Nazar's ribs when... *a shot.* Schilder stopped thumping and rolled off Nazar, clutching his chest and howling. Nazar struggled to his feet, panting like a dog after a street fight and staring down at Schilder and the tiny gun in his hand. He looked at CJ, who waved his 9mm, reminding him who had the biggest gun and beckoning him to hand it over.

Nazar nodded compliance and went to lay his gun on the table. But at the last moment, he angled it down and shot Schilder again, and that was it. The digerati prince in the peacock jacket lay motionless, his empty eyes staring at the ceiling, his celebrated forehead oozing blood. Nazar skidded his gun across the table to CJ, sending it plowing through spilled diamonds and scattering them on the floor. It was a Baby Browning in engraved nickel with a pearl handle. The sort of gun that belonged in a femme fatale's handbag in a 1940s movie, not a sleazy Iranian's phone pocket. Preston gawked at it but said nothing. CJ gave it an admiring glance, then slipped it in the fanny pack hidden in the folds of his pirate's outfit.

"Thanks for not killing me," he said as he tucked it away.

"Asshole." Preston spat it out. Not at CJ, at Nazar.

"Me?" Nazar turned on him. "I'm the asshole?" He pointed his finger. "You were nothing. A West Point dickhead with a rent-a-gun outfit. I cut you the breaks. My contacts. My money. That's what started all this." He waved around at Preston's superyacht. "I created you. We were brothers. Then you connived with this Jew."

Preston hung his head. "For what it's worth, I felt bad about it... but with the indictments..."

"Damn you, Preston. After what we've been through together, you think I'm stupid enough to let those halfwit *federales* catch me. Yes, I did a deal with Ashford. It kept you alive and this deal on track."

"Sooner or later, they'd have gotten you somewhere…"

"Oh, really? I've got news for you, pal."

But whatever the news was, Nazar left it unsaid, settling for a chuckle, an angry man's chuckle, but a winner's chuckle nonetheless, and given the circumstances, that wasn't right. But it did give CJ his answer, that final zig, the elusive *what* that Ashford had tacked on the end to guarantee those diamonds. Nazar was chuckling because there was *somewhere* beyond the long reach of the FBI, a country where a federal indictment was nothing but a sheet of paper for wiping a dirty backside. Nazar's problem was that he'd burnt his bridge to Iran. In the land of his ancestors, he was a Westernized whore, a stone-to-death candidate. But Ashford could fix all that. He was a seasoned Middle East hand, speaking fluent Farsi with contacts in its militias, its government and intelligence services. So what if Nazar turned up with a gift? How about the technology to level the playing field with the US Navy?

"Sanctuary," CJ said. "Ashford's trade for the diamonds. Texas and an Iranian passport." Nazar's eyes flashed up at him—no more chuckling. "And it would have worked too. Only Preston and Schilder decided to knife you in the back. So Ashford called the deal off—only he forgot to tell you—and sent me instead."

"You fool," Nazar said. "The mullahs would hang me."

"Not if you have the GPS location of a weapon that can turn the Persian Gulf into a no-go zone for the US Navy."

"What!" Preston took a pace closer to Nazar and CJ's hand shot up, warding him off.

"What did they do on that freighter?" CJ said. "Winch up the container somewhere off the coast of Iran, so the mine slid out, then reset the seals?"

"You little shit…" Preston lurched at Nazar, but CJ's gun arm went straight up to his head. "The ship dropped off the grid. He told me it was a black box thing."

"It's all bullshit," Nazar said, appealing to Preston. "The mine's useless without the activator, and the mullahs don't want war anyway."

"You're right," CJ said. "They're not going to use this. Their scientists will reverse engineer it. In two years, they'll be rolling off an assembly line. Those GPS coordinates in your head—they're worth all the oil in Arabia. You'll be the prodigal son, a national hero, a little Satan turned angel. As for you, Preston, they'll be no crippled warship, no tumbling dominoes, no rich pickings, only notoriety. You'll be the most famous American traitor since Benedict Arnold. Congratulations."

Congratulations.

A wave of nausea flooded up through Preston's guts. It wasn't the money he'd lost, the federal contracts with eye-watering strings of zeroes. It wasn't the failure either. He'd had plans fail before and he'd always recovered. But this time, it was different. The shame of what he'd done was suffocating him. There'd be no coming back from this. Even if by some miracle, he could escape the inevitable, a bullet from Brink's gun exploding through his brain, he'd never recover. Lieutenant Colonel Vance Preston. Yes, that was he, a once-proud officer of the US Army. For sure, he'd lied, cheated, murdered, blackmailed and bribed. But he was a patriot. Wars happened anyway. America was a child of war, its lifeblood pumped by armed conflict. So why not cash in and lend a helping hand to get one started?

But this…

Treason.

He'd provided Iran's Revolutionary Guard with a weapon far more useful than the nuclear bomb they coveted. They could never actually use a nuke even if Israel and the US let them develop one. But an access-denial munition like the EM-88 could flip the balance of power. God hadn't answered their prayers. So a greedy US Army lieutenant colonel had stepped up and played God in his place. Brink's bullet was imminent. This was it. Preston's last stand, his final snapshot, his takeaway from life on earth was this: Nazar's smug grin.

But no…

There was still a chance he could stop it happening. Nazar hadn't revealed the exact location to anyone. Brink was right. He couldn't afford to.

"Kill him," Preston said, turning to CJ. "You can't let them get that mine."

"Take the diamonds," Nazar said. "And kill him. That's what you were sent to do. Domino is stopped already. The carrier is safe. Kill him and your job's done. The diamonds are a bonus."

"You fool," Preston said. "He can kill us both and take the diamonds anyway. You have nothing to trade." He looked at CJ. "Do it! Kill him first. Let me know that at least. I don't want to die a traitor. Then kill me and take the diamonds." Surely Brink would do the right thing. He'd fought side by side with US Marines. He couldn't possibly let those raghead mullahs get a weapon like this.

"He is right, though," Brink said, sounding a long way short of convinced. "Domino is stopped already. So if I kill you, I'm done for the day."

Preston was aghast. He looked back at Nazar, his slimeball smirk an unbearable provocation. He screeched and leapt on him, smashing him backwards, his hands on the Iranian's throat. They tripped on Schilder's body and hit the floor, Nazar taking the brunt of it with Preston's weight on top. Nazar got off a punch, cracking his attacker's injured jaw. Preston cried out, but he didn't stop. He roared the pain out through bared teeth, leaning into Nazar's throat with straight arms. Preston was expecting a bullet at any second. Brink was bound to do something. Stop them, break them apart. But no referee appeared, and Preston's world faded into a mist of rage. Two men in a fight to the death. Nazar clawed at him, his fingers and nails gouging the American's arms and face, but Preston didn't flinch, holding on until the Iranian went limp. Preston fell off him, stunned by what he'd done. He'd killed men before this, but never with his bare hands. He dragged himself away from the body and slumped on his side too weak to stand. He looked up at Brink, who was peering at Nazar's body, his gun loosely held at his side.

"Nice work," he said. "Are you ready to join him now?"

Preston nodded. He had no illusions about his future. Brink had come to kill him and he would certainly complete his mission. But oddly, Preston was unafraid. At least he'd die clean. Moments before, he'd felt dirty.

The treason word had done that. But killing Nazar had purged it, redeemed him. The fact of dying was not so important. We all got to it sooner or later. But that last taste of life, the moment you let go, that matters. Preston went to pull himself up, but he didn't make it, slumping to his knees halfway.

Brink leveled the gun at him.

Preston reached out a defensive hand. "Let me take it on my feet," he said. "Not on my knees."

Brink lowered the gun.

Preston summoned all his will and pulled himself up straight. He looked around the room, at the bodies, the diamonds, the activator, and finally he looked at Brink, his nemesis. "I'm ready," he said.

"No last words?"

Preston shook his head. But then it came to him, not words but a realization… a stay of execution, maybe even a full pardon. "How fast does a freighter go?" he said.

Brink's face wrinkled up and his eyes narrowed. "As last words go, they're not especially memorable, are they?"

"Try these instead… how much would that EM-88 be worth to allied intelligence?"

CJ glanced at the dead Iranian and back to Preston.

"But you just killed the only man who knows where it is."

"It's offshore from the Iranian province of Sistan and Baluchestan."

"How does that help? That's two hundred and fifty kilometers of coastline at least." Preston waited. Brink was smart. He'd add this up, and sure enough, he lowered his gun. "The black box thing?"

"Exactly. Like you said, they must have slid it out of the container. To do that they'd have to stop the ship, and that would give away the location. So they blacked out the AIS. I was following its progress when it vanished. I called Nazar. He lied, of course. Then a couple of hours later it popped up. I can time-stamp that. We can narrow the window down to a few miles. The US Navy could sweep that in an afternoon."

"So they get the EM-88, and you don't get a bullet. Is that the deal?"

Brink raised his gun and stuck the barrel against Preston's head.

"I had nothing to do with Alex's death," Preston said, his euphoric moment dwindling. Maybe he'd read Brink all wrong. Maybe he was so crazy he didn't give a damn about who got the mine. "The guys on the ground in Iraq called the shots. I'd never have risked you and Alex. You were my best guys."

Brink lowered his weapon. "I'll think about it. In the meantime"—he waved his gun around the room—"all this needs cleaning up, and I need to take care of the goons at the door. If you cooperate—and don't push your luck—maybe we can work something out." Brink took a lighter from his bag and tossed it over. "Grab some of that notepaper, light it and hold it under the smoke alarm."

Preston was happy to oblige. Setting off the fire alarm would bring their security stampeding through the hangar to the conference room. But Preston knew it couldn't be that simple. He lit the paper, and when the fire alert was blasting, Brink triggered an explosion with his phone. Then he burst open the door. Tony was staggering out of the smoke by the entrance. Brink shot him, and he dropped on the spot. No one else had survived the blast. Now the only way off the Owner's Deck was through the hangar doors by sea. Brink swept the diamonds off the table into his knapsack and threw the activator in after it. Then he nodded at Nazar.

"Drag him out to the sub." There were a few more diamonds scattered on the floor. Brink picked them up and pocketed them before grabbing Schilder by the leg.

When they had dragged the bodies out through the smoky hangar and stuffed them onto the back seats of the sub, Brink took the pilot's seat and operated the winches and doors. Preston, sitting next to him, recognized the phone app he was using, obviously surrendered by his spineless technician.

The sub swung out over the water and eased down onto its gentle waves. Brink operated the controls effortlessly. Having been trained on military-grade amphibious equipment, he was hardly going to need a set of diagrams to figure out a civilian sub, and its motors soon whined into life. The shriek of alarms faded as the sub ducked under the water.

So the day was done. More or less. Only one question remained.

Would Brink take the deal and let him live?

He was speculating about that when Brink said, "Here"—he picked up the knapsack at his feet—"put this on your side." He leaned over and dropped the bag into Preston's footwell. "I need this side clear to work the foot controls."

Preston bent forward to position the knapsack against his seat. That was when he saw it.

Hope.

That's how it hit him. Maybe he didn't have to count on Brink taking the deal after all.

A screwdriver.

There it was jammed between his seat and the door frame. Not so big, but big enough. It must have been dropped by that worthless technician. Preston fiddled with the knapsack, tucking it behind his legs. Then he pulled himself up slowly, dragging his hand by the side of the seat.

God bless that son of a bitch technician.

Ashford's townhouse was in a complex that was newish but built to look oldish, white village style, more Andalusian than Majorcan. The units were tiered on a hill overlooking the sea between flights of steps. So the only access to the front door was by foot, either from the lane that dead-ended at the top, or from the street at the bottom where an ungated entrance opened onto a parking area. An empty lot adjoined the property, wired off and overgrown. Ashford's place was halfway up the steps, making any kind of surprise approach impossible. But they had an ace. Jeanine. By the time they'd thrashed out the options, they were a team.

Not exactly. Jeanine wasn't going to kill anyone. The way she looked at it, she was helping Paz survive. She'd tried to talk her out of it and failed, and she wasn't going to let this young woman die. Her role would be small, but crucial in saving her life. Ashford was expecting Paz alone. Jeanine running interference was a complication he could not possibly have foreseen.

Jeanine stood at the top of the steps looking down. The lighting was patchy and the townhouse gardens on one side and the empty lot on the other offered all sorts of hiding places. But that wasn't an issue. Jeanine wasn't hiding. She was advertising. Eyeballs and attention. That was the goal. That was why she'd made a fuss parking the car at the top, shunting it into a hedgerow and summarizing the damage with a string of colorful expletives. The role wasn't so difficult. She'd attended more than a few drunk and disorderly calls in her time as a police officer. Now she had to play a drunken American tourist making her way back to her rental after a long day at the fiesta. So she was wearing a headscarf, although she'd learned from Paz that it was called a *khimar*. As for the rest of her attire, that wasn't remotely Moorish, and definitely not *purdah*. She had taken off her bra, undone a few shirt buttons and swapped jeans for skimpy shorts. The knapsack on her shoulder finished the picture. It was heavy and made her walk lopsided, and it went *chink-chink* as she navigated the steep path, one drunken step at a time.

At the first terrace, she stopped. It was lit and she had a show to put on. She adjusted her knapsack, removing an open bottle and taking a slug before continuing her wobbly progress with painstaking care. Her eyes were pointed at the uneven steps ahead. But they were concentrating on the edge of her view frame, especially the dimly lit stretch around Ashford's entrance, where a hoodie soon emerged from the shadows, a silhouette, probably a man, judging by its stature.

"Hey…," she called out, waving the bottle. "They throw you out of the party too?" With such an ominous figure lurking in the darkness ahead, no woman in her right mind would have continued on down the steps. But that was the point. So off she went, stepping with the same ponderous precision, eyes down, but looking elsewhere… and soon finding Paz on the other side of the fence in the empty lot. Jeanine had dropped her off a mile up the lower road half an hour before, and Paz had made the rest of the way on foot. Her challenge now was to hop over the fence without drawing the attention of the hoodie. Cue Jeanine…

She stumbled theatrically, nearly landing on her face, her bottle spinning out of her hand and shattering on the steps below.

"Shit, damn…" She pulled herself upright, close enough to the hoodie now to make out his face. Paz was over already and edging up the steps. He must have heard something as his hand slipped under his hoodie and he went to turn, but Paz was on him, cracking his head with the butt of her pistol, and down he went. Jeanine searched him while Paz taped his wrists. She stuck his gun in her bag and gave Paz his keys. Then she checked his phone, stopping Paz as she was taping his mouth.

"We need his face," she whispered, angling his head up into the light to activate the phone's facial recognition. She checked the contacts while Paz finished bundling him up, and she was soon messaging Ashford.

She's alone. Unarmed. Got the stuff. Sending her up. Car down by the parking. Need to check.

They dragged the hoodie to the fence and dumped him over it into a thorny bush.

"Okay, I'm ready," Paz said, scanning the steps to Ashford's place. "I've got this now. Thanks." She turned back to Jeanine, looking anything but ready, and gave her a hug. "I'll always owe you."

And with that, she was on her way, slipping into the shadows of the bushy palms decorating the townhouse gardens. So that was it. Jeanine was done. She had to climb those steps back to the car and wait, except that she didn't. That gutsy look on Paz's face was fake, and Jeanine had seen right through it. Underneath it was terror, the kind that breeds mistakes. She was steeling herself. She'd see it through. Jeanine didn't doubt it. But at what cost? She drew her gun and started back, but two shots rang out before she made it. The door was half-ajar. There was a hallway beyond it, side-lit from a room.

No one. No sound.

She stepped into the hallway, dropping into a crouch, then checked the room with the light. A small kitchen. Empty. She cleared the room opposite it too. A bedroom. Then she edged along the wall and into a split-level dining and lounge area. Ashford was on the floor by a fireplace, and Paz was sprawled on a sofa. Both were bloodied and motionless. She rushed to Ashford first. He was still a threat until she ruled it otherwise. No need to check his pulse. He'd rigged his last deal. Paz had made no mistake about that one shot, straight in the face.

Jeanine went to her and saw at once that she was going to live. She'd been shot in the leg and there was a lot of blood loss, but it wasn't squirting out. It was stoppable. There were two wounds, entry and exit. So unless the bullet had hit her thigh bone and fragmented, there'd be nothing in there to fish out. Most likely, Ashford had ambushed her, but she'd dived to one side and gotten off a lethal shot. Now she was wide-eyed with shock. She was staring at Ashford's smashed-up face. Jeanine couldn't say if the shock was caused by her wound or the reality of killing a man for the first time. She used the same tape they'd used on the hoodie to bind the wounds on her leg, applying it over the jeans and making sure it was tight. The tape was waterproof, and after the cloth underneath it was saturated, it would staunch the blood flow long enough to ensure her survival. The priority then was getting her out of there. Jeanine sat her up, holding her head between her hands, their faces inches apart.

"Paz, you can do this. Come on… get up."

But she couldn't do it, her blank eyes staring straight back into Jeanine's. With no other choice, Jeanine hooked her arm over her shoulder, pulled her up and started to walk, hoping Paz might make a step or two. But her feet trailed on the wood-tiled floor, and Jeanine had to take all her weight. Up they went into the dining area and out into the night where they made it up a few steps before stumbling and falling on the stairs. Jeanine wiped off her grazed hands and leaned Paz against the fence of a neighboring house.

"We're never going to make it like this," she said, sucking at the cool night air and surveying the task ahead. Nothing else for it. Jeanine had learned the so-called fireman's carry somewhere along the line. But that was theory. This was for real. She squatted down and somehow got Paz draped across her shoulders. That turned out to be the easy part. The hard part was standing up and walking up three flights of stairs. Paz was slim, but she was as heavy as all hell, with each stone step a mountain. And by the time Jeanine reached the top, the burn in her thighs was white-hot and tears of pain were streaming down her face. She laid Paz on the back seat and drove off, her legs still shaking as she opened up the gas. A while later, when the lights of the city were behind them, a weak voice came from the back seat.

"Jeanine?"

"I'm here."

"I did it. I did, didn't I? I did it."

Jeanine glanced back at her, then went back to the road.

"Yes, you did, girl. You did it. And so did I."

With the nighttime gloom of Davy Jones' locker setting the mood and drawing a canvas for CJ's dark thoughts, the Explorer Sub hummed onward. The company in the back seat was a big help too, Schilder in wide-eyed wonderment, the bullet hole in his forehead a third eye peering into the netherworld, and Nazar slumped against him, his head lolling like a drunken buddy on Schilder's shoulder, his tongue choked out between his teeth. In front of them, Preston sat immobile, his chiseled features pale and thanatoid, staring into the bubble of light beyond the bubble of glass. CJ was sitting next to him, checking the instruments and controls with diligent attention and noting with scant interest the marine life that nosed up to their buzzing ball of light. But all his piloting stuff was a sideshow, running on cruise control. What was really going on in CJ's head was an echo of his own voice, finding him all the way from Nevada...

Should I kill him?

By any accounting system, Preston was overdue a bullet in the brain. He had so many outstanding items on the ledger it was barely worth the effort of itemizing them. CJ's mission was all but accomplished—the Domino threat had died with Nazar, and so had the prospect of an Iran armed with China's most advanced undersea warfare weapon. But Preston was right. The EM-88 in the hands of allied scientists would secure the US Navy's ability to keep international waters safe for commercial maritime traffic. Beyond that, there was something else dangling here... a man and his fate. CJ had speculated about his own choices and resolved to change his life back in Nevada—to break free of his past. Maybe Preston was a change candidate too. The American had been enraged by Nazar's duplicity, but that wasn't the spark that touched him off. Not the fact of it, but its nature. The Iranian's had the EM-88. They were supposed to get their ass kicked. Instead they'd gotten China's silver bullet. Nazar had sacrificed America on the altar of his own survival, and Preston had done the right thing. He'd throttled the bastard to death.

"What do you think, Alex?" CJ said, continuing to stare stoically ahead. Preston snapped his head towards him, half light flickering patterns on his pallid cheeks. CJ ignored him. "Back there… he stepped up. Bit of a surprise, that. And Naval Intelligence could sure use that mine. Or shall we stick to the plan and waste him? There's plenty of fish here need feeding." Preston's forearm was on the wrest between them, his hand trembling. CJ glanced at him. "You see that?" he said, pointing at the glass where its curve refracted the instrument lights into a patch of glow. "Looks like nothing to you, right? Dials and LEDs?" He waved his hand at the dashboard. "Truth is… it's Alex. Look, here's his nose, his eyes. The doctors told me it was a hallucination and they put it down to a wiring problem, regrown brain cells short-circuited by guilt. Survivor's syndrome, they called it. But that's a load of BS. Look…" He waved his hand at the glass again. "There's the blood dripping from his throat. And I hear him too. He laughs a lot. We always had a good laugh even when it got tough. But he's not laughing now… he's deciding." CJ broke off, staring at the sub's control panel. "Looks like we're here." He nodded at the dashboard as he worked the controls. "Lovely gear. Inertial navigation. Very classy."

The sub broke the surface—it was still night—and the glass canopy opened like a clam offering up its meat. CJ dimmed the lights, but he didn't cut the engine. There was no sign of the *True Grit*. They were offshore a few coves to the south. CJ climbed out of the cockpit and stood on the deck.

"Out you get?" he said.

Preston clambered out, and CJ pointed towards the beach.

"How far is that, do you reckon?"

The sky was star-studded with enough of a moon to light the coast and shimmer in rivers of silver on the shifting waters.

"A mile. No more than two," Preston said. "This sub's got an eight-hour battery life. There's plenty left."

"This sub's not going anywhere. I'm going to founder it right here. When they find it, it'll look like you took Schilder and Nazar for a ride, but something went wrong."

"You're killing me?"

"You've got fake IDs, right?"

"What?"

"Offshore accounts… a fire-exit package for the day when it all goes tits up? Well, this is that day. Option one: you get a bullet in the head and join your mates here. Option two: you disappear. The world assumes you died with them, and your body was washed away. But in fact, you will assist me to locate the EM-88. After that…"

"You put a bullet in my brain."

CJ shook his head. "You can live out a new life under your new identity. I'm giving you a second chance. You have my word, on one condition. You're out of this business. Play golf, drink scotch… all good. Any more war games, and I'll find you and I'll kill you."

Preston looked over the bodies in the sub, then turned towards the shore.

"But how do we get to the beach if you founder the sub?"

"Swim."

"You expect me to swim that? I'm fifty-four."

"But you're in good shape. Besides, you'll be swimming for your life. It always helps." CJ pointed to the rocky capes, silhouettes at either end of the bay. "We're outside the bay. There's a current, and the tide's against us for another half an hour or so. The first four hundred yards will be tough. If you make that, I reckon you're good. It's a chance anyway. Alex never had one. Think about him—stroke after stroke. Then, when you crawl out on that beach exhausted, you'll be a better man." Preston stared at him, fearful blue eyes limpid in the moonlight. "Am I going to need this?" CJ pointed to the gun in his belt. "Or are you going to do the right thing?"

Preston nodded agreement and stepped onto the pontoon on the beach side, casting his eyes back and forth towards the beach as if measuring the challenge. He took a long breath and bent forward, crouching like a diver at the start of a race.

One, two...

On three, his body snapped down towards his legs and his arm shot backwards, and CJ felt blunt steel cutting into his thigh and slamming against bone. He yelped, grabbing the wound reflexively and arching his body forward as Preston jerked up straight, the back of his head smashing into CJ's face. He stumbled back, making a grab for Preston as he keeled over. But on a rig this size, there was only one place to go, and CJ was soon drilling into cold water in a roar of bubbles.

He didn't fight it. No struggle. Letting his body's buoyancy take control. Willing the calm he needed to soothe his pounding heart. As the bubbles cleared, he took a stroke and broke the surface. The sub was already on its way, its glass dome closing, the three bandidos now only one. He ripped off his pirate's outfit, pulled the screwdriver out of his thigh and bound it tight. Preston had missed the femoral artery and there wasn't too much blood. Even so, an open wound would bleed plenty in the water and he had to staunch it to make the swim to shore. He felt his nose. Tender, but its pain buffered behind a wall of insensitivity. He used both hands to click it back, then trod water, readying himself for a tough swim with an injured leg. Preston was heading north, back to the *True Grit*, and as CJ watched the sub, he remembered Nevada and that muddle of thoughts scribbled on a napkin.

Can a man change his fate?

That was the question he'd been reaching for. So had Preston finally delivered the answer? CJ had given him the chance, a road to redemption, albeit in the form of a rough water swim. But Preston had turned his back on it. Something in his nature had stepped up and made the call. The wrong call. Not that he knew it yet. He was in that sub congratulating himself, no doubt. After all, he'd escaped. He'd bested Brink and gotten his knapsack with the diamonds and the activator, and—as he was soon to discover—the tactical explosives, which CJ hadn't needed on the yacht. Preston's catalog of crimes had run out of pages.

CJ took out his phone. He soon picked up a signal, and Preston's yellow submarine disappeared in a flash of orange, the explosion intensified by airtight seals and gorilla glass built to take huge pressures. Metal, machinery, glass and diamonds, it was all winging skyward above a smoke cloud backlit by a crackle of flame. CJ watched and waited until the sea had erased all trace, leaving an acrid afterburn on the onshore breeze.

CJ soon picked up an easy stroke, arms only, his injured leg tight against the other to avoid drag and limit the blood loss.

Can a man change his fate?

He thought about that on the long swim to shore. And as dawn broke and he pulled himself out of the water and onto the rocks of an empty beach, the answer came to him.

It doesn't matter.

His old boss had taught him as much. The important thing is to never stop trying.

Epilogue

With Easter over and summer's busy tourist season still in the wings, Palma Airport was uncharacteristically quiet as CJ and Jeanine hurried through departures, heading towards the security gates. It was an odd moment, and neither of them had the right words. So there was not much being said with most of the talking left to something physical, a smile, a squeezed hand, a one-armed hug. They stopped a ways off from the line at the security checks, and Jeanine turned to face him.

"It always hits you, doesn't it?" he said.

"What?"

"This… the goodbye. You know it's coming, but even so."

"Is that what this is?" she said. "I mean… do I have to ask you?"

"You're getting on a plane. You live in LA."

"And you live…?"

CJ shrugged and looked around, his eyes catching a departures information board studded with locations. One of those, maybe.

"The question's not where for me, it's what," he said. "I've made promises to myself and others, and I keep them. I'm old-fashioned like that."

"Promised what? More of the same?"

"I think you're misunderstanding."

"No, I get it. We had fun. Now it's over. Time to move on. Well, good luck with that. But maybe you had a chance here. You're healing. So instead of more of the same, how about moving on and leaving all that bad in the past where it belongs?" CJ shuffled and huffed, his eyes avoiding hers and flitting around the terminal like an emergency exit would be handy. "So tell me… I want to know." Jeanine bore down on him, stepping into his space. "Don't I deserve that? What damn promise is worth trashing this?"

CJ gave up. There was no way to avoid it. So he met her gaze, his face softening with regret like a doctor with bad news for a waiting-room spouse.

"It's just that… I promised Aidan I'd take him to a baseball game."

"What?" Her face clouded, puzzled eyes querying.

"The forty-something… Alex's team. I swore I'd take him, and by God I'll do it…" CJ stamped his foot, adding a little theater. "And to hell with everything else."

The light flickered on, a smile creeping across her lips despite her efforts to shut it down. "You son of a bitch." She cracked his ribs with her fist and pulled his mouth down on hers.

ABOUT THE AUTHOR

Michael Woodman was a thriller-writing sensation in his teens, signing multi-book deals with major publishers straight out of high school.

His spy novels ended up on bestseller shelves on both sides of the Atlantic, but their young author was oddly troubled. His hero went on dangerous missions to exotic locations, but Michael had never been anywhere or done anything, and he wanted a thriller-writer's bio like the authors who inspired him. So he quit writing imaginary adventures and took off looking for real ones.

Since then, he has traveled in over 50 countries and had extraordinary careers and adventures on four continents. He now lives in Spain with his wife, Elizabeth, and he's back at the keyboard with a new hero for a new age.

The Saint of Baghdad, his first thriller in 50 years, was critically acclaimed and became a #1 bestseller on Amazon charts within months of publication.

Find out more at michaelwoodman.com.